"If you keep insulting me, this kiss won't ever happen, Red..."

"Don't call me that," Margot whispered. "Please?"

"This kiss." His calculated gaze didn't make her feel any better about the situation. "How long does it need to be? How deep? Where do you want my hands?"

Margot's mouth dropped open. "That's not how kisses work! You can't just map out the kiss. That takes all the romance out of it!"

"Oh, so you *want* romance?"

"Yes! No! I mean. I didn't say that!" Her face flamed.

"I was joking," he said, just before his lips brushed hers. His tongue slid across her bottom lip and then he deepened the kiss.

Her lips softened beneath his gentle coaxing, his hard thighs pressed against hers as a deep hunger awakened within her.

Oh, this was bad.

So bad.

And very, very, good at the same time.

Praise for The Bet Series

THE WAGER

"Rachel Van Dyken is quickly becoming one of my favorite authors and I cannot wait to see what she has in store for us in the future. *The Wager* is a must-read for those who love romance and humor. It will leave a lasting impression and a huge smile on your face."

—LiteratiBookReviews.com

THE BET

"I haven't laughed this hard while reading a book in a while. *The Bet* [is] an experience—a heartwarming, sometimes hilarious, experience...I've actually read this book twice."

—RecommendedRomance.com

"If you need a funny, light read...I promise you this is a superb choice!" —MustReadBooksOrDie.com

"Friends-to-lovers stories...Is there anything better? And when told in a fun, light manner, with a potential love triangle with lovable characters; well, how can you not enjoy it?"

—TotallyBookedBlog.com

Acclaim for the Eagle Elite Series

ELECT

"Secrets, sacrifices, blood, angst, loyalties...This book has everything I love!...Rachel Van Dyken is a fabulous author!" —GirlBookLove.com

"Takes you on a roller coaster of emotion...centers around the most amazing of love stories...Nixon has definitely made it to my best-book-boyfriend list."

—SoManyReads.com

ELITE

"This is by far the best book I have read from this talented author." —Book-Whisperer.blogspot.com

"Four enthusiastic stars! This is just so fresh and different and crazy and fun...I can't wait for the next book, *Elect*...Judging by [*Elite*], this entire series is going to be fantastic." —NewAdultAddiction.com

THE
Playboy
BACHELOR

RACHEL VAN DYKEN

FOREVER

NEW YORK   BOSTON

Copyright © 2017 by Rachel Van Dyken
Excerpt from *The Bachelor Contract* copyright © 2017 by Rachel Van Dyken
Cover design by Elizabeth Turner
Cover copyright © 2017 by Hachette Book Group, Inc.
Hachette Book Group supports the right to free expression and the value of copyright. The purpose of copyright is to encourage writers and artists to produce the creative works that enrich our culture.

The scanning, uploading, and distribution of this book without permission is a theft of the author's intellectual property. If you would like permission to use material from the book (other than for review purposes), please contact permissions@hbgusa.com. Thank you for your support of the author's rights.

Forever
Hachette Book Group
1290 Avenue of the Americas
New York, NY 10104
forever-romance.com
twitter.com/foreverromance

First Edition: August 2017

Forever is an imprint of Grand Central Publishing.
The Forever name and logo are trademarks of Hachette Book Group, Inc.

The publisher is not responsible for websites (or their content) that are not owned by the publisher.

The Hachette Speakers Bureau provides a wide range of authors for speaking events. To find out more, go to www.hachettespeakersbureau.com or call (866) 376-6591.

ISBN 978-1-4555-9873-1 (mass market edition)
ISBN 978-1-4555-9874-8 (ebook edition)

Printed in the United States of America

OPM

10 9 8 7 6 5 4 3 2 1

To Kristin, Jill, Jessica,
Liza, and Lauren—
thank you for helping me NOT lose
my mind with this book and
making it amazing!

ACKNOWLEDGMENTS

I'm so thankful that I'm able to do something I love!

God is so good and I'm in constant thanks every day that I get to wake up and write—something that literally keeps me up at night because I'm so excited to do it!

My family, Nate, Thor—you guys are the best boys I could ask for. Nate, thank you for taking Thor when I need writing time and for helping me basically write every single book—and for letting me cry when I'm frustrated over a character NOT listening to me. You're my sanity, my partner and such an amazing friend. I'm so happy that our son has you as an example!

My editor, Amy—I feel like these books have really pushed me; thank you for not letting me settle and for making me a better writer!

Erica—the best agent ever! I always look forward to our talks and I know these last few years have been nonstop.

Thank you for always having my back and being such a wonderful friend. I know that my books are in the best hands—and I'm so thankful to have you in my life!

Lauren Layne, aka wife, don't you EVER lose your phone. I think we text more than anyone else I know—but it's always completely necessary for my sanity—thanks to bae for letting me borrow her, and next time I'm in New York I expect whiskey.

To Jill, my amazing PA/friend/sister/publicist/brain—you do all the things and I'd probably be lost rocking in a corner without you!

Rockstars of Romance—thanks again for another incredible tour and blitz, you guys are always so on top of things. Lisa, you are so fun to work with and I'm so grateful for you!

Liza, Kristin, Jessica, thank you for reading all of the words and not hating them, even when I text you early in the morning and go, *Have you read the chapter yet? Does it suck?*

Angie, Dannae, Heather, mi familia ;) Love you girls so hard!

And all the Rockin' Readers. Guys, seriously, we have the best group on Facebook. It's like family and I love you guys so much! Thank you for always encouraging me and helping me with my projects!

Finally to all the readers, bloggers, and the amazing people who allow me to do what I love. Thank you for reading. You have no idea how much I appreciate your loyalty!

If you want to be kept in the loop with all of my releases, text MAFIA to 66866 and you'll automatically be signed up for my newsletter!

THE

Playboy

BACHELOR

PROLOGUE

Phoenix, Arizona
Summer 2006

Margot tried not to stare at him.

Then again, so did every other girl at the country club.

With a smug smile, she sat back into her deck chair while a loud splash sounded to her right. At least twenty people were at the barbecue, laughing, eating, swimming.

And then there was Margot.

Reading.

She peeked over the edge of her book one more time.

At least she promised herself it would only be one more time.

Her best friend loved the attention.

She hated it.

Maybe that was why they worked?

She read, and Bentley basically charmed the world with his smile and that small dimple near the right side of his mouth.

Her stomach fluttered.

She really needed to stop thinking about his smile, because that almost always meant she'd start thinking about his perfect lean physique and perfect hair.

Everyone was under his spell—herself included, which just made it that much worse.

They were friends.

Best friends.

Nothing more.

"Are you even reading that?" Brant said as he plopped down next to her. Bentley's twin was equally attractive, but for some reason it was always easier for her to talk to him. Maybe because he never made her feel like there could be something more.

His stares never lingered like Bentley's.

Ugh. Maybe she'd been reading into things too much lately.

"I'm totally reading." She swallowed the lie and stole another glance at Bentley.

His deep laughter rang out and then his searching eyes found hers, locked on to her with an intensity that had her heart pounding and her stomach in her throat.

"You should tell him," Brant said under his breath, as Bentley made his way over to them.

She feigned ignorance. "Tell him what?"

"That you're in love with him."

"I'm not."

"Are too."

"Brant—"

"—Good luck!" He winked, gave her a playful pat on the head, and sauntered off in the direction of his brother. They did a weird head-nod thing, which looked way cooler than it should have, before Bentley finally stopped in front of her.

She cleared her throat and pretended to be reading her novel—the exact same page she'd been on since the minute Bentley Wellington had walked outside with all the arrogance in the world. He wore his confidence well.

Just breathe.
Breathe, stupid!
In through your nose.
Out through your mouth.

He was her best friend, for crying out loud! She knew how to have a normal human conversation with him without passing out.

Why then did it suddenly feel different?

Charged?

Yup, her romance novels really were starting to alter her sense of reality.

"Hey, Margot."

Lips trembling in a nervous smile, Margot glanced up and managed to squeak out, "Hey, there."

Hey? There?

She inwardly groaned while Bentley chuckled low in his throat and pulled up a chair next to her.

Around them, the annual Fourth of July barbecue for the country club both of their families belonged to continued as though her world hadn't just been tilted on its axis by his proximity.

The barbecue was a forced tradition that had gotten worse over the years, mainly because everyone around her seemed to be growing into their bodies, the girls with the beautiful, bouncing blond hair and perfectly toned arms and curved hips. The boys with their sensual lips, six-packs, and muscular arms.

And then there was Margot.

As if to prove a point, a piece of fire engine–red hair worked itself free of her bun and tumbled across her shoulder.

Bentley's eyes locked on the piece of hair, and before she could tuck it behind her ear, he reached out and rubbed it between his fingers.

"I love your hair," he whispered.

Margot's mouth gaped open as a searing heat surged through her and finally settled on her cheeks. "It's my conditioner."

Kill me now. My conditioner? Really?

Bentley smirked then dropped his hand. "Another romance novel? You've been devouring these things like chocolate lately." He leaned in. "Is this your cry for help? Do you need a little romance in your life?"

It was hard not to focus on the shaking in her hands or the fact that the only person she wanted romance from was staring at her the way she'd always dreamed. "Sometimes fantasy is better than reality."

"You sure about that?" he fired back, scooting closer to her until their thighs touched.

"You tell me."

His blue eyes lit up with surprise before suddenly focusing on something behind her.

Within seconds, she knew why.

"Jennifer." Bentley smiled and his slow, appreciative perusal wasn't lost on Margot as he finally stood and held out his hand. "How's your summer?"

"Horrible. My mom's a bitch and I'm bored." Jennifer stomped her heel into the ground and then glanced at Margot. "Oh, hi, Marg."

Marg. She hated that nickname.

"Hey, Jenn—"

"Ugh, did you know that I'm grounded after last night?" She smacked Bentley on the chest with her purse. "I hope it was worth it."

Rejection slammed into Margot so swift, so hard, that breathing was almost impossible.

Last night?

He'd been with Jennifer last night and now he was hitting on Margot?

Bentley stiffened next to Margot and then gave a casual shrug as he stood and snaked an arm around Jennifer's shoulders. "I'll be more careful next time."

Next time.

As in: There was going to be a next time.

As in: Whatever had just taken place between them was nothing but another stolen moment where Margot's hopes were crushed beneath Bentley's expensive shoes.

Tears burned.

Margot refused to let them fall.

"I'll see you later, Red." Bentley winked at Margot. "We're still on for later, right? Your house or mine?"

Huh? They hadn't made plans.

And by the look of it, Jennifer was pissed.

Straightening a bit, Margot shrugged and said, "How about we go to yours this time?"

Last weekend they'd spent two nights in a row watching a horror movie marathon—probably not the kind of marathon that Jennifer and Bentley had participated in, but Jennifer didn't need to know the details. Right?

"Cool, see ya!"

She sighed longingly after Bentley and Jennifer.

Her book was long forgotten.

"So not a complete crash and burn, I take it?" Brant's voice scared the crap out of her, and she nearly toppled out of her lounge chair. "I mean, you're smiling way too big for it to be fake." Brant made his way around the chair and sat again, crossing his arms.

"No, in fact we're hanging out later."

Brant's smile fell. "Just be careful."

"Careful? He's your brother and my best friend. Trust me, I know him."

"Not everything, though." There was an edge of warning to Brant's voice. "Just...be careful, that's all I'm asking."

"Yeah, thanks, Dad. I'll get right on that."

Brant pressed a hand to his chest. "Ouch."

They fell into fits of laughter as Margot's grandmother's voice rang out.

"Margot!" her grandmother yelled from the door. "Margot!" She sounded frantic. "Margot!"

Grandma almost teetered over into the pool as she made her way toward Margot and Brant. They shared a look before rushing to her side.

"What happened?" Margot asked.

Grandmother exhaled and then frowned.

"Grandma, what's wrong?"

Her grandmother tugged at her pearl necklace and shook her head as she leaned heavily on Brant. "I need you to go retrieve your parents." She handed Margot the keys to her brand-new Mercedes. "And don't you worry a bit about me, I twisted my ankle. There was a hole."

That explained the hobbling. If there was a hole, Grandma would find it.

Or a mailbox.

Or a telephone pole.

Or anything that resembled danger to her person. Her grandmother refused to wear the glasses she desperately needed; it was as simple as that.

"Okay." Margot nodded. It wasn't like she was doing anything important other than lusting after a boy whose only fault was that he was too good-looking for words—and liked blondes.

"I got her." Brant smoothly led Grandma to a chair. "So, Mrs. McCleery, where was the hole?"

Margot suppressed a smile. Brant, like Bentley, could charm anything with a pulse. Her grandmother was probably loving the attention.

She tucked the book back in her purse and slowly made her way to the parking lot.

It took ten minutes to get downtown, where her parents were already waiting outside their office building. They had been called away from the club to address an emergency at the office, and since Nadine Titus, an old family friend, was headed that way, she'd offered them a ride.

"Hey, guys." Margot unlocked the doors as her parents piled in the back. "Everything okay?"

Her mom looked furious, her dad calm.

"Fine," they said in unison.

Margot rolled her eyes. She loved her parents, she really did, but they rarely shared the burden of their work with her. They wanted her to be a regular teenager.

Too bad that ship had sailed long ago. She was a red-headed book nerd who had only the Wellington twins as best friends and wouldn't know what to do in a social situation if they weren't with her, thus the book she'd brought today.

She pulled out onto the road and glanced in the rearview mirror at her parents as they held hands and shared a kiss. Her mom looked up, and horror registered in her eyes as she screamed, "Margot! Watch out!"

Everything went black.

CHAPTER ONE

Present Day

Bentley groaned as the woman, whose name he'd already forgotten a few hours ago, spread her toned thighs over his body and rode him. The scent of her vanilla lotion clung to the air as he slid his hands up and down her hips.

She was just another nameless face.

Another willing female in a long list of women who wanted to have a piece of the notorious playboy Bentley Wellington.

Because that was all he was to her—all he was to anyone. And most of the time? He was completely okay with it—he had to be. A familiar tightening threatened to choke him. He feigned boredom until he could get the unwanted emotion under control.

And covered his fake yawn with his hand as she started to increase her speed, her breath coming out in small, fake pants.

With a smug-as-hell smirk, he winked. "That the best you can do, Sarah?"

"It's Christine!" She smacked his chest and panted as she

rode him harder, her skin slapping against his in a way that should have felt good but instead irritated the hell out of him. "You're a complete asshole!"

He gripped her hips and quickened her movements with deep thrusts. "But..." Another punishing thrust. "I'm a handsome asshole." Her lips parted on a moan. "Right?"

"The last thing you need," she said in a breathy whisper, "is for me to stroke your ego."

"Aw." He made a face and pulled free from her body. Bored. Angry that she was speaking. And maybe a little bit sick of himself if he was being completely honest. "Play fair. I'm always in the mood for a good stroking and a willing hand."

Her bright blue eyes flashed before she rolled off his sweaty body and out of the bed. "I'm leaving."

"That was fun," he called after her. "We should do it again sometime."

She screamed in fury, and two minutes later he heard the door slam.

Frowning, he sat up on his elbows. Whatever. Where one left, there were at least a hundred waiting in line for a glimpse or even just one small taste of what he had to offer.

His sexual appetite was huge—and legendary. His twin, Brant, was better at relationships—or at least he had been until the incident that had pushed him into a drunken state that even Bentley hadn't been able to pull him out of.

But unlike his twin, Bentley hated anything that sounded long-term. Besides, the last real relationship he'd had hadn't ended well.

He gulped as a memory of red hair flashed in his line of vision. Sometimes it felt like she was still sitting next to him, teasing him, touching him.

It didn't matter anymore.

What was done was done.

Besides, she was a long-term girl.

Long.

Term.

Like a contract he would never be able to get out of. And the last thing he needed was to allow someone in—someone who would want to share all his burdens or, worse, ask questions.

The door opened again and clicked shut.

"Back for more?" He chuckled and pulled the covers over his naked body, waiting for whatever her name was to come back in and finish the job she'd started. Damn it, he could have sworn her name really was Sarah.

He snapped his fingers. No, no, Sarah was the night before. Amazing mouth. Jet-black hair.

He hardened again just thinking about how she'd used her long silky hair to—

A shadowy figure stomped toward his bedside with clenched teeth and a furious look in his eyes. "Shouldn't you be on your way?"

"My way?" Bentley repeated, fisting the sheets with his hands. His grandfather was a giant pain in the ass. "To hell?" Another nonchalant shrug, because that was what his grandfather was used to. The youngest twin by a few seconds, the one who would never amount to anything—not for lack of trying.

"Don't be a jackass." His grandfather's mouth twisted into a disapproving frown.

"Prudence McCleery spent ten thousand dollars for your services." Grandfather's voice sounded calm, but he was still clenching his fists and his cheeks flashed red. "Today is the day you were supposed to arrive at their country estate and make good on your promise."

"Right." Bentley hadn't forgotten. How could he, when he'd been nearly scarred for life two weeks ago as every rich and single woman in the greater Phoenix area had bid on him? In an effort to help save his lovesick brother and the woman he loved, he'd agreed to participate in the bachelor auction their grandfather was convinced would save the face of the family business. The stockholders had needed a reason to need the Wellingtons, and Bentley and his brothers had given them a damned good one.

They were the new face of Wellington, Inc., and people loved them for it. Besides, Bentley's participation had helped his image—which in turn made his grandfather momentarily happy.

Momentarily being the key word.

He'd assumed some bored, rich trophy wife would take him home, have her way with him, then slap him on the ass and send him on his way.

Instead, a woman with bright green eyes and equally bright white hair had lifted her paddle—and purchased him for a weekend getaway.

She'd looked familiar.

And then her name was called.

A name that caused a slow burn to invade his body as he tried to suppress every single ounce of the guilt and longing that he'd fought to keep locked away all these years.

She'd bid on him for her granddaughter.

And suddenly, the past, his past, became the present as images of a girl with red hair burned his vision.

And continued to do so for fourteen days straight.

Bentley hadn't had a choice—for the first time since they were children, his brother Brock was smiling, laughing, and disgustingly in love.

It had been worth it.

It was *still* worth it.

And it was only a weekend.

"I tried." Grandfather's shoulders slumped. "I tried to do right by you boys. Maybe, maybe I was just too focused on Brock to realize how horrible you and your brother have turned out."

"Thanks?" Bentley offered with a grimace. It wasn't like he didn't work for what he had. He just didn't have to work very hard—a fifty-million-dollar trust fund had a way of doing that to a man.

After all, people worked to make money.

They worked for success.

And he already had all of those things.

A nagging voice shattered his confidence, the same voice that reminded him how he used to be a man who had dreams—an actual purpose—direction.

And that same voice reminded him that his life was a boring, useless cycle of using women and hiding who he really was from the world.

Because the last time he had tried to be himself...

Hell, the last time he'd actually *felt* like himself, had trusted someone else, he'd put all of his eggs into one giant basket.

His world had shattered.

It wasn't worth it.

It would never be worth it.

Grandfather glared at him. "The VP of marketing stepped down this morning," he said hesitantly. "I want to hire within."

Bentley froze; his heart hammered against his chest. On the outside, he was calm, rational, thoughtful, but on the inside, he was freaking the hell out. "Oh?"

He'd spent the better part of his teen years trying to impress his grandfather, not to mention his time at college, and once that crashed and burned he'd simply given up.

"Yes." Grandfather leveled a perceptive stare at Bentley, interrupting his dark thoughts. "I don't suppose that would be something you'd be interested in? Although if you are, you'll have to take 'fucking' off your list of hobbies in order for me to actually process your résumé."

Bentley smirked. He'd been pissed when he'd filled out his résumé, mainly because he didn't think it was necessary for someone who owned part of the company to have to fill one out in the first place. "It was a joke."

Grandfather narrowed his eyes. "It wasn't funny, nor was it professional."

"Brant thought it was funny."

"Your brother doesn't count." Grandfather's mouth twitched like he wanted to smile but thought better of it. "So... what do you say?"

"Are you hinting that you'll give me an actual position within Wellington, Inc.?"

With a heavy sigh, Grandfather nodded once. "The board, of course, won't like the idea."

"They can go to hell." Bentley clenched his teeth. The board never liked any of their ideas. Mainly Bentley's.

"It might help your image"—Grandfather's body was rigid as he spoke—"to be seen doing charity work. The board isn't impressed with your floozies."

Bentley stiffened.

Because he knew exactly what type of charity his grandfather was referring to and her name started with an *M*.

Hell. It would do more than help. But he had a life in Phoenix. One that on most days, he actually enjoyed, or at least liked.

Seeing her.

Being with her again.

It brought everything back to the surface. Everything he'd fought like hell to keep buried in the past.

"Or don't make good on your promise with the auction and keep sleeping with every woman who will spread her legs for you in hopes you'll get them pregnant and pay child support."

Low blow.

"I'll go." Bentley sighed. It wasn't like he had a choice, not if he wanted the job, not if he wanted more purpose outside of what he already did for the company, which was basically just smile for pictures when they had charity events and business dinners.

His grandfather was finally, finally, giving him a chance to prove himself, and he wasn't going to fail.

He'd always wanted more.

And now he was getting it.

Three days?

A weekend?

He could do anything for a weekend. And then the job would be his and he'd leave.

A small, annoying voice reminded him that was what he had done before.

He'd left.

But he'd had his reasons.

Just like he had his reasons now.

"Of course you will." Grandfather straightened. "You're going to be late."

"Does it matter?" Bentley snorted. He was already irrationally angry, and directing the anger at his grandfather when really he should have been directing it at himself.

"Punctuality always matters." Grandfather stood. His

thick gray hair was swirled into one sweeping curl that fell across his forehead. Bentley and Brant might be playboys, but his grandfather had an Instagram page dedicated to that very curl. And he was pushing eighty-eight.

Grandfather lifted a brow. "Well, boy? Aren't you going to pack?"

Bentley clenched his teeth until it felt like they were going to crack. "I'm naked."

"Ain't nothing I haven't had the great displeasure of seeing before." He moved to the doorway. "Now get your shit together before I cut you off and give your trust fund to your brothers and hire Brant for the VP position."

"You wouldn't." The words rushed out before he could stop them.

"I would."

"You hate me."

"I love you." Grandfather sobered. "You're twenty-seven, Bentley. Time to stop playing around and actually take responsibility for your actions, starting with Prudence McCleery's granddaughter. All you've got to do is give the girl a weekend that'll put a smile on her face. It's not like she's a stranger to you anyway."

Hah.

Well, she was now.

Ever since the day he walked out of her life.

"Margot," Bentley whispered without thinking.

"What was that?" Grandfather cupped his ear.

"Nothing." A vision of luscious red hair that went on for days, bright green eyes, and freckles burned before him. At sixteen she'd been breathtaking but quiet, too shy for someone like Bentley.

Hell, she'd been too good for him.

Too nice.

Too proper.

Too perfect.

And now...too sad.

He gulped. How the hell was he supposed to cheer up a woman who'd shut herself away from the world?

CHAPTER TWO

His eyes whispered a promise his words had failed to convey," Margot repeated out loud as the sound of her fingernails tapping against the keys of her computer filled the room. "'*I love you*,' *he declared, tucking his beaver hat under his arm as he took a step toward her waiting invitation.*"

She hesitated and contemplated the computer screen. *I love you*? Was that it?

She had exactly forty-seven chapters of historical crap.

Crap she had thirty days to fix if she had any hope of meeting her deadline.

She glared at her computer and tried again. The scene was pivotal; it had to be perfect, it needed to be believable.

Then again, what was believable about a rich, rakish duke falling for one of his scullery maids only to discover she was really part of the ton? Even if she came from a good family, it would still be frowned upon. The story wasn't historically accurate, and it bothered her, but it was romantic, and that was why she'd decided to write it.

It was a horrible idea.

But that was what sold.

Rakes and Rogues.

And the poor, sad wallflowers who somehow magically became the object of their affection.

It was complete BS.

She'd been that wallflower.

She *was* that wallflower.

And nothing, not one thing, had set her apart from the other girls. Men might say they wanted character, but they wanted something different. They claimed they wanted the girl next door, child-bearing hips, whatever. Their actions, however, said it all.

Skinny.

Botoxed.

Implanted.

Airheads.

Margot slammed her hands against the keyboard and stood in a huff.

It was *his* fault.

Because he was late.

Not that she wanted to see him anyway.

She could live an entire lifetime without seeing him and be perfectly happy.

Liar.

She tried to focus on the words she'd written, but her mind had other plans. She didn't want to remember that day. She never thought about it. She didn't allow herself to go there. Except now, now, it was all she could think of.

"Your parents didn't make it." Grandma clenched Margot's hands tightly. *"But you have me. You'll always have me."*

And Bentley.

Her best friend.

But he never came.

She'd lost three people that day.

And so many pieces of her heart, it was a miracle she was able to survive surgery.

Her grandmother meant well, most of the time. Margot didn't blame her for being overprotective and worried. In a moment of complete insanity, her grandmother, God bless her, had bid on one of the country's most notorious playboys in an auction set up for cancer research.

Unfortunately, her grandmother had won.

Margot still remembered the phone call from that night.

"I've landed you a man!" her grandmother yelled loud enough for half the country to hear. *"Paid a pretty penny for him, too! Oh, muffin, you'll love him, he's strong, and—"*

"You bought—" Margot pressed her fingertips against her temple *"—a man?"*

"He was spendy, too." Grandmother slurred her words a bit. *"Cost at least half of what I was willing to spend, though."*

"Half?"

"Ten thousand dollars is a bargain!"

Margot choked.

Grandmother laughed.

"Are you drunk?"

"I had the whiskeys, yes." Her grandmother sighed happily. *"Such a delicious burn. Did you know Titus Enterprises just bought out Honey Whiskey, Inc.? Nadine's such a dear, she even brought me a few bottles. Has her sights set on McCleery Whiskey, too, but we'll cross that bridge when we get there."*

"Grand—"

"You know him! This man."

"The man you paid ten grand for? That man?"

"Yes. Your old friend."

Oh no, that was even worse. She knew the man her grand-mother had bought for her?

"Thanks, but I don't need you to buy me a man. I can find my own man," Margot said through clenched teeth.

"How's that working out for you, love?"

"I'm busy!" she snapped.

"You're sad."

"I'm—" Margot flexed the toes of her left leg and tried not to stare at the right. *"I'm not sad."* How many times had she said it before? She wasn't sad! She was successful! *"I'm fine. I have my books. I have my house. I have my work—"*

"You have wild tomcats, too, and cats are a bad omen."

"How much whiskey did you say you had again?"

"Whiskeys. Plural," Grandmother corrected with a hic-cup. *"Now, he's going to report to the estate in two weeks. He'll arrive at nine in the morning, I told him to be punctual. And you're to give him the downstairs blue room during his stay."*

"His stay?" Margot yelled. *"He's not staying any-where!"*

"Of course he is," Grandma said in soothing albeit slurred tones. *"It's part of the package. Hah, not his pack-age, but the package. I bought you a Wellington!"*

Margot gasped.

"I know! A full weekend! Think of the possibilities!"

"Did you say Wellington?"

Please God, she thought, let it be Brant. He always had a teasing smile for her. Besides, Brant didn't tempt her; he didn't promise to be there and then abandon her during the darkest moments of her life. At least let it be Brock. Brock, the serious one. No, it wouldn't be Brock, didn't he just get married?

"Bentley Wellington!" her grandmother shouted with glee. *"Lovely man. When he keeps it in his pants, which, let's hope for the sake of my great-grandchildren he doesn't—"*

Tears burned the back of Margot's eyes as she blinked away the blurry vision of a boy she'd always wanted.

And never had.

He was a man now.

Featured in Forbes, *among other magazines.*

He dated supermodels, celebrities, gorgeous women.

Her ex–best friend.

The one who didn't even visit her in the hospital.

The one who pulled her out of her shell in high school only to drop her the minute she wasn't pretty anymore.

She was exactly the type of girl men like Bentley Wellington turned their noses up at.

She glanced down at her right leg. The amputation had been done right below her knee, so while her thigh looked normal, the prosthetic clearly marked her as damaged goods.

"Oh, must go, I'll fill you in later on the more pertinent details." Her grandmother hung up before Margot could protest.

Two weeks later she still hadn't figured it out. Why would Bentley agree to be auctioned off? It made no logical sense. He was either bored, stupid, or doing it for good PR. God knew he needed it, since he'd allegedly been having an affair with a senator's wife; not that she was the first—or the last— of his conquests. The boy she'd known had clearly grown up to be a sex addict.

Though he'd already been well on his way to charming every single female in the city when their friendship had ended.

She'd called.

She'd waited.

She'd made numerous excuses.

And still. Nothing.

Which just proved the point. Bentley was friends with the beautiful, the pretty, the people that made him look good.

It was probably why Brant was always so hesitant about her relationship with his brother. He knew that Bentley only wanted something from her, just like he only wanted something from every girl he hung out with.

Sex.

A good time.

She groaned into her hands.

And now she was going to be stuck with him. For an entire weekend!

Margot shook her head at the memory of Bentley's smile and wandered over to the window. A sense of dread filled her as a red sports car sped up her driveway, scaring the crap out of every small creature in its way and kicking up enough dust to make the road nearly impossible to see.

Bentley Wellington had arrived.

CHAPTER THREE

He'd driven like hell to get to the damn mansion in time.

But he was *still* late.

And if there was one thing he remembered about Margot, the woman loved rules, and shirts tucked in, polite smiles, and sweet good-byes.

Etiquette.

The woman loved etiquette.

And God, he'd loved being the guy to throw her off her perfect little path. Not a day had gone by where he didn't tease her until they both laughed so hard they cried.

He was always tugging that tight bun loose and dipping his hands into her thick, luscious red hair.

Bentley shuddered as he finally allowed a few memories out, one, two, maybe three and then they were going back on lockdown.

She wasn't his to want.

Not then.

Not now.

"What are you doing?" Margot covered a yawn with her

free hand while Bentley toyed with her left hand, drawing small circles across her palm.

"Looking at your lifeline."

"Is it long?" She nearly hit his head when she peered over their clasped hands. "What? Why are you looking at me like that?"

Because I could love you, *he thought.*

Because at eighteen you make me think I could do anything if you smiled at me like that.

He knew saying those things would freak her out, so he settled for: "Because you look way too excited over the fact that I'm touching you."

She rolled her eyes and shoved him away, but not before a pretty blush stained her cheeks.

His fingers strained to touch those cheeks.

Instead he grabbed the remote, scooted away, and pressed Play. "All right, you ready for the movie?"

It was one of the last times they were together.

Before the accident.

Before he disappeared from her life.

And she from his.

All he knew about her now was that she wrote books and kept to herself, which made sense. He'd teased her relentlessly about her reading, and now she had a very successful career as a writer. It made sense.

It wasn't hard to picture prim and proper Margot with a tight librarian bun sitting behind a computer typing out romantic scenes. She'd always been a romantic, and a romance novel addict.

He rang the doorbell, tugged off his black Prada sunglasses, and tapped them impatiently against his leg.

When she didn't come to the door, he double-checked the address his grandfather had texted him.

It was the right house.

Maybe he'd luck out and she'd answer the door, tell him to go to hell, and kick him to the curb.

Finally, the door creaked open, revealing just how dark the inside of the house was.

A feminine hand with red fingernail polish slid elegantly across the door frame, and then the woman attached to that oddly pretty hand appeared.

And Bentley Wellington, certified playboy, knew he had been completely and royally screwed by lying down on the altar of brotherhood and sacrificing himself in order for Brock to be happy.

He was screwed.

Sad?

She looked anything but *sad*.

She looked...

Angry.

Spirited.

He gulped and then narrowed his eyes. "I think I have the wrong house."

"Do you?" she asked in a husky voice that wreaked havoc on certain parts of his anatomy.

Bentley grinned. Maybe this wouldn't be so bad after all.

And then, without another word, she slammed the door in his face.

"Hell." He should have expected that.

He knocked again.

Once.

Twice.

Then resorted to pounding.

"Damn it, open the door, Red!"

With a whoosh the door opened wide, revealing her voluptuous curvy body in all its glory.

He swallowed and tried to find words. After all, he was good with words, almost as good as he was with his hands.

"I don't want you here," she in that husky sexpot voice. "And I'm one hundred percent sure you're here because you have no choice. So this is how this is going to work." She shoved a key in his hand, the metal digging into his palm. "You can come and go as you please, lie out by the pool, eat my food, watch TV, and do whatever bored millionaires do—and when this whole disaster is over with, we'll go our separate ways. I'll tell my grandmother I had the time of my life, and you'll do the same and continue sleeping your way through the greater Phoenix area and—" she sighed, finally sucking in a breath "—and, well, I think that's it."

He opened his mouth to speak when she turned back on her heel and called over her shoulder. "By the way, you're late."

"About that—"

"Your room is that way. It's the one on the left, can't miss it. It's blue." She said the word slowly like he had a learning disability then pointed to the right of the stairs. "I'm not cooking for you."

"Red—"

Her hips swayed as she limped up the stairs, and his gut clenched as his eyes fell to her legs. Her right leg seemed almost stiff.

Frowning, he tried to recall details from the accident that had taken her parents' lives. He'd heard she'd shattered most of the bones below her right knee and her parents were killed instantly, but beyond that, he'd been too engrossed in his own life, his own demons, to get all the grisly details of that day.

Demons that flared to life the minute her parents lost theirs.

If he was being completely honest—they'd always been there, but they'd hidden in the shadows until Margot's accident and then they pounced, attacked, ripped him to shreds, and left him a bloody mess.

She wasn't the only one hurting.

But he knew he couldn't compare their pain.

And at the time, he'd taken the only option given to him.

By the time he was healthy again, he'd looked for her, only to find out she'd moved out of the city.

And it was easier.

Ignoring her.

Ignoring the past.

Ignoring his mistakes.

So he did what he did best, what he did when he needed a distraction, when he wanted to ignore the pain—he fucked any girl that batted an eye in his direction and forced himself to forget just how much Margot had inched herself into his life.

He fucked to forget.

And as he gazed into her emerald green eyes, he finally realized: You couldn't forget a woman like Margot.

No matter how hard you tried.

The skin on her neck burned bright red under his perusal.

He grinned.

Some things...never changed.

"I hate it when people are late," she said more to herself than anything and then flashed him a glare that would send most men running. "Don't stare."

"I was just—"

"It isn't polite." He could have sworn her heard her mutter *jackass* under her breath.

"So I'll just see you at lunch?" he called after her quickly disappearing form. She hobbled a bit, but she still managed to take the stairs pretty fast.

Was she still injured from the accident? Even after all this time?

"I eat in my room." she said once she reached the top of the stairs. Then she disappeared from sight.

"What the hell just happened?" Bentley muttered, key in hand, sanity left somewhere between the door and the stairway, and pride a bit wounded that she hadn't once given him the impression that she cared he was here after all these years.

Everyone cared.

They always said they didn't care.

They lied.

They did.

They always did.

He represented money, power, sex, although he knew it was the sex part that got him the most attention.

Bentley gazed up at the tall spiral staircase and waited for any sort of sound that indicated she was coming back.

He waited for a good five minutes then begrudgingly went back to his car to grab his things. Damn, the house was monstrous for just one person. He gazed up and smirked when he saw a curtain fall, hiding the woman who had just been spying on him from a second-floor window.

Just like he thought.

They *always* cared.

CHAPTER FOUR

It wasn't fair.

It wasn't right.

That he should be so handsome. But wasn't that just the thing she wrote about on a daily basis? The guy who made the girl's heart slam against her chest in an unnatural cadence. Her pulse hummed, and yes, she did in fact feel the intense need to flex every muscle in her body in order to keep herself from touching him to make sure he was real.

His hair alone.

God, his hair.

Why?

Why would God bless a man with hair that thick? That wavy and tantalizing? Shots of caramel mixed in with the nearly black tresses, falling in a haphazard fashion over his forehead. The dimple was deeper; his blue eyes were even clearer and more mesmerizing than she'd remembered.

And his body?

She shuddered and took a steadying breath, in and out, in and out. He was just a man. With broad shoulders, and full lips. His mocking smile burned. How dare he stomp in here like he owned the place? And stare!

His stare.

Her cheeks burned. She'd always dreamed of the way his hypnotic eyes looked at her—made her want things she had no business wanting.

The accident had stolen so much more than her parents.

It had stolen her dream of ever being with someone who was able to look at her like she was still her. Still a desirable woman.

Whole.

Instead, men treated her like she was broken, fragile, disabled.

Just thinking about it made her want to punch something. Once she had looked forward to seeing Bentley's smile. And now? Now she just wanted him to go away.

His gaze had lingered on her leg; she'd felt it. And she'd seen it. Her stomach did flip-flops, and not the good kind.

She put her hands on her hips. Well, he'd better know how to cook or he was going to starve to death.

Not that she cared.

At all.

He could die for all she cared.

A fleeting wave of guilt washed over her. Okay, maybe that was too far, but still. She worried her lower lip and glanced out the window only to see the man himself glance up at her with a knowing wicked grin.

With a gasp, Margot dropped the heavy gold curtain and stumbled backward. Hands shaking, she allowed herself a few moments to organize her jumbled thoughts and the irritating way they all pointed toward the man who would be living with her for the next few days.

His smile was the same.

Okay, that was a lie. The smile resembled the boy she once knew, but all traces of that boyish charm were gone, replaced with this red-hot manly vibe that she barely recognized.

Not that she wanted to even acknowledge the way he made her feel.

He was still a horrible person.

And an even worse friend.

He reminded her of everything she tried to keep in the past: the accident, her pain, the feel of the uncomfortable hospital bed, and the sheets that scratched against her skin.

He had walked out of her life years ago.

Why now? Why would her grandmother do this to her now?

What type of auction sold a grown man as a companion for a weekend?

And a millionaire on top of it? Didn't he have more important things to do?

He was either really charitable, or he'd done something so horrible that he needed to get back into his grandfather's good graces. Yeah, her money was on the latter.

Huffing out an exhale, she marched over to her desk and pulled out the chair. She had a deadline to make.

But as she stared at the cursor blinking on the blank screen before her, all she could think about were Bentley's lips, the way they curved into that deliciously sinful smile, spreading across a row of perfect—and more than likely, capped—teeth.

Because, really, who had teeth like that?

She was never going to finish this book if her thoughts kept straying toward Bentley Wellington's teeth.

"Focus," she scolded herself. "You're a grown woman. You can—"

A knock sounded at her door.

Nobody *ever* knocked on her door.

Ever.

Even her grandmother knew not to disturb her if the door was closed. That was why they invented texting! Anger surged through her. He'd been here, what? Five minutes? And already he was ruining everything that kept her sane. Peace and quiet, the hum of her computer. She held in her anger, digging her fingernails into the desk, and waited.

He knocked again—this time louder.

"Go away," she barked, her heart in her throat.

"No," came his quick reply.

Rolling her eyes, she stood and winced with pain as she adjusted her prosthetic, then marched over to the door and jerked it open. Bentley breezed past her like he owned the place. And anger was quickly replaced by fear; but, really, weren't they, a lot of times, the same thing? "What do you think you're doing?"

"Oh, I thought you remembered." He ran a hand over the back of her favorite chair, his fingertips drumming across the green leather before he called over his shoulder, "I'm an explorer at heart."

How could she forget?

More like he wasn't used to hearing the word *no* and thought she was just playing hard to get. Besides, this wasn't one of her romance novels, right? Where the drop-dead sexy guy realizes what he lost and accepts the broken woman for who she is. Her heart deflated a bit, sadness twisting into unjust anger.

Directed at the only person available.

Him.

"Explore," she replied, fighting to keep from yelling at him, "elsewhere."

His lips twitched; his eyes raked over her as though he could see every inch of skin beneath her clothes. It would have worked. Maybe if she was a different person. Whole. It would make her feel good, like a woman.

Shoving the longing she felt away, she gritted her teeth. "Stop that."

In two strides, he was at the window tugging open the dark curtains, exposing her body to more sunlight than she'd been exposed to in years. "There, that's better."

Panic gripped her as she stomped over to the curtains and tugged the fabric as tight as she could, once again blanketing the room in blessed darkness. Sunlight meant that he'd be able to see her missing leg that much more, and it was hard enough having that reminder between them. Her pain. Her loss.

His abandonment.

"Leave."

He looked down and frowned. The light had been enough for him to see her limp up close and personal. It had hurt like hell to walk up the stairs without as much as a grimace and now, now his eyes were trained on her leg like he was trying to put the pieces together and found they didn't fit. "What's wrong with your—"

"I said get out!" She shoved his rock-hard chest as panic swelled in her body. What type of sick person pretended not to know about her injury? Bentley Wellington, that was who. He damn well knew what happened. "Now!"

"Red—" His eyes widened in confusion.

"Never come into my room again," she said in a hoarse whisper as she fought to keep herself from bursting into tears. People always had the same reaction. What happened? Does it hurt? Will it ever get better?

A memory of her mom's face flashed, causing her to

stutter-step against Bentley. He caught her by the elbows, his eyes full of pity.

God, she hated pity.

Besides, he was a whole lot of years too late to be giving her such a concerned look.

She'd rather he look at her with disgust than pity. She'd had enough pity to last a lifetime.

Margot jerked away and lifted her chin. "Please, just go."

Sighing, he released her and quietly left the room, clicking the door shut behind him. Her body trembled for a few seconds after he'd left. Maybe because she hadn't been touched by a man in—a very long time. Or maybe because he was exactly how she remembered: hard in all the right places, gorgeous, unavailable, and spoiled.

Margot marched over to the window to make sure the drapes were pulled and then examined the room. It was dark again. It was safe. It was home.

She needed to feel safe. Safe in the darkness. Safe from the stares and whispers, and most of all, safe from the only guy who had ever seen past the timid, shy girl she used to be.

"Hey." The beautiful boy held out his hand. "Are you okay? I saw you fall."

Embarrassment smacked her in the chest, nearly knocking her over onto her butt again as she blinked up at Bentley Wellington.

The Bentley Wellington.

The most popular guy in her high school.

From one of the richest families in the United States.

It was her freshman year, and she'd finally gotten her braces off and grown into her lanky arms and legs. Maybe he had noticed?

The only Wellington boy who ever gave her the time of day was his twin, Brant, but Brant was nice to everyone.

"Yeah." She found her voice and stood with his help. His hand was warm. And strong. "I probably shouldn't...read and walk."

"It's a safety hazard for sure." His grin widened. "What's your name?"

She should have been insulted.

After all, their parents were a part of the same country club, and she'd gone through middle school with him sitting behind her in at least half of her classes.

And he didn't even know her name?

"Margot," she answered, trying to keep the wobble out of her voice. "What's yours?"

His stunned expression was priceless. She bit down on her bottom lip to keep from laughing.

Did she imagine it? Or did Bentley's chest puff out a bit as he took a step closer and said in a low voice, "Bentley Wellington." He tilted his head. "Then again, you already knew that, didn't you?"

"Guilty." Her cheeks heated. "But it was worth it to see your face."

Who was the girl saying all of these things?

Flirting?

"I deserved it," he finally admitted, taking a step back.

"Bentley!" a whiny voice shouted, drawing his attention away from Margot and toward a gorgeous brunette in a short white sundress. "Hurry up!"

"You sure you're okay?" he asked again, his hand reaching out to cup her shoulder like he actually cared, like it mattered to him.

With a jerky nod, Margot managed to give him his answer. Her smile was forced as he slowly pulled away and rejoined the group of friends he'd been walking with.

Once he joined them, laughter rang out, and then a few of the girls glanced back at her and whispered.

She didn't care. She normally did.

But not today.

Because Bentley Wellington had just proved he was more than his good looks and easy smile.

He had a heart.

It was the start of their friendship.

One that gave her confidence and courage to step outside her comfy little shell. Only nobody warned her that the minute you start to finally trust—you risk losing it all.

He'd taught her that lesson.

Never again.

A door slammed downstairs.

Margot jumped a foot and shook the memory from her head as she slowly moved toward the door and pressed her forehead against it.

She was proud of herself for waiting at least another five minutes before allowing the warm sting of tears to fill her eyes and run down her cheek.

CHAPTER FIVE

Well, she was a hell of a delight, now, wasn't she? Her fire-engine hair matched her winning personality, that was for damn sure. Bentley stared at her bedroom door, then retreated down the stairs, angered by her rebuff and mildly intrigued as to why she limped—and why she seemed so upset when he asked a completely innocent question.

Her face had contorted with pain, as if she was still in it. Which was crazy, right?

What type of accident left a woman in pain ten years later?

He wasn't sure if her pain was more emotional than physical, or maybe both. Not that it was his problem if she wanted to live out the rest of her life as if it was already over.

A nagging voice reminded him that he'd abandoned her all those years ago. He'd been her best friend, and he'd just walked away. Something he'd rather not think about, hadn't *let* himself think about, but something that this weekend made impossible to ignore any longer.

She blamed him, probably as much as he blamed himself.

His goal in high school had been to get Margot to smile, that was it. And then suddenly, that one goal morphed into more smiles, more time together, until they were inseparable.

Best friends.

It had never been part of his plan to fall for his best friend, and then, just when he had gained the nerve to tell her—he almost lost her.

And the thought that he could lose her—forever—had caused such crippling anxiety that it had taken his entire family to pull him out of it.

And once he was finally able to function...

...he still couldn't face her.

The thought of her in that hospital room was enough to set off the panic again.

So he ignored her calls.

And when he couldn't take it anymore—there was Jennifer, and then Miranda, and Ashley.

He'd found his cure.

Women and alcohol.

Too bad it never lasted.

And he usually woke up with a hangover and irritation that the woman sleeping next to him wasn't who he wanted—who he imagined when he closed his eyes at night.

His dick gave a hopeful jerk at the picture his mind had just painted. God, he needed a distraction. He wandered through the house and ended up in a state-of-the-art gourmet kitchen. This opened up to a dining room lined with windows that overlooked the expansive grounds.

An inviting pool was nestled near the foot of the hill that the house sat on. Bingo. At least he'd have something to do other than sit on his ass. With an exhale of relief, he turned to go back to the room where he'd placed his bags only to have his phone ring in his pocket.

Grandfather.

Of course, because the man hadn't done enough?

"What?" he barked out.

"Manners, Bentley."

Kill me now.

"What did you need, Grandfather? I was late, as you predicted, and she's a sad, miserable human being, as *I* predicted. Haven't you tortured me enough? Because I've gotta hand it to you, I'm pretty good at finding the positive in any situation, and the only positive I'm coming up with right now is that the house is big enough that I can avoid her."

Grandfather chuckled. "She's not used to people."

"No shit." Bentley snorted.

"Language, Bentley."

Bentley leaned against the countertop and clenched the edge of the granite until his knuckles turned white. "Just get whatever lecture you have stored up in your head over with."

"Eager to be with Margot, are you?"

"Right." He drew out the word. "I can't wait to get off the phone so I can go fuck the red queen upstairs. You read the papers. Do I look desperate? Hell would need to freeze over before I touched someone that..." The first word that came to mind was *broken*, but was that it? Was she broken? Or was she just a cold, hard unforgiving woman who wanted to make the whole world feel whatever pain she was suffering? "Frigid."

A soft gasp caught his attention.

He turned around and tensed as Margot slowly backed away from him with her hands up, maybe in an attempt to block his words, but he knew they'd already done their damage.

"Shit." He shook his head, "Margot, wait, I didn't mean—"

Her eyes were swollen. Had she been crying? "You just stay away from me!" She thrust her finger at him like it was a weapon.

Bentley glared right back at her. "Hold on, Grandfather." He pressed the phone to his chest. "We need to talk."

He tried to meet her eyes, but she shifted her gaze to somewhere over his head. "No. I don't think that's a good idea, in fact none of this is a good idea. Just...stay away."

Bentley remained silent. Great. He'd walked right into that one. It wasn't like he wanted her company anyway. At least that's what he told himself.

"Promise me!" she said in an urgent tone. "Promise me you'll stay away from me." Her glassy eyes were like a direct punch to the gut. "After all, you're good at that... staying away."

Her sharp words hit their mark, making it hard him to breathe. So he deflected, he did what he'd always done, he turned the tables back on her to keep her from seeing the blood from the gaping wound she'd just torn open. "Is that what you want, Margot?" Bentley immediately recognized the familiar helplessness and anxiety welling up, storming inside him. Clearly, she brought out the worst in him. Still. "For everyone and everything to stay away? To what end? You do realize there's a big badass world out there? With actual people in it? Who have conversations? And don't hole up in their houses with all the blinds closed mourning the loss of something that happened a decade ago?" He knew that firsthand. Isolation only fed the anger. And maybe he was reaching, but what other reason could she possibly have for shutting herself off from the world?

He knew the minute he'd pushed her too far. Her face went ashen white, and then she charged toward him. She jammed a finger in his chest and then, as if having a second thought about it not being good enough, slapped him across the face and turned on her heel.

"Do you hit all your guests?" he asked in a mocking tone.

Ignoring him, she limped to the fridge, pulled out a bottle of water, and walked past him again.

"Red—"

"Don't call me that," she barked and then left the room, but not before getting in the last word. "Leave me the hell alone!"

Well, one thing was clear as hell—she still had that notorious temper when pushed too far. He hated how sexy she was when her eyes flashed and her cheeks pinked.

"So this is going to be really fun," Bentley said to his grandfather once he pulled the phone away from his chest. He rubbed his right cheek and winced at the stinging skin. Where the hell did she learn how to slap so hard?

Grandfather sighed. "She's had a hard life, son."

Bentley sucked in a dark laugh and did a half circle. "You're kidding, right? She lives in a mansion and has enough money to buy a small country. Right, her life is *so* hard. She's not the only one who's lost someone. Now I know why her grandmother had to buy her a companion. Well, she didn't pay enough. No job is worth this."

He braced himself for an argument, but his grandfather merely listened and then said, "Sometimes, we are blinded by our love for people. So blinded that we allow them their justifications and reasons, only realizing too late that by not pushing—we've helped them become a little less human."

"You've just explained the woman perfectly. She's insane. She slapped me. In the face." Bentley sulked toward the stairway.

"Where else would she slap you?"

Visions of her hands all over his body slammed into him in rapid succession.

"That's not the point," he argued, suddenly exhausted. "She needs professional help."

"I'm so glad you agree." Grandfather said in an eerie tone. "I think you're just the man for the job."

"Job?" Why the hell did the word *job* sound like a death sentence coming from his grandfather's mouth?

"Job." His grandfather coughed. "Or, duties."

Oh hell, now his grandfather wanted to pimp him out.

"Be honest." Bentley smirked at his reflection in the oven. "Did you hire me out as a gigolo? No judgments, but you do realize I leave a trail of broken hearts in my wake, right? Every. Single. Time."

"Funny, I imagined most of the women you slept with didn't have hearts. You know, since they're clearly missing a good brain." He chuckled.

Bentley rolled his eyes. "Hilarious."

"I find myself quite funny, yes." Grandfather coughed. "I've decided to up the stakes."

Stakes? What game was his grandfather playing? "Come again?"

"The stakes required to secure your future," Grandfather explained. "Naturally I'll allow you to interview for the new VP position if you stay the weekend."

"Interview? Did you just say *interview*?"

What the hell? "I thought the job was mine!"

"I said the board wanted to hire within and that you'd have to fix that ridiculous résumé, not that the job was yours…at least not yet."

"Yet." Why the hell was his grandfather suddenly interested in his life now? Not years ago when he actually needed him, but now that he was a grown-ass man who didn't need or want the attention.

"There is a manila folder in the top drawer of the guest bedroom downstairs, the one that Margot should have said you could stay in. Open it and complete the tasks. You don't have to complete all of them—think of the tasks like suggestions...*strong* suggestions. Cheer the girl up. Stay a full month, out of the limelight you love so much, out of trouble. A bit of quiet will do you good, and a month with you might just help the girl start living again."

"Pardon my language, but why the fuck should I care about her?" But even as he said the words he knew he didn't mean them. He cared. He'd *always* cared. Too much.

"I thought you wanted the job at Wellington, Inc."

"I'm not sure it's worth it." Liar.

"It comes with a corner office, a signing bonus, and anything else your heart desires...but you have to stay with the girl a month, and Bentley, you have to try."

There was that word again.

Try.

As if he had spent his entire life doing the opposite, when all Bentley felt like he'd been doing since his parents died was try. Try to impress his grandfather, try to keep his brothers happy, try to keep himself happy at the same time. Try not to have a nervous breakdown or an anxiety attack in public.

Try, try, try.

Hell, he hated that word.

"That's it, then?" he asked. "I either leave and take my chances at an interview with a potential board member who hates me, or I stay for thirty days and you hand the job over to me on a silver platter?"

"That's it."

"Easy," he lied. "I can do anything for thirty days."

Anything but charm a girl who hated him, a girl he'd abandoned when she'd needed him the most. Right. He could do anything. But that? That would take a miracle.

"What if she still hates me after the month is up?" Most women fawned all over him—while Margot looked ready to shank him every time he opened his mouth.

"*Still?*" Grandfather was quiet, and then said, "I was under the impression you used to be friends—at least that's what her grandmother says."

Well, hell. "People grow up."

"Do they?" Grandfather asked rhetorically, most likely lifting his eyebrows in that judgmental and arrogant stare that forced a lesser man to crumble.

Bentley sighed. "I just want to know that there aren't any other loopholes. Say I can't make her happy, say she kills me before day thirty; I want to know that on my gravestone you write VP of marketing."

Grandfather let out a hearty laugh. "She's not going to murder you."

Bentley laughed drily. "Well, if she does, give Brant my cars."

Grandfather joined in real laughter. "Bentley, one more thing." He blew his nose. "Son, try not to fall in love with her."

Bentley ended the call with an easy laugh and made his way to the bedroom in search of this mysterious list of tasks.

He trudged over to the one and only dresser in the room and jerked open the top drawer.

As promised, a large manila folder sat in the empty drawer with his name printed across it in large black block letters.

He mumbled a prayer of thanks when there was only one sheet inside, with neat boxes next to each item.

The list was handwritten.

On Titus Enterprises paper.

Fucking. Hell.

Grandfather had called in reinforcements. Nadine Titus, known as one of the most powerful and richest women in the country, had recently joined forces with his grandfather, making both of their companies, Titus Enterprises and Wellington, Inc., basically a monopolizing empire.

She was an eighty-eight-year-old menace who in her spare time liked to play matchmaker.

And because *her* grandsons were all perfectly happily married.

She was a bored, rich menace.

Who was currently dating his grandfather.

Her familiar, feminine handwriting didn't put him at ease, although he was relieved to see only five tasks written out on the paper.

He could probably complete five tasks blindfolded.

Number One: Do not under any circumstances, kiss, seduce, or make advances on Margot. But every day, until she finally opens her door or receives them—try bringing her flowers from the garden. Do not force them on her. Note that accepting the flowers means she keeps them at her desk or in her room. Throwing them at your face, stomping on them, or burning them doesn't count. Once she's accepted the flowers, you are free to kiss her. Only then. Try to do this backward and you may just end up with an injured penis or, worse, none at all!

Margot would *burn* flowers? And maim him? Seriously? His mouth wasn't going anywhere near her. Even if the idea did have merit: her skin, his lips. He shook away the image of her red hair spread out across his bed.

Suggestions.

He had to force himself to remember these were suggestions from an insane eighty-eight-year-old woman and his equally insane grandfather.

The first item wasn't going to be the easiest to accomplish after their third fight of the day, but he knew women in and out. She'd accept the flowers. He just had to accompany them with something she really wanted. In his experience flowers had always been a sort of peace offering, so the suggestion wasn't too far from the mark. Then again, the last time he'd given a girl flowers, it had been based on the assumption that he'd get to see her naked.

The problem was that he had no idea what Margot truly wanted. Did she still like books? Poetry? Swimming? A cold sweat broke out across his brow as he kept reading, his confidence dwindling by the second.

> Number Two: It would be romance suicide if you told her about the list in your hand, as in, she'd probably kill you in your sleep. Remember these are suggestions. Don't tell her you are following a list of silly instructions—it would make her feel like she's just a job, and it would make you look like a paid whore.

Solid word choice.

His gaze fell back to the list.

> This item needs to be handled delicately. Give her a new, meaningful compliment once a day until her

cheeks glow with the knowledge that what you say is true. Unless you own a woman's heart, you will never truly have her. Give her compliments that mean something. You'll know when she finally believes you, because her demeanor will change. If it doesn't—you're an idiot and doing it wrong.

A headache pulsed between Bentley's temples. He'd be more likely to get a black eye than have her believe any of his compliments, because he wasn't stupid—he knew most of his compliments were empty and self-serving.

With a frown, he read on.

Number Three: You cannot force love. Nor can you force a friendship, especially if it's been broken in the past.

Love? What the hell was wrong with these two? The last thing he wanted was for Margot to fall in love with him. Although having Margot's friendship again wasn't a bad idea at all. Damn them.

Try a picnic. Force her to go outside. In the sunshine.

Number Four: Make her laugh. A real laugh. The laugh must bubble up from the soul, and we want there to be tears with this laughter. Laughter, after all, can cure anything.

Number Five: Give her something priceless. We're not talking about diamonds or furs. The gift must have meaning. It must be received willingly, cheerfully.

Thirty days.

You have thirty days to be her friend, her confi-

dant, and everything in between. Regardless of how
things end, you will still get your job.

   This is a binding contract. At the end of the thirty
days the marketing VP position at Wellington, Inc.,
will be hereby granted to Bentley Wellington pro-
vided he completes all five tasks...

Bentley's eyes glazed over at all the legal language until
he scanned the bottom of the page. It had been signed by
both his grandfather and Nadine Titus, in the presence of
Margot's grandmother, Prudence McCleery.

The worst part?

The other witnesses were his brothers, Brock and Brant.

So that's what he got for helping?

"Hell." He slammed the paper against the dresser and ran
his hands through his hair. He was going to murder them.
Would it have killed his twin, his homie in the womb, to
call? Send a text? Drop a note, saying, *Oh, and by the way
you're completely fucked. Have a nice thirty days in hell!*

He'd just seen Brant the night before.

The tight-lipped bastard hadn't said a word. Though he
did look paler than usual. And that was another thing.

If Bentley was here, Brant was in the city alone, which
begged the question: Who the hell was making sure his twin
wasn't out getting drunk and arrested every weekend? Nobody truly knew the extent of Bentley's babysitting, and they
would be in for a rude wake-up call over the course of the
next few weeks.

Bentley made a mental note to text his eldest brother and
fill him in. At least Brant was a creature of habit: same bars,
different women. Easy.

But babysitting Brant and cheering him up was easier
than this.

How the hell was he going to tame the redheaded Beast?

And damn it, he was more than a little bit leery if that made him Beauty in this scenario. Because he knew just as much about romance as he knew about love.

Which was absolutely nothing.

CHAPTER SIX

Later that night, Margot opened her bedroom door and scanned the empty hallway. It was past midnight. Maybe she'd get lucky and Bentley would be drunk off his ass downstairs or sleeping off a hangover. Either option would be fine as long as he stayed the hell away from her.

He hadn't knocked on her door again.

In fact, he'd been deathly silent.

At one point, she even pulled back her curtains to make sure his car was still parked outside.

Unfortunately, a splash of cherry red glistened from below, mocking her. Of course he'd have a sports car, because what type of millionaire womanizer would he be without one?

He was either the easiest houseguest in history or he was planning his attack for later. She ignored the shiver that ran down her spine, just like she ignored the heaviness in her breasts when he'd stared too long at her cleavage earlier that day.

Bentley hadn't ever been the type to just give up, but then

again he hadn't been lazy and unkind back then. How many times had he confided in her that he wanted to change the world? Beneath his gorgeous exterior had been a consistent need to prove himself to everyone—especially his grand-father.

What changed?

And why did she suddenly feel guilty when it was Bent-ley who'd left her? Not the other way around?

Guilt had no business in her life, especially guilt over him. Besides he was literally being paid to be here with her.

She frowned. Well, technically, he wasn't getting paid.

He was doing this for charity.

Yet somehow this whole thing made her feel like the charity.

Just great.

How the hell did a grown man get conned into such a thing? That was the question, because Bentley had never been the type of man you could force into anything.

Clearly, she had hit a new low in her life if her grand-mother was paying good-looking men to shack up with her and actually hinting toward sexual escapades and unplanned pregnancies.

Shivering, she took a step out in the hall, and her feet immediately touched something that lay right outside her door.

Blinking against the darkness, she managed to squat down and pick up the offending object. A bouquet of flowers?

She inhaled the light, sweet fragrance, and a smile tugged at her lips before she forced it away.

Did he really think she was that starved for attention that a pitiful bouquet of wildflowers would get her into his bed?

Not that flowers meant an invitation into Bentley Wellington's bed.

Her skin heated.

The curse of being a romance author meant that you read meanings into everything, overanalyzed all things, and when a man brought you flowers you immediately started imagining all the reasons behind it—because it was her job to know those reasons, to portray them on a page, to make them believable.

But this? This wasn't a novel. This was reality.

She dropped the flowers like they were burning her, only to pick them back up again—but not because she was keeping them, because she was going to at least throw them in the trash. After all, she hated a mess.

Yup, that was why she was clenching them so tightly in her right hand and why she kept glancing at the pretty blue petals.

If he knew her at all anymore, he'd know that flowers only reminded her of funerals.

And abandonment.

Flowers had filled her hospital room until she thought she was going to choke to death on their scent.

To Bentley flowers were a gesture.

To Margot? A pretty reminder of everything that went wrong in her life, and all of her reasons for shutting people out.

Her toes slid over the threshold of her door into the hallway. The floor let out a low creak under the weight of her body. Clenching her eyes shut, she waited for Bentley to pop out of one of the rooms or suddenly appear, but nothing happened.

Margot exhaled in relief, and then very slowly and quietly made her way to the stairs, careful to avoid the creaky ones.

The lights had been turned off—at least he did that much, not that she really cared about the electricity bill—but it gave her the impression he wasn't completely mindless and stupid.

With hurried steps, she limped into the kitchen and dropped the flowers into the trash can with a flourish before kicking the can and making a beeline for the fridge, thankful she didn't have to look at the jackass's face. Because she was sure that would wreak havoc on her dreams.

The last thing she needed was a vision of his cruel smile and penetrating eyes before she slept. The nightmares from the accident were bad enough without him making an appearance. And now she had him to thank for the fact that she was thinking about flowers again, about funerals.

"Margot dear, what color?" Grandma whispered.

Through her tears all Margot could think of was: This shouldn't be happening. I shouldn't be picking out flowers to place on my parents' grave. And why? Why the hell did it matter what color they were?

Her mother had loved flowers. Thus the garden that wrapped around the east side of the house. And now her mother's favorite flowers would be covering her grave.

Margot shoved the memory away and opened the fridge door. As light seeped into the room, she quickly located the orange juice, pushed the carton open, and took a few giant swigs.

An eerie sense of awareness trickled down her spine as she swallowed the last gulp and set the orange juice back on the shelf then closed the door.

"Can't sleep?" a sexy-as-hell voice said to her immediate left.

"Shit!" She stumbled away from the fridge and braced herself against the granite countertop with both hands, but not before banging her hip into the blunt edge. Yeah, that was totally going to be a bruise by morning. "You scared me."

Bentley lazily leaned against the opposite wall, muscled arms crossed, arrogant mocking grin firmly in place. Why did he have to look like that? *Why?*

He pushed away, taking one step toward her then two. He stopped once he was a foot in front of her. "You don't like me."

"No."

"You used to."

She stiffened. "*Used to* is the key word there, Bent."

It slipped.

His nickname.

His full lips curved into a smug grin. "I haven't changed that much..." He glanced down at his rock-hard body then back up at her.

Understatement of the century.

Everything had changed.

Everything.

From his perfectly sculpted face to the muscles that bulged all over his body. Oh, he'd changed, all right. From a boy to a man. But the change that affected her the most was the fact that every time he opened his mouth, she was taken back to a time when she would have done anything just to listen to him talk. She'd hung on his every word. But Bentley had taught her a very hard lesson when she'd needed it the most.

Words are just words—empty promises—unless there's action behind them. And Bentley? He wasn't a man of action. He never had been.

"You're arrogant." She finally found her voice.

His T-shirt bulged over muscled forearms and swollen biceps. Eyes heated, he opened his mouth and drew a breath.

Whatever he was going to say, she beat him to the punch. "You're spoiled." She kept talking, refusing to give him any opening to defend himself as she held up a finger. "You think you're God's gift to women. You screw anything that allows you between their legs, and you have no respect for yourself or me or anyone for that matter, and you're—"

He clapped a hand over her mouth. "I didn't ask for a damn list."

She shoved his hand away and glared. "We'd be here all night if you did."

His eyebrows shot up like he was surprised she had fight in her, and then his gaze slowly wandered down her body, lower and lower, until she felt herself start to break out in a cold sweat. Oh God, could he see her leg in the dark? Could he tell? She wasn't wearing shoes. All he had to do was look down, though the pajama pants she wore might just save her.

She muttered a prayer of thanks when his head snapped up, but his dangerous smile had her swallowing in nervousness. Bentley leaned in, and whispered, "Nice legs, Red."

She glared up at his sculpted lips and fought to keep the tears from falling at his compliment.

Either the bastard really had no idea about her injury or he was just playing a cruel joke on her—but she'd never known him to be cruel.

"So you hate flowers?" he said, changing the subject, and gave her a sliver of space between their bodies.

"Yup." She clenched her teeth together. God, her throat felt like it had a basketball lodged in it.

"Hmm." He ran a finger down her neck. She flinched and jumped back. "Doesn't like to be touched, prefers the dark, and hates living things." His smirk was like a weapon, deadly to a mortal female. "Vampire? Zombie? Ghost?"

"Or," she countered as she sidestepped him, "you're just not as good-looking as you think you are."

"Or you're just playing hard to get like always."

She shook her head; the thought was hilariously stupid. Hard to get? When had she ever been hard to get? When they were in high school she'd practically drooled all over his lap whenever they hung out. "I'm not your type."

"Female"—he said the word with a sensual edge—"is my type."

"With that hair I would have thought you swung both ways." She lifted a shoulder carelessly. "My bad."

The walls between them were once again erected.

His eyes bulged, and then he cursed and walked off. "Good night, Red."

She didn't answer.

The minute he rounded the corner, she slumped against the counter.

Humiliation built up inside her chest until all she wanted to do was cry. But Margot had shed enough tears for a lifetime already. He'd said *legs*.

Plural.

Well, the joke was on him.

Since she really only had one.

Or one and a half.

She wasn't sure what was worse: the fact that he really had no idea about her injuries—meaning he'd never even checked up on her all those years ago—or the fact that years ago she would have killed for him to give her a compliment like that. To look at her with that smoldering gaze he often reserved for girls with bright blond hair and chirpy voices.

Even his compliment missed its mark, because the arrogant bastard had no idea the reason she limped was because her prosthetic fit poorly, and she was too embarrassed to go to the doctor and get one that was easier to walk in, because that meant leaving the house.

It meant asking for help.

Besides, she didn't walk much.

She sat.

And she swam.

Margot exhaled a rough sigh and glared at the dark hall where Bentley had just disappeared. She needed to focus on all the bad, not the way he looked at her, and not the easy way he handed out compliments as if she were something special.

Because any compliment wouldn't make up for the fact that he could be a complete prick when he wanted to be.

Margot drummed her fingertips against the countertop and waited to hear the click of his door shutting behind him.

It didn't.

Did the man seriously not shut his door at night?

And why did it bother her so much?

Rolling her eyes at herself, she slowly walked around the stairwell and peeked down the hall at the wide-open door and the half-naked man standing almost fully in front of it.

His black T-shirt went flying.

Tight, skinny jeans that should have gotten caught on his legs were next as he jerked them to the floor, giving her an amazing view of his firm ass.

His fingers paused at the waistband of his boxer briefs.

Her breath hitched, lips parted, as he very-slowly pulled them down and turned slightly to the side.

She was painfully aware of her own heartbeat drumming against her chest as her eyes strained to take in every masculine, beautiful part of him.

No wonder.

That was her only thought.

No wonder women fall all over themselves.
No wonder he's always had it easy.
No wonder.

Heart in her throat, she took one last look at him and then limped back to the stairs, her uneven gait a painful reminder of how different their worlds were.

And how important it was to keep them separate.

CHAPTER SEVEN

A smile curved his lips as Bentley put his hands behind his head and stared up at the boring white ceiling.

She'd watched him.

And not by accident.

He'd seen her reflection in the window, had been tempted to turn around, but instead he'd decided to give Red a little striptease—test her to see if she was completely immune to him.

Instead, she'd placed a hand to her chest, her mouth had dropped open, and her eyes had bulged damn near out of her head.

For a fraction of a second, he'd almost turned completely around, but there would be no point in making her even angrier, especially with the next fucking thirty days hanging over his head.

Maybe he could convince his grandfather to count the fact that she'd almost smiled when he'd taken off his clothes. No way—the old man would just take his request as another instance of Bentley not living up to expectations.

Growling, he punched and then fluffed his pillow stuffing it underneath his head, and closed his eyes.

*   *   *

"No! *Stop!*" The feminine shriek had Bentley falling out of bed with the sheets tangled around his ankles. Cursing, he jerked on his jeans, not even bothering to button them, and took the stairs three at a time.

"Please!" Margot screamed. "Please! I didn't mean it! Come back! Please!" Her screams shook the entire house.

He knocked on her bedroom door.

What the hell am I doing?

"Margot!" He flung open the door and charged toward the bed and the woman screaming around and tossing in it. "Margot!" Bentley reached out and touched her shoulder only for her to scream again. "Wake up, honey. Wake up, it's just a dream." He shook her harder and then her swollen eyes snapped open—locking on to him like a vise.

The temptation to run was so strong.

Because eyes like *that* saw too much.

Eyes like Margot's made a man want to fight wars. They made a man want to confess his sins—and Bentley Wellington had too many to list, and enough common sense to realize that a woman like *her* would never understand.

"Are you okay?" he finally asked.

She shook her head and swallowed, clenching the sheets with her hands and tugging them up to her chin like she was afraid he was going to strip her.

He rolled his eyes. "I'm not going to take advantage of you."

Yeah, she didn't look convinced.

"Look." He ran a hand through his hair. "I have no idea

what you've read about me, but I'm not into that...the whole 'scream and whip me in bed'...I don't get off that way, and I sure as hell don't screw women who aren't willing."

Her face shuttered—like she flicked off every emotion a human should possess and, in its place, put on a mask of complete indifference. "Thanks."

"It was nothing."

"You can go now." Voice hollow, she pointed at the door.

"But—"

"I'm tired." Her lower lip trembled.

He wouldn't have noticed had he not been obsessed with her lips and the way she sucked on her bottom one with her teeth when she was nervous, turning it cherry red.

"Does this happen often?" he asked.

"Please don't," she whispered. "Don't ask questions you really don't want the answers to. You didn't care all those years ago, so please don't pretend to care now."

"Margot." Fuck, she was frustrating as hell. If she only knew how much he cared. The agonizing days alone in the dark, fighting his own anxiety about hospitals and death...trying to gain enough courage to even step foot in the right direction.

"I'm going to the hospital." Bentley nodded his head and stood. *"I have to. She's going to think I left her and..."* His knees knocked together before he collapsed against the chair.

Brant shook his head. "They won't let you out."

"Then I'll break out!" Bentley yelled. "Cover for me or something."

"We'd get caught and you'd just be stuck in here longer...I'll figure something out, just...you need to get better."

"I am better!" he screamed. *"It was a onetime thing, all right? I just, I heard about the accident and I snapped, but I'm fine. Look."* Bentley threw his hands in the air. *"I'm not going to shank anyone or hurt myself. It's anxiety, not depression. Huge difference!"* He was lying. He was still terrified of what he would do once he was back in the real world.

Once he was alone again.

Bentley shook the memory from his head and locked eyes with a terrified Margot. "I'm just trying to help."

"Ohhh..." Her smile was fake. Beautiful, but fake. "Is that what you're doing at my house? And here I thought my grandmother spent ten grand so that I'd have my best friend back." She turned on her side and pulled the covers over her head. "You can go now, Bentley. Go save someone who needs to be saved. I'm fine. I was fine when you weren't there for me back then—I'm pretty sure I'll survive now."

He stood and stared at the red hair that peeked out from under the white sheet; the stark contrast between the two drew his eyes more than he would have liked.

But what kept him still as a statue was the loneliness in her voice, and the way she hid herself not just from the world—but from anyone, everyone. And the horrible part? She didn't realize it. She had no fucking clue.

"It's not enough," he said in a gruff voice. "Being fine isn't enough."

"It is for me," she said in a muffled whisper.

"Don't lie. Not to me."

In a dramatic flourish, she pulled the sheet back from her face and scowled. Damn, she was pretty, even when she was trying to scare him off or yelling at him, which was basically 99 percent of every encounter they'd had since he'd stepped foot inside her home.

"Go away."

"Going." He lifted his hands in the air and slowly backed away toward the door, but not before glancing over his shoulder and adding, "For the record, they're emerald green."

"What?"

"Your eyes. Apparently my memory's complete shit since I always thought they had specks of yellow in them. But they don't. They're like emeralds, angry emeralds."

"Are you drunk?"

"No." He shrugged. "Just making a completely impersonal observation about my new roommate for the next thirty days."

Margot froze.

Bentley cursed himself for slipping.

"Thirty days?" Margot whispered in a hoarse voice. "Did you just say thirty days?"

"You should get some sleep." Bentley slowly started backing away.

"You aren't staying here thirty days, Bent."

"The hell I'm not." He smirked. "The rules have changed. Just ask your grandmother. Besides, I bet you always wanted me as a roommate…think of all the benefits. I can wash your back in the shower, scratch any…itches you may have—"

"—Bentley, if you get anywhere near my body I'm going to kick you in the balls, got it?"

"How hard of a kick are we talking here?" He eyed her up and down. "Because I seem to remember you faking a case of the hives so you wouldn't have to participate in gym class."

Margot rolled her eyes. "Doesn't really matter how hard the kick is when the package is that—" she tilted her head and smiled "—small."

Bentley's eyes narrowed. "You really want to start something you can't finish, Red? You're stuck with me for the next month...maybe you shouldn't pick a fight you can't win."

"I don't need to win," Margot fired back. "I just need to survive."

"So is that what you're doing? Surviving?" He was pushing her too far.

Her eyes widened as her cheeks colored a bright red. "It won't work."

"What won't?"

"Whatever you're trying to do. I don't have friends or company for a reason."

"I know." He finally turned to fully look at her. "*You're* that reason."

She stared him down like he was Satan himself. "Bentley, I've talked to some of the best shrinks money can buy—what makes you think a man who fucks his way through life and doesn't even remember most Friday nights is going to be the one to have a breakthrough?"

He straightened. "Maybe because the man who fucks his way through life understands desperation when he sees it reflected in someone else's eyes—even if they are a different color than he remembers. Good night, Margot." He turned on his heel and walked out the door.

CHAPTER EIGHT

After less than twenty-four hours under the same roof as Bentley, Margot was seriously contemplating calling her grandmother and faking a miraculous healing of the mind. Not that Margot's mind was broken, but her grandmother worried about Margot's aversion to all things that she used to love—everything but books.

Her mom had loved the garden outside.

And her dad had basically just loved life.

So it felt wrong going outside, enjoying the life that was stolen from them because she hadn't been paying attention.

It was easier to stay locked inside.

And every time she was tempted to step outside to do anything other than swim, it was like her leg pained her more, convincing her with this terrifying sense of dread that if she did step outside, she wasn't honoring their memory.

Not that she'd ever admit that to Bentley of all people.

The more she thought about it, the more she realized it was the principal of the matter. Why should she get to enjoy anything, when she was the one living while her parents were dead? Buried. Cold in the ground. She should be punished.

The phantom pain returned to her missing right calf.

Like it always did when she thought about the accident.

The screeching sound of brakes, the shattering of glass, metal twisting.

Her skin broke out in a cold sweat.

With a huff, she sat up in bed and attached her prosthetic. Her skin was pink where the surgeon had amputated— probably because she'd been putting more weight on it than she was used to.

Another strike against the playboy. Not only was he mentally taxing—he was physically hurting her without even realizing it.

Sighing, she followed the leg with a pair of jeans that weren't too tight, and then added a T-shirt and tennis shoes. Everything was covered, and if he didn't look too close, he shouldn't notice the leg.

Or lack thereof.

The problem was going to be trying to last another twenty-eight days without him noticing. The last thing she wanted was Bentley's pity. He'd already looked at her like she was broken—it would just get worse if he knew the true extent.

The last thing she wanted was for him to apologize for abandoning her, and for that apology to be out of guilt, rather than because he was truly sorry.

Thirty days.

What the ever-loving hell was her grandmother thinking? When she'd texted her grandmother to complain, the only response she got was:

Surprise.

Right.

Surprise.

As in, *Yay, aren't you so glad that I bought you a man and then somehow convinced him it would be a good idea to hang out with you and cheer you up?*

Margot cursed herself for opening up to her grandmother a few months back—telling her that she was stressed and having a rough day. People were allowed to have rough days! Her grandmother asked her if she was happy; she'd said yes!

She didn't need cheering.

In fact his presence was literally doing the exact opposite of what her grandmother probably wanted.

It was making her remember.

When all she really wanted to do was forget.

Her old life was gone.

Now she had a new one—one that wouldn't even fit a portion of Bentley's ego.

Her bedroom door mocked her.

Taunted her.

And she was reminded all over again about his intrusion and the way he dared judge her and his ridiculous offer of advice.

She shook with anger. It was so insulting, and humiliating, the fact that he was right—she *was* hiding from the world. At least partially. But it wasn't because she was depressed or in a bad place. It was just easier not to have to deal with all the stares, the disgusted looks, the memories.

Ugh.

Her stomach grumbled. She couldn't starve, though the idea did have merit, because at least then she wouldn't have to face him again.

But she'd eaten her last protein bar yesterday.

And unless she wanted to chew on some Laffy Taffy for breakfast, the stash in her desk wasn't going to help her.

Squaring her shoulders, she jerked open the door and made her way down the stairs and into the kitchen and gasped.

Two places were set on the breakfast bar. Her eyes landed on a plateful of scrambled eggs, and to the right of it, toast and bacon.

Damn it. The man learned to cook. Back when they were friends, he couldn't even make a sandwich without ruining it. And now? Eggs. She had eggs.

Wildflowers rested on their sides in the middle of the table. Dirt still caked the stems. Did the man even know how to pick a flower?

Bentley looked up from his spot at the bar and patted the seat next to him. "I wasn't sure if you liked eggs. Actually, I wasn't sure if you fed off the blood of humans and were actually able to even digest food, so I took a chance in hopes you won't stake me."

"Funny."

"I'm hilarious" was his dry-as-hell answer.

"You cook now?" Her mouth watered at the sight of the fluffy eggs. The last time she'd made breakfast had been when her grandmother visited—a month ago.

"I cook."

"You cook," she said more to herself than anything.

"I think we established that. Twice now. But by all means say it again, only maybe this time, say it more breathlessly. There's nothing better than bacon and sexual innuendos in the morning."

She was tempted to toss the eggs in his lap and smear butter all over his face. Though he'd probably think of it as an invitation.

Bentley always did confuse flirting and fighting.

Before she could reach for the spatula, Bentley was already piling food onto her plate—enough to feed at least four of her.

"That's too much." She stared down at the bacon as steam billowed off her plate.

"You're too skinny." He was back to reading the newspaper she wasn't even aware had been delivered and taking a sip of coffee. "Eat."

"This won't work." She crossed her arms. "Feeding me doesn't make me friendly."

"It was worth a shot." He paused. "It worked for my stray dog."

"Wow, how nice, being compared to a canine." She fought back the urge to stab him with her fork.

"She's a really pretty bitch." He grinned over his newspaper. "Like someone else I know. All bark, no bite, but a hell of a—" he winked then eyed her slowly up and down "—coat."

There it was again. The flirting. Why was he really staying for longer than the weekend? What was his angle? Because it sure wasn't out of the goodness of his heart. Life wasn't a romance novel with a happily ever after. He wanted something.

"I'm curious." She dug into her eggs. Not because she wanted to, but because she couldn't take the smell anymore, and drool was about ready to roll out of her mouth. "Do you compare all women to animals, or am I the only lucky one?"

"I dated an Ashley once."

"And when you say 'dated'?"

"I screwed her in the bathroom of a club," he said in a bored voice. "Twice." He set the newspaper down on the counter and lifted the coffee to his lips. "She reminded me of a cougar. Does that count?"

Margot shoveled more eggs into her mouth and reached for the orange juice to keep herself from choking.

"Are you ignoring me now?"

Margot almost leaped out of her chair. How long had she been sitting there mentally going through all the images he'd just prompted to flow into her mind? The bathroom stall, a woman, Bentley's mouth.

Maybe she did need to get out.

Or start writing nonfiction instead of romance. Her imagination was way too vivid; it was hard enough sitting next to him and feeling his body heat. Great. She said *heat*.

Her heat.

His heat.

Damn it!

"It doesn't count." She wiped her mouth with a napkin and tried to calm her shaking hands. "Just like this doesn't count as a normal friendly conversation. We're not friends anymore, remember?"

"Good, because I didn't ask to be your friend."

Her heart sank. This was why you didn't let people like Bentley Wellington into your life. Even though she knew he was bad news, she'd still hoped...and there it was. He might have abandoned her. She might hate him. But she still always hoped he'd come back.

"Fine, because I didn't want that anyway. I don't want any of this."

Liar.

"And you think I do?" It was probably the first honest thing he'd said to her, which of course made her even more curious and hurt.

After Margot bit into a piece of the best bacon she'd ever had in her entire life, she turned her full attention to Bentley. "No choice, huh?"

He set his coffee down. "I was threatened."

"That makes two of us."

"My grandfather hates me and I was tricked."

"My grandmother wants me to have unprotected sex with a stranger."

Bentley started coughing and choking. "Wrong pipe."

"I think I win." She took one more bite of bacon and slid off the chair.

"Wait," Bentley called. "Aren't you going to take your flowers?"

She eyed the wildflowers as anxiety washed over her. She had no idea what his angle was, and that made her more nervous than anything. A man who was forced to be with her wouldn't randomly bring her flowers, right?

"Come on." He held out the flowers, his eyes drawing her in as he raked his gaze over her body appreciatively. "I picked them for you." His sexy grin was enough to make her crumble.

It had the opposite effect he probably wanted. Because it just reminded her that the only reason he was looking at her like that was because he clearly didn't know the truth about her leg. Tears burned her throat until she felt like she was going to suffocate. Either he really was attracted to her and was in for a very rude awakening, or he was doing what he did best. Charming his way back into her life by way of a sexy grin and empty compliments.

With a fake cheerful smile, she took the flowers from his hand and tossed them in the trash.

Bentley stared at her then back at the trash. "Are you serious?"

"They were dirty."

"Because they were outside!" he argued.

She shrugged and spun on her heel when he called out.

"Where are you going?"

"Upstairs," she answered firmly before turning around to face him. "To work, which I'm sure is a completely foreign concept to you."

Bentley's expression hardened. "Going back to the dungeon with your blinds closed and panties in a twist?"

"You know so much about women, Bentley Wellington, it's a shock so many land in your bed."

"Half of them are drunk," he said in a teasing tone.

She froze. "Seriously? You think that's funny? It's not."

"Sorry." He sobered. "I was kidding. I would never take advantage—"

"And yet here you are." She threw her hands up into the air, nearly knocking herself off balance. "Taking advantage of me."

"The hell I am!" he roared, jumping to his feet. "Do you think I have nothing better to do than babysit a depressed shut-in who refuses to even step outside the doorway for fear the sun's going to burn her vampire skin? A girl who can't even accept flowers or a fucking compliment without attacking? What the hell happened to you?"

There it was.

But if she answered him, she'd have to admit that something did happen—and she was definitely not interested in discussing her injury with him. And the elephant in the room would grow, because she'd be forced to face the truth of why he left.

Maybe he was never her friend in the first place.

Maybe, even back then, he was using her like he did every other girl that landed in his bed.

"I'm not a vampire." Of course, that was what she decided to fixate on. Everything else he said hit its mark too well, leaving her dizzy with anger.

"No shit."

"Whatever." She gave him her back and took a step up the stair, but her bad leg, or what was left of it, suddenly gave out—which only happened if her muscles were too tired.

Bentley's arms were underneath hers before she could even think to reach for the railing.

"You okay?" His breath tickled her ear. Why did he have to feel so warm? Thick, muscular arms wrapped around her body.

And for the first time in years, she felt safe.

Jerking away from him, she kept walking, head held high, all the way to the top of the stairwell.

"You're welcome for breakfast." His hard voice followed behind her.

She slammed her door.

And tried to calm herself down.

Because for a minute—it had worked.

The food.

The conversation.

The flowers.

He'd always been easy to talk to. And now he knew how to cook.

Worst-case scenario, he was going to somehow find a way to weasel himself into her life and then leave her. Because that was what people did—they left.

CHAPTER NINE

W ell, that went well," Bentley muttered to himself, his body still humming with awareness. Her skin smelled like sugar.

The kind of scent that fills the house when you're making candy or caramel popcorn.

Great. He was comparing her to food.

Like the dog comment wasn't bad enough.

It had slipped.

The ugly words.

He'd always been the type that was more comfortable projecting his own issues onto other people—in some twisted hope the attention would shift to the other person.

It never worked.

Nothing really did.

Except loads of sex.

And doing what he did best.

Ignoring anything that brought him back to that moment, to that moment in his life when everything went black.

"Bentley!" Brant pounded on the closet door. "Open up!"

Bentley rolled his eyes and continued assaulting Jessica's mouth with his as he slowly lifted her skirt and gripped her thighs. "Go away."

"Bentley." *Brant's voice was panicked.* "I'm not kidding, man, something happened."

"Something's happening now." *Jessica grinned against his mouth as he reached for his pants.*

"It's Margot," *Brant said with a hoarse cry.*

Bentley froze in place.

Jessica kept kissing him.

And then he shoved her away, fixed his jeans, and opened the bedroom door. He knew in seconds that something was very wrong.

Because his brother had tears in his eyes.

And he couldn't remember the last time he'd seen his brother cry.

"I'm not sure if she's going to make it." *Brant reached for Bentley.*

Bentley shoved him away. "What do you mean if she's going to make it? Where is she?"

Brant shook his head.

"Where is she?" *Bentley yelled.* "Margot! Margot!" *He was hysterical as he started shoving the perfect little vases from their equally perfect table. Flowers and glass littered the floor until his own brother tackled him to the ground.*

Police.

Sirens.

Domestic disturbance.

Jail.

And a lingering feeling that the only person in his life who really knew him was gone.

So why live?

There wasn't any point, was there?

A car ride home.

A lecture.

And one bottle of pills later.

He pounded his fist onto the counter as the taste of acid burned the back of his throat. The eggs were cold, the bacon discarded. His stomach rolled. He made it as far as the kitchen sink before he puked up everything he'd just eaten.

Anxiety had always been a complete bitch to him, making it so that if he was too keyed up he couldn't keep any solid food down. Which meant he needed to get the hell out of here before her dark moods and memories of what he thought was her death killed him.

He was good at that. Running away.

Bentley stumbled out of the house and walked around the back, body still shaking with the memory of waking up in the hospital room right across from Margot.

And not even knowing it until he was moved to a different floor.

It might as well have been worlds away from her.

His grandfather kept it hidden from the media.

And told Bentley that if he was seen wandering the halls he'd cut him off completely. It was for his own protection, he'd said.

Protection, his ass.

With a sigh Bentley moved through the back garden where he'd earlier picked flowers and down the stairs to the back porch.

The glistening pool shone in the distance.

Sink or swim?

Hell, he felt like he'd been doing nothing but sinking since he arrived. She was everything and more than he remembered—he just never realized how violently the memories would assault him.

Or how badly it would hurt when she looked at him like he'd destroyed her—when all he'd ever wanted to do was kiss her.

Twenty-eight days.

Of hell.

And then he'd go back to his life—and leave her in the past for good. There was a reason he'd buried all of those feelings that went along with Margot—because some people were too important to risk losing twice.

The water in the pool glistened.

Bentley sat on one of the white plastic chairs and let the warm air wash over him as he took deep, soothing breaths.

Soon, the anxiety started to melt away. He just had to focus on getting the woman to accept some damn flowers, go on a picnic, accept a gift— He burst out laughing.

Right, he just had to, you know, solve world hunger and cure cancer at the same time. How hard could it be?

She was his ticket to bigger things. To better things.

To finally moving on.

To a life that meant more than what he had.

God, listen to him! Barely two days with the woman and he was sounding like a depressed asshole!

"Think, Bentley, think." He ground his teeth together as he tried to figure out a way to reach her without losing his mind.

What did he even know about her now?

She clearly still hated him.

Hated flowers.

Wrote books for a living.

Books?

Was that his way in?

He quickly pulled out his phone and got on Amazon. At this point he was willing to try anything.

CHAPTER TEN

It was too quiet.

And not the good type of quiet you find on a nice summer evening when you crack open the window and fresh air fills the room.

It was a bad quiet.

It was a Bentley Wellington quiet.

Like he was just waiting to pounce.

Two days had passed since their fight over breakfast, and for the most part, he'd left her alone.

For the most part.

She'd learned that the best way to avoid him was to stash food in her room and make sure that she kept the door locked.

So basically she was a prisoner in her own house—which wasn't any different than usual, but this time she was essentially locked in her room. Which meant no swimming.

It was really all she missed other than the amazing movie room downstairs. She had everything she needed in her room.

She'd probably die in this room.

She wondered briefly how long it would take someone to find her.

God, when had she turned into this depressed, crazy person? All she needed was a bazillion cats and a shopping cart to complete the image. It was like Bentley's arrival reminded her of how lonely she really was.

With a defeated sigh she typed one more chapter, then scanned the clock on her computer...

It was eight o'clock.

Too early for bed.

And too late to still be working, since she'd already put in over twelve hours that day.

She cracked her neck just as a soft knock sounded at the door.

Right on time.

At least she'd give him that.

Every night he dropped a fresh-picked bouquet of flowers outside her door. And each time they left a little dirt spot on the hardwood. She was pretty sure he did it to be irritating.

With a yawn she opened the door only to jerk back.

In one hand, Bentley had a bouquet of flowers, in the other about ten paperback books.

"Can I help you?" She leaned against the door and waited.

He grinned and then shoved the stack of books at her. "Hold these?"

"Wait—"

He held up a hand and then waltzed right into her room and deposited the bouquet of dirty flowers right on her nice, clean white bedspread.

She let out a growl of frustration. "What part of 'Leave me the hell alone' do you not understand?"

"Um, let me see..." He tapped his perfect jawline with his right hand. "All of it?"

"Take your dirty books and leave." She shoved the stack back into his chest and huffed.

"Dirty?" He frowned. "Did you even look at them?"

"Fine. Your illustrated children's books with really fancy pictures and one-syllable words like *cat*." She grinned, proud of herself at the insult as he rolled his eyes.

"Look." He nodded his head.

Curiosity got the best of her. She looked at the stack of books and let out a little gasp.

Jane Austen. *Jane Eyre*. James Patterson, to name a few. Some of them she'd read before, while others were new to her. "I don't understand."

"Common ground," Bentley said in a low voice. "I figured that the only thing we have in common other than being forced into this situation"—he shrugged—"is that we both like books. I thought it could be a fresh-start present. You know, since we already broke the proverbial bread and you threw things at my face."

Her lips twitched. Ugh, why did he have to be funny?

And good-looking.

"You don't read."

"Says who?" he countered.

"Says..." She let out a frustrated sigh. "You always used to make fun of my reading."

"It's called flirting, Red. How else was I supposed to get you to talk to me? Ask about the weather? Pull your tight little bun every day?"

"You did both of those things."

He held up a book and waved it in her face. "Until I found common ground and asked you about reading."

"You said you failed reading, as if it was an actual class offered to freshmen, and asked me to tutor you."

His eyes briefly flashed with heat before he turned away. "And since I was too hard to resist—"

"—I always resisted," she felt the need to point out. "Besides, it's not like you liked me"—she swallowed—"in that way." *Breathe, in and out.* "We were just friends, Bentley."

"Weird. I remember having vivid daydreams about my *friend.*"

Her head jerked up just in time to see him lick his lips and stare at her mouth like he was hypnotized.

No.

Don't let him in.

Not again.

"Thanks," she mumbled. "Now, please leave."

"Did you just say 'please'?" His mouth dropped open before he winked and took the remaining books from her hands. "Now, where do you want me to put them?"

"Wait—" She reached for him but it was too late. He was already at one of her bookcases, which wouldn't have been such a big deal if it wasn't the same bookcase with a picture of her parents.

And Bentley Wellington holding her hand in the background.

He froze and then a grin spread across his face. "So, just how long have you been fantasizing about me, then?"

"That's it. You need to go." She tried grabbing the books from his hands, but he jerked away from her. He set the books on the nearest shelf and grabbed the picture. "I have to admit, I never took you for a stalker...How many more pictures do you have of me, Red? Be honest."

She'd kept this photo because it was the last photo she had of her with her parents and her best friend.

Her parents were in a loving embrace, while she and Bentley were laughing in the background.

She had been looking at him instead of her parents.

Story of her life. She'd always been looking at him.

Bentley chuckled and pointed to her sixteen-year-old self. "You know, I would have probably kissed you if you'd asked. I always was curious what it would be like."

It was too much.

The man holding the picture wasn't the same person as the boy she'd had a crush on. Back then Bentley was dangerous—hadn't Brant warned her time and time again? But the man facing her now was downright deadly.

"I'm pretty sure," she said as she jerked the picture from his hands "that teen pregnancy wasn't on my life goals list." He didn't look hurt but his eyes went cold. "Besides, you're Bentley Wellington, the guy women sleep with when they're bored with their husbands or don't have anything better to do. What would make you think I would ever feel anything for you except for pity?"

He jerked back as if she'd slapped him.

Too far, Margot.

Even he didn't deserve that.

But he'd thrown their friendship in her face—again. As if he'd been doing her a favor back then—and maybe that was where all her own hostility was coming from.

When their eyes met again, his dripped with hatred. "And to think, this pitiful man was going to offer to fuck you— after all, it must burn, knowing you'll be a virgin the rest of your life."

"*Out!*" she screamed. "Get out!"

"No need to shriek," he sneered. "I'm gone."

He slammed the door after him. The picture fell to the floor and cracked, but for some reason Margot thought it felt an awful lot like her heart had broken, too.

And she only had herself to blame.

CHAPTER ELEVEN

If avoiding a woman who lived in the same house as him was an Olympic sport, Bentley would have been a gold medalist.

It had been a day since their fight in her room.

Since he'd let his anger get the best of him.

Since she'd made him feel about as useless as his grandfather did.

It seemed every time they tried to have a decent conversation, one or both of them lashed out. The only thing he couldn't figure out was how she knew exactly which button to push with him.

Because she'd hit her mark.

And it had burned like hell the rest of the day.

Because for some reason he didn't want her looking at him the way everyone else did. Like he was useless, replaceable, only out for a good time.

"Fuck this." He'd been moping for a whole day. He'd needed to get outside before he lost his mind.

He numbly jerked his T-shirt over his head, then pulled

both his jeans and boxers down and jumped in the pool naked.

The very nonheated.

Cold.

Frigid-as-all-hell.

Pool.

He surfaced from the water and smoothly moved from one end of the pool to the other, his body gliding through the water in even strokes.

Already, his stomach felt better even if the heaviness was still there. How the hell was he supposed to reach a woman who refused to accept food from him? Who looked like she was in pain when she smiled at him?

Who didn't just shut him out...

...but found ways to attack him in the process?

Bentley knew that he deserved some of her hatred. It was one of the reasons he was pissed about the whole scenario to begin with. He knew it wouldn't be easy, but he never thought she would be this unforgiving, or have such a strong memory.

He wasn't sure if he should feel guilty over the fact that she still hated him and was still hurting, or thankful that he wasn't the only one who still remembered all of their time together.

He kept up the same pace for a good ten minutes and forced all thoughts of Margot completely from his mind.

Which meant there was only space for the water and the memories.

"Oh come on, you're never serious." Grandfather chuckled. *"It's what makes people love you. You've got your grandmother's sense of humor."* He pulled out a cigar and lit it. A cloud of white smoke engulfed his head. *"Now, why*

would you want to go to graduate school? You've never been into your studies."

True. Bentley had basically fucked and partied through most of college at Yale, and only Brant knew the real reason why. Bentley needed constant distraction, and the sex and drinking worked; it helped relax him, kept his mind off of all of the things that made him snap back in high school. But something had shifted at the end of senior year. Or maybe life just clicked? His usual vices weren't working as well. Frustrated, he'd left a frat party and on his way home saw a hurt dog; it was limping, and in really rough shape.

Immediately he went into action.

Distraction.

The kind where he was more focused on someone else's pain than his own.

He'd looked for a collar but found only blood where a collar and name tag should have been. Anger surged through him as he'd picked up the dog, taken it home, given it a bath and a meal, and then realized—that was what he wanted to do.

Being a vet was a completely valid occupation, right? Besides, what else was he going to do? His eldest brother was taking over Wellington, Inc., and his twin was going to school for business.

Why not do something different?

He slept the best he'd ever slept in his entire life that night.

Only to wake up and form a plan.

Over spring break he'd gone to his grandfather's office first thing to tell him the good news.

"Vets." Grandfather shuddered. "They aren't even real doctors."

Bentley bit back his retort and stared his grandfather down. "The point is that I finally know what I want to do."

"No." Grandfather shifted in his chair. "You think you know what you want to do, just like you thought you wanted to go to Harvard only to end up at Yale, just like you switched from Social Sciences to Business to Communications. No, I'm putting my foot down. Give it a few years, and if you still want to do it, you can use the money from your trust."

But that was years away. Now that he'd finally figured out what he wanted he didn't want to wait.

"Bentley, I love you, but you're not serious. You'll be bored out of your mind, and then you'll have quit just one more thing." His grandfather's face twisted with pain. "Besides, I don't think it's good for you to be under so much pressure, the stress for that type of med school could be—" he gulped "—harmful."

Harmful.

Bentley opened his mouth to speak, then shut it. Searching for the right words before blurting out, "That was years ago. I'm totally fine now. I cope with my anxiety just fine."

"Coping means you're getting by. What happens when you get a bad grade, what happens when you lose interest or fail? I can't see you go down that road again." Grandfather tensed. "Bentley, I know you, son. You get a wild hair, and then you quit. I'm sorry, but I can't invest in seeing you hurt yourself, not again."

The rejection hurt like a bitch.

Truth typically did.

Because Bentley would be lying if he said he wasn't afraid of the very same thing. That fear kept him away from trying because what if . . . the what-ifs killed him.

But this . . . this felt different.

What was worse was that his grandfather couldn't see the difference in Bentley's eyes, or hear the sincerity in the way he spoke about finally having a purpose, a dream.

And at the end of the conversation, his grandfather winked and said, "Why don't you go pour yourself a drink and tell me about that new girl you're with. God knows, she'll only last another day before she tries to get you to marry her. Be careful, most of them are only after those good looks I passed down to you boys."

And that was it.

The end of the conversation.

Darkness settled like a blanket around his shoulders, weighing him down as he pushed himself through the cold water.

He opened his eyes just before he slammed headfirst into the wall. Then, with a deep breath, he sank to the bottom of the pool.

And waited.

While the silence of the water washed over him.

And once again, he could feel that lingering what-if. The temptation to ask himself, *What if I gave in again. What if I snapped?* Because that's what anxiety did to a person: it played mind games, it made you overanalyze every single thing, and it made you wonder about your own sanity and your own place in the world.

He promised himself he'd never go back to that place in his life—the place where he thought his best friend was dead just like his parents, the place where he wanted to be dead, too, because, for one crazy moment he'd snapped, and all the emotions he'd been keeping at bay came rushing in and dragged him under.

He rarely allowed himself to remember. He couldn't risk it.

Lucky for him, Margot had a way of tugging those memories free. Just being here with her forced him to take a good hard look at his own life, and he hated what he saw. Because the same sadness in her eyes was reflected in his, the same anger, the same pity, the same guilt. He just didn't know why she looked that way. And he couldn't allow himself to care.

He should have stayed away.

He should have told his grandfather to go to hell.

His lungs burned with the need for air.

A purpose. He needed a purpose beyond coping with lingering anxiety and thoughts of all things Margot.

Margot.

Red hair.

Huge eyes.

Swollen lips.

She forced him to ask the question he always avoided at all costs: What the fuck was he doing with his life?

Would he ever be happy? Even with the new VP position within his grasp, was that what he really wanted? To turn out like Brock and spend his life pleasing his grandfather and jumping through every damn hoop until he was wearing the exact same suits, golfing on the weekend, going to all the right restaurants?

His lungs burned with the need to exhale and then suck in more air, but he kept his lips sealed.

And wondered.

In the lingering silence of the pool.

If he died.

Would the world even notice?

And what was worse...what the hell kind of legacy would he be leaving behind?

Women.

Sex.

And more women.

What the fuck had happened to the guy who wanted to be a vet? Easy. He was shamed, broken down, beaten, and afraid.

His confidence was shattered in every way that counted and he was constantly judged by one mistake.

Bentley glanced up at the glistening ray of sun as it spread through the pool, and parted his lips.

CHAPTER TWELVE

She was going to burn in hell.

And she was completely okay with it.

As long as hell had naked men with beautiful glistening bodies and abs that seemed to go on for days. She'd been stuck on a love scene and started pacing her room when she glanced out the upstairs window and saw movement by the pool.

Her breath hitched as Bentley pulled off his boxers and jumped in the water. A smile played on her lips as he broke to the surface and started swearing about the frigidly cold water.

Whoops?

She was suddenly glad she never told him about the heater being broken. Then again, they lived in Arizona. Why heat the pool when the sun typically did a good-enough job?

Though it hadn't been as warm as it normally was.

His fault.

Not hers.

He should have asked.

Not that they'd exactly been on speaking terms since their last fight. She knew she'd hurt him. But he'd hurt her, too.

Was it even possible to hurt a relative stranger?

It was.

Because as much as she tried to convince herself how different the old Bentley was from the new Bentley, being around him again reminded her of how much she'd missed him.

The friend who watched horror movies with her. The friend who made fun of her romance novels then secretly read them to her over the phone at night until she fell asleep.

The friend who often held her hand just because he said his was lonely.

The friend she'd always wanted to kiss.

And she had to wonder if he was missing her, missing the way they'd used to be. Was that what the flowers were about? But he'd already stopped offering them to her.

A small part of her missed them, because as much as she hated to admit it, she appreciated the gesture. Great, he'd been there a total of what? Three days? And already she missed flowers? Flowers that reminded her of funerals?

He didn't even pick them right!

Now it was as if he was a houseguest that stayed far, far away. He'd given her exactly what she asked for. And she kind of hated him even more for it. Because at least when they fought, he treated her like she wasn't broken—and she felt like her old self again. When they fought, she forgot all about her handicap. Funny, how it would be Bentley who would be the one to make her so angry she couldn't do anything except find a way to win every argument.

So much for her grandmother's plan.

At least her consolation prize was watching the man swim in the nude.

Bentley's body was chiseled like a god from Olympus, all gold and smooth as it flowed across the surface of the pool. The writer in her knew it was so clichéd, but it was true. She could write a hell of a duke if he looked like Bentley. She mentally started making notes, then pressed a hand to her chest and forced herself to breathe in and out as he continued his fluid movements, only to stop.

And sink under the water.

Margot counted to thirty seconds.

And then forty.

And then...

Panicked.

Taking the stairs one at a time, she tried to hurry her gait. When she finally hit the ground floor, she tried her best to rush through the house and hobble out the back kitchen door.

"Don't be dead, don't be dead!" she yelled. "Bentley!"

No answer.

He was in impeccable shape! She still remembered watching him swim at the club, his muscles gleaming in the water. The man was incapable of drowning. Unless he had a cramp. Oh no, what if he had a cramp? What if he hit his head? What if he died and she never got the chance to tell him she was sorry? For everything. For yelling. For hating him. For still hating him for what he did to her.

The water didn't even have one ripple as she moved to the pool and looked for something to throw in to him.

"Oh God." There he was, a blur in the bottom of the pool. It had been nearly two minutes, maybe more?

With jerky movements, she pulled the prosthetic off her right leg, set it aside like she'd done numerous times when she went for a swim, and jumped in.

Her lungs nearly burst when the cold water hit her skin. Margot opened her eyes to see Bentley sitting still as a statue at the bottom of the pool, arms outstretched, eyes closed.

She swam toward him as best she could, and hooked her arms beneath him before using her good leg to shoot them to the surface.

When they reached the top, he coughed out a breath, chest heaving, and then blinked at her as if she'd lost her mind. "Can I help you?"

"You!" Margot choked out, still grasping his naked skin with her hands. "You were drowning!"

"I was?" His chest heaved, his lips were a bluish pink.

"You were!"

"The hell I was!" His response was defensive, all masculine arrogance wrapped up in one tightly toned package. His eyes darted from right to left before finally settling on her mouth.

"You were down for more than two minutes!" She slapped him in the chest then did it again since he didn't flinch. And then one more time since the bastard was smiling!

"Aw, Red, were you worried about me?" His grin widened even further as his hands snaked around her body and pulled her tight against him.

"No." She clenched her teeth and shoved against his chest. "I just didn't want to go to prison over your murder!"

"Oh, so that's what this is." Bentley winked. "You don't want to get blamed for drowning me. Imagine what your grandmother would say. She pays ten grand for my presence. I fail at cheering you up. And you drown my sorry ass in your million-dollar pool."

She narrowed her eyes and poked him harder in the chest; her finger lingered against his warm skin, and then her palm. "You have to admit it's a good idea. Maybe I'd get away with it."

His eyes locked on hers. "Maybe."

I will not smile.

Margot shrugged, her hand still on his chest. "I doubt anyone would miss you."

His eyes flashed like she'd hit a nerve. "You're probably right. I have a very severe Gatsby complex...I live to entertain the world only to die with nobody by my side."

Guilt nagged her as the truth of his words rested between both of their wet bodies.

And then she realized, way too late, if she didn't keep him talking, he was going to realize she had one leg, not two. She hated the idea of moving, of pulling her hand away from the spot near his heart where she could count his beats and know he was alive. Even if he was an arrogant ass, he was alive. And he felt good, so good.

"Maybe you should get a cat," she suggested cheerfully as she slowly removed her palm and tried to keep him talking.

Bentley licked his lips and slowly parroted, "A cat?"

"So you're not lonely."

"I know the reason. I'm just curious why you'd suggest a cat for a bachelor."

"I may be a dog." She narrowed her eyes. "But if I'm a dog, you're a cat. Arrogant and lazy."

"There was a compliment in there somewhere if I search hard enough, right?" His arms tightened around her body.

Not good. She could feel every hard line of his body. His hands slowly slid down to her hips.

She sucked her lower lip between her teeth as a mixture of anxiety and heat washed over her. Her prosthetic may as well be a beacon—the chair blocked only part of it. She'd been insane with worry, and she hadn't thought past saving him.

Saving him.

Ah! What was she thinking? Men like Bentley never needed saving.

Her eyes darted back and forth between the leg and Bentley.

His eyes were questioning and then he was turning his head, just enough to see part of the prosthetic.

"*No!*" she yelled, grabbing his face between her hands and smooshing his cheeks together like she was a crazy aunt getting ready to pinch them.

"No?" The word came out muffled, since her hands were still squishing his face. God, he felt good, he even smelled good, not like chlorine but with a hint of pine and soap.

"Kiss me," she blurted, releasing her hold on his cheeks enough so he could talk without sounding like his tongue was swollen. "Now."

"Let me get this straight." His grin was so aggravating she wanted to scream. "You rescue me when I don't need rescuing, insult my reputation, offer to buy me a cat—"

"I didn't offer to buy you a cat."

He pressed a finger to her lips and kept it there. "And now you want me to kiss you?" He removed his finger and whispered, "I need a good reason. I know it doesn't seem like it, but I rarely kiss women on the mouth—it's too personal."

She frowned. "Well then, where else do you kiss them?"

He bit down on his bottom lip and looked down. Thank God at this angle it would be easy to miss what she so desperately wanted to keep hidden. "Oh, you know." Voice husky, he slid his hand further down the side of her hip and then trailed a finger across her stomach. "Places."

"I hate you."

"Hate's never a good enough reason, Red." He shrugged and started pulling away. His hands hadn't even left her and already the loss of his warmth was crushing.

Not yet. He couldn't see the prosthetic yet. Not when they were having a moment—however misguided. Not when he was looking at her like that. Just not *now*. She wanted the fantasy. She wanted the book boyfriend with the happily ever after for at least a few more seconds. It was inevitable he was going to see the missing leg.

And then, the pity would come.

And she would hate him all over again.

"I'm writing a kissing scene!" she blurted, mentally kicking herself for screaming it in his face. "And the guy's a complete jackass. Since my only experience with jackasses is you . . ." Her voice was shaky, just like her body. Could he tell how much she wanted him? How much she hated that her response was this—raw. "I-I figured you were the only one who could show me what it's like." *Good one, Margot. Do you really have to sound so . . . desperate?*

"What what's like?"

"A kiss. From a jackass."

"Got the jackass part." He treaded water and then grabbed her by the arm and pulled her deeper into the pool until they were on the opposite end, his body pressed against hers. At least his eyes were still locked on her face. "And you've never been kissed?"

She rolled her eyes. "Not by someone like—"

"If you keep insulting me, this kiss won't ever happen, Red."

"Don't call me that," Margot whispered. Was she so weak that she'd forgive his abandonment for one kiss? "Please?"

"This kiss." His calculated gaze didn't make her feel any better about the situation. "How long does it need to be? How deep? Where do you want my hands?"

Margot's mouth dropped open. "That's not how kisses

work! You can't just map out the kiss. That takes all the romance out of it!"

"Oh, so you *want* romance?"

"Yes! No! I mean. I didn't say that!" Her face flamed, and she sagged in defeat. Admitting she wanted romance kind of felt like she was on the losing end of the little battles they'd been having, like she was giving him an in. And if he got in, he'd only hurt her again.

"I was joking," he said, just before his lips brushed hers. His tongue slid across her bottom lip and then sucked it for a few seconds before he slid it into her mouth and deepened the kiss.

Her lips softened beneath his gentle coaxing, and his hard thighs pressed against hers as a deep hunger awakened within her.

Oh, this was bad.

So bad.

And very, very good at the same time.

Heat flared beneath her skin as his thumbs pressed against her hips, his hands holding her in place as if he was afraid she was going to disappear.

He broke off the kiss, his eyes cloudy, distant. "That was my first kiss on the mouth in a month."

"Oh." She had a hard time breathing out the word. It was embarrassing enough how hard she was inhaling and exhaling, like she'd actually done something other than bobbed there and let his tongue invade her mouth while he strummed her body like an instrument. The man had barely touched her, and she felt him everywhere. Between her thighs, against her skin, in her mouth.

"Can you write that?" He dipped his head, capturing her lips again, this time more aggressively as he floated backward and took her with him.

No. No. He was too close, his hands wandering too far south. Her plan was completely backfiring as he peppered kisses along her jawline and then across her neck, like he couldn't get enough of her.

Like she was enough to begin with.

Her heart skipped a panicked beat when his hands continued moving down. She kissed him again on the mouth and pulled his hands up to her hips, only to have him deepen the kiss.

With a hungry growl, he gripped her ass and then slid his hand down her right leg, only to freeze once he was met with nothing but a stump where the rest of her leg should be.

With a cry she swam backward, nearly slamming into the wall.

"Margot." He panted. "My God. What happened? Did you lose it in the accident?"

"I lost *everything* in that accident." Her voice broke and she felt tears brimming in her eyes. God, she didn't want to talk about this. "Stop looking at me like that, Bentley. I don't need your pity. Just leave me alone.

"Look at you like what? I'm just trying to make sure I didn't hurt you." He swam toward her and looked down. "Are you okay? I didn't mean to—"

"Of course not!" She laughed bitterly. "Of course you didn't mean to touch my stump—no man ever does! Because it's disgusting! I get it. Trust me. I get it more than you could ever possibly imagine, now get the hell out!"

"Margot—"

"*Go away!*" she screamed through tears as Bentley treaded water, a look of confusion on his face.

"Margot," he tried again, reaching for her, "I'm so sorry."

"No." She shook her head. "You don't get to be sorry. I killed my parents. It's my fault. And then you..." Anger surged through her. "You left me! You may as well have died, too!"

He jerked back, pain twisting his features.

"Go. Please. Just…go." Margot found the strength to look away from the pain she'd obviously caused. The past was always painful, or maybe it was just their past, their past together.

She heard movement and looked up to see Bentley heave himself out of the pool, his jaw clenched.

She gasped, forgetting he'd been naked when he jumped into the pool.

She should turn around.

Instead, she was shocked.

Because if anything was a mood killer—it was her missing leg.

And yet, he was fully erect as he stomped toward the house damning her to hell all the way.

She smiled when he slammed the door, as a flicker of hope grew in her chest.

Then died the minute her eyes fell to the prosthetic.

Who was she kidding?

CHAPTER THIRTEEN

Bentley stomped into the house, dripping wet. He tossed his clothes on the bed, went into the bathroom, and turned on the shower full blast.

What the hell?

How could his grandfather not have told him?

No wonder she walked with a limp. His hand still burned with the shock of reaching for her thigh and sliding his fingers down only to meet water.

Anger surged through him.

Not at her.

At himself.

And his grandfather for leaving out that minor detail.

She'd lost part of her fucking leg!

At sixteen!

And her parents.

No wonder she was so angry.

According to her, Bentley had abandoned her in the hospital. Why the hell had everyone kept this from him? Brant had to know!

But they shouldn't have had to tell him.

Because he should have been there.

He shouldn't have been so focused on himself, on his own grief, his own fear at what seeing her would do to him. Because at the time, all he could think was *If I see her alive, and something happens to her again…*

…I'll wish I were dead.

They'd gotten too close.

He still had a hard time explaining why, after he knew she was out of the hospital, after he was free to do whatever the hell he wanted, he'd hesitated.

He only had himself to blame. And his own fear.

And Brant's constant reminders that Margot was happy, fine without him, that he'd talked with her and she was in good spirits. That she didn't even ask for Bentley.

Not once.

God, it had sucked so bad to hear that. To hear that she'd talked to his twin but not him. That she hadn't even mentioned Bentley once.

Bentley slammed his fists against the shower wall as the hot water ran down his back. He should be thinking about her pain, her obvious grief, but instead memories of their kiss assaulted him. Her plump bottom lip, the lingering taste of her sweet cherry ChapStick as it clung to his tongue.

"Shit." He was so hard he couldn't think straight. She'd been so soft against him, and for a few brief moments the white flag had been waved between them and he'd taken exactly what he'd wanted from her.

Not because he'd seduced her.

But because she'd *asked*.

And he had been too shocked and turned on to say no.

The minute he'd pulled Margot into his arms, he'd had a hell of a time hiding his arousal. When she innocently brushed her body against his, he'd nearly exploded with the need to have her against the pool wall.

His tumultuous feelings weren't helping things...pity for her, pity he knew she didn't want, lust, anger at being forced into this situation to begin with...

Hell.

And to think, before she'd jumped in the pool, he'd been toying with all those thoughts from his past. He would never end his life, but he'd been spending a hell of a lot of time thinking about all the things he didn't have, rather than focusing on what he did. He'd been feeling sorry for himself.

Which only made him feel like more of an asshole.

He had two legs.

He was healthy.

He'd lost his parents as well, but he'd been too young to remember.

She lived with the guilt of feeling like she killed her parents.

At sixteen.

Hell. Nobody deserved that type of soul-sucking guilt.

He closed his eyes against the memory of her taunting right before the kiss, and once again his body pulsed with need for her.

The throbbing in his body refused to go away.

His mind was hell bent on reliving that kiss. So when he should have been apologizing, or seeing if Margot was okay, he grabbed himself in order to find a quick release.

But nothing about the kiss had been quick or fleeting.

He couldn't remember the last time he'd responded so intensely to a woman. Like his body recognized something in her it desperately needed.

He gripped himself and swore. But when he closed his eyes, all he saw was her horrified and angry expression.

Lust gone.

He rested his forehead against the cool tile and tried to think of a way to cheer her up—only for his thoughts to settle on the list his grandfather had left.

An hour later, he was in the middle of one of the largest gardens he'd ever seen, with the unbearable Arizona sun sizzling on the back of his neck.

Margot was holed up in her room again.

With the door locked. He'd tried opening it only to hear shouting from the other side.

He needed to apologize—for his panicked expression, and for the fact that he knew his reaction had hurt her feelings.

It wasn't pity.

It was fucking human decency.

And even with as many times that he'd been called a jackass in his life—he really did have a heart, even if he managed to ignore it 99 percent of the time.

The garden was expansive; clearly she had a gardener, because the woman rarely went outside—unless she was trying to save poor drowning millionaires.

His lips twitched.

She really did deserve flowers.

Every day of her life.

*　　*　　*

"Go away!" Margot hissed, for about the hundredth time.

Would the man never give up?

He'd been knocking for the past fifteen minutes.

She had work to do.

Her computer mocked her in the corner—okay, so she'd completely ignored her writing since returning to the house.

She was too sick to her stomach.

Too angry.

At herself.

At her body.

A tear slid down her cheek before she could wipe it away. Was it so wrong? To want someone like Bentley to see her as more than just a girl who lost her right leg?

To see her as a woman who was still worthy of kisses?

Even if they weren't his?

Not that she wanted his.

Liar.

He'd take her heart, promise not to break it, then leave her for the next girl.

Bah.

"Margot..." Bentley said her name again, knocked, then yelled louder. "Margot, open the damn door!"

He wasn't going to go away.

Why was it that when she wanted him the most he left, and now, now that she had him, he wouldn't leave!

"I'm not going to go away!" he yelled as if reading her freaking mind.

Rolling her eyes, she limped over to the door, turned the lock, and jerked it open only to have wildflowers thrust in her face.

It would have been sweet, the fact that he was still trying even though she hadn't accepted any of his bouquets.

It may even have been nice.

Had a bee not attached itself to one of the petals, panicked at the proximity of her nose, and committed suicide by stinging her top lip.

"Ow!" she wailed, swatting the bee to the floor as flowers went everywhere. "Ow, ow, ow, ow!" Eyes watering, she pressed a finger to her already swelling lip while Bentley scooped her up into his arms and carried her into the bathroom. "What are you doing? Put me down!"

"Are you allergic?" He cupped her face gently with his hands.

"Depends," she mumbled as her lip started to go numb. "Was that a ploy to kill me?"

"I had no idea that sneaky bastard was in there. I promise." He cursed under his breath and went to the bathroom sink for a few minutes before returning with a wet washcloth. "I know it's hard to believe now, what with your face swelling up to the size of a pregnant watermelon"—she scowled—"but I was trying to cheer you up."

Margot gulped and glanced away as her cheeks heated. "Oh."

"I don't think I've ever given a girl flowers so many times," Bentley said then winked at her. "Clearly, you can see why."

She smiled, or tried to, but her lip was so swollen she was sure she looked anything but friendly. "How bad is it?" She removed the washcloth.

Bentley bit down on his bottom lip and hid his smile. "It's . . . hardly noticeable."

"You're lying."

He nodded his head. "Absolutely."

She groaned.

"It's not like anyone's going to see you except the cat you still haven't bought me," he teased.

Margot snorted and stood to look in the mirror. Once she made her way over to the sink, she dropped the washcloth and gasped. "I look like I belong on that plastic surgery show! The one where they show all the mistakes people make with Botox before almost dying!"

Bentley moved to stand behind her. He touched her

shoulders and then slowly slid his hands down her arms until they were pressed against her hands on the granite counter. "At least both of your lips match now."

Her eyes narrowed at him in the mirror. "Excuse me?"

"Your bottom lip." He reached around her and thumbed the lip in question. "It's slightly larger than the top." Voice husky, he whispered in her ear, "Believe me, I know, I measured it with my tongue."

Her breath hitched.

"And now..." He removed his hand from her lip and nodded at the mirror. "They match, er, kind of."

She grinned and then grimaced since the grin made her look like she was a circus clown. "Thanks for the flowers."

"Anytime." Something about his expression gave her pause, like he actually wanted to be talking with her—that it wasn't part of this ridiculous auction charade, but that he genuinely wanted to cheer her up, make her feel better.

Warmth spread throughout her body.

"Maybe next time you give me a gift you can include a scorpion," she teased.

"I'll be sure to hunt one down after dinner." He held out his hand.

She frowned and then placed her hand in his. "What? You want to shake hands? Over the scorpion hunt?"

He tugged her against his rock-hard chest. "I'm sorry that I panicked." She tried to pull away but he was too strong, so she stayed there, against his warm chest and sexy scent. "I was surprised. It won't happen again."

She gulped.

"And for the record..." His eyes lowered to her legs.

She squeezed her eyes shut in a stupid effort not to show him how much his words affected her.

"You still have sexy legs."

Her eyes snapped open.

"Both of them," he whispered. "Just because one holds battle scars doesn't mean it isn't beautiful." He seemed to hesitate and then pressed a kiss to her cheek. "Survival always is."

He walked away from her.

Just like she'd asked.

He left her alone in the dark, gloomy room.

Just like she'd begged.

And he shut the door.

He did everything she'd asked of him.

And for the first time since he arrived—she wanted him to argue, she wanted him to push past the barriers she'd thrown between them. Because Bentley had done the impossible.

He made a half . . . feel like a whole.

CHAPTER FOURTEEN

Bentley!"

Was he hallucinating? Or was Margot actually yelling his name in a *Hey, return to my cave of doom and I won't kick you out* way?

He'd been headed down to the kitchen to start lunch or to find something that would occupy his mind when her voice rang through the upstairs hallway.

"Yeah?" he called back without moving from the stairs.

She didn't answer.

Right, so he really was hallucinating. Great.

"Sorry." She startled the shit out of him, and he almost fell face-first down the stairs. He gripped the railing and turned. Margot's face was flushed red, her top lip still huge. "I'm going to punch you if you laugh."

"Sorry." He coughed to hide his laugh and crossed his arms so he wouldn't reach for her. It seemed now that his body knew what her touch was like, it craved more. Just great. That was what he needed—he'd always shied away from commitment of any kind, and she wasn't the type you could just screw and leave. His throat went completely dry at the realization that kissing her would turn into sex, sex would turn into more sex, and more sex would turn into pain. For both of them. Besides, this little cease-fire wouldn't last. "What's up?"

She put her hands on her hips. "Why do you keep picking wildflowers?"

"Is this a trick question where if I answer wrong you get to push me down the stairs or yell at me more?"

"What?" She frowned. "No."

"In that case..." He wasn't technically supposed to tell her he had a list that was helping him romance and cheer her up—and his pride wouldn't let him admit that he had an old woman giving him romance lessons, so he went for vague. "I picked flowers because women like flowers. Right?"

"I'm allergic to flowers," she said in a deadpan voice, and then sneezed and shoved them against his chest. "It's the thought that counts, though, right?"

"Are you flirting with me?" He moved closer to Margot, only to have her stumble backward.

"No!" she denied, her cheeks turning a pretty pink. "I was just telling you, for future reference, if you want to do something nice...don't bring flowers to a girl who's allergic to flowers, especially not flowers carrying kamikaze bees."

"Noted," he said, taking the flowers back from her, his hand falling to the side awkwardly. Why did it feel like he'd just got rejected on his first date?

Hell.

"So." She nodded. "I should probably go back to... work." She swallowed and didn't budge, her eyes locking on his like she wanted to say something more.

He reached for her arm. "Do you ever work anywhere other than your office?"

"No." She pulled away. "My creative process is very..."
She licked her lower lip. Damn it, he was hungry for another
taste. "...precise."

"Precise?"

"I like ritual. I'm a creature of habit. Everything in my
room creates the perfect environment for me to be creative."
Her chin lifted, just daring him to defy her.

So he did.

Because that was what he did best.

And honestly he'd rather fight with her than go back
downstairs by himself, because he'd already learned that being alone with his thoughts was a really dangerous thing.

He needed distraction.

He needed Margot.

Which was why he took a step toward her and whispered,
"Show me."

"Sh-show you?"

"Yes. Show me your ritual, and maybe if you're lucky
I'll lie down on your bed while you explain all about your
creativity in the bedroom. I'll even keep my mouth shut the
entire time."

She snorted even as her cheeks pinked.

"What? Don't believe me?"

"You like the sound of your own voice way too much."

"Now, Margot, why wouldn't I like the sound of my own
voice? I've been told it's addicting..."

She burst out laughing. It was the nicest sound he'd ever
heard. "And I'm sure every time it was by a girl with dollar
signs in her eyes and dreams of broken condoms in her future."

"Why else would I carry my own condoms? Can't trust
theirs not to have holes poked in them. Now that we've got
that out of the way..." He grasped her shoulders and turned

her around. "Lead the way. I promise I won't lock the door behind me and try to take off your clothes." Was it his imagination, or did her body shake? "Unless you want me to."

"No," she said quickly. "Sorry, but you'll never see me naked."

"Way to let me down slowly."

"I'm more of a rip-off-the-Band-Aid kind of girl."

"Oh, I see, you're more into instant pain than long bouts of pleasure..." He grinned at her back.

She stumbled a bit then glared over her shoulder. "You say things like that on purpose, don't you?"

"Maybe."

"You're a manwhore."

"Finally." He trailed a finger down her exposed neck where a few pieces of tantalizing red hair kissed her skin. "Something we agree on." He'd be lying if he said her barb hadn't hit home. Why was it okay for him to admit it to himself, but it hurt when Margot said it?

She jerked away from him and continued into her room. He followed. And locked the door behind him.

Margot froze and then slowly turned to face him. "You said you wouldn't lock the door."

"I lied."

Her eyes bugged out. "If you touch me I'll use my stapler on your balls."

Bentley laughed. "Relax, I was teasing. It's only a joke." Her expression was unreadable. "And apparently I'm not funny. So where do we start?"

Margot raked her gaze over him and then pointed at her computer. "That's where I work."

He tilted his head. "Shocker. You work at a desk. Why hadn't I thought of that?"

"Probably because you don't work?"

Frustration welled up from deep within Bentley. What the hell kind of impression did she have of him if she really thought he sat around on his ass all day?

"Actually..." He cleared his throat. "I organize most of the charity functions for my family—not to mention I'm more the face of the company than Brock, since he hates functions. Brant, well, lately he hates life, so it's all me, but thanks for the insult." He shrugged. "Though years ago I *was* a marketing intern."

He almost missed her confused look before she turned away.

"What? What was that look?"

She waved a hand at him then sat in one of the recliners by her desk. "Sorry, I have to sit, my leg, it—" She averted her eyes.

"I'm sure it hurts to stand for long periods of time," he said gently.

She nodded, and then glanced back up at him. "Why marketing?"

Bentley froze.

Nobody had ever asked him that before.

Not even his grandfather.

He was so used to lying, so used to using his charm to avoid questions just like that one, but for the first time, he wanted to tell someone the truth.

"Why writing?" He deflected her question with one of his own. "Is it because you love books so much?"

"Fine." A pretty smile spread across her face. She was on to him. Of course she was. "You know I like books."

"I'm pretty sure that's how we met. You dropped your book on the ground; I, being the Prince Charming that I am, handed it back to you and let my fingers linger a little longer than necessary because I was curious."

"Curious?"

"About how soft your skin was."

She gulped. "And?"

"I was right."

"Right about what?"

He liked this side of her, the side he remembered: wide-eyed, beautiful, flushed. "So you write because you like books?"

Her eyes narrowed. "You're the king of subject changes, you know that, right?"

"Some things never change, do they, Red?"

Her eyes flashed before she looked away from him and down at the ground. "And some things...have no choice but to change." After clearing her throat she glanced back at him, "I like words. I like creating worlds and making people happy. To me it's not a job."

Her words struck a chord in him. Marketing would be a job.

Being a vet would have been a passion.

"Not all of us are so lucky." Once again he was weighted down by the shit from his past.

"Your turn." She crossed her arms.

"Can't we go back to talking about your skin again? I liked that topic."

Her eyebrows arched.

"Fine, it was the only internship they had after graduation. I needed a job so I wouldn't—" He caught himself.

"So you wouldn't what?"

Kill himself with boredom? No, that wasn't it. He needed a job so that he could prove himself, and so that he wouldn't focus on the crippling anxiety that tended to attack when he wasn't screwing and drinking his way through life. Work actually helped with that—just never as much as a willing woman or bottle of whiskey.

"Do what twenty-one-year-olds do, I guess?" he said lamely. "I needed a job, and I knew I could get it."

"But—" She was still frowning at him, her eyes piercing in their assessment. "Do you love it?"

He let out a bitter laugh and walked over to the window, pulling back the curtain enough so that light could filter into the dark room. "The only thing I love is women. The more, the better."

And suddenly the cease-fire shattered in front of him, because he'd given her a dick answer. Because as much as he wanted to tell her the truth, he was leaving soon.

Going back to his passionless life.

Fuck.

A tense silence wrapped around the room.

"You should go," she finally said, sadness blanketing her face. And he knew he was the one who put that look there. She'd opened up, she'd shared, and when it was his turn to prove he was more than a womanizing playboy, he'd defaulted. "I have a chapter to write."

"A kiss to write," he corrected, trying to regain ground. "Don't you mean a kiss?"

Margot stood abruptly, limped to the computer, and took a seat. "Ah, the kiss—our kiss—sorry, I completely forgot about it. Must not have been memorable."

Bentley gritted his teeth and followed her to the computer. "Not. Memorable?" The hell it wasn't! *He* still remembered it, and he'd kissed countless women. Holy shit. Was he a horrible kisser now?

She lifted a shoulder in a shrug as she ran her fingers over the mouse pad and stared at the screen. "I'm sure most women wouldn't agree with me. Why don't you go find one of them and leave me alone?"

"The hell I will," he growled, grabbing the back of the

chair and spinning her around. "Pity your top lip's too numb to remember this."

He closed his mouth over hers.

Sucked her lower lip like he was dying for a taste—which he was.

And then punished her with a kiss that had his body anticipating its release. Pulling back, he blew cool air across her wet lips.

She blinked at him in a daze, and he ran quick nibbling kisses down her neck, returning to her lips seconds later as his hands slid to her stomach and then down to her thighs.

She squirmed toward him.

"That." He stood. "Write that."

A pencil flew by his head, hitting the door before he unlocked it and pulled it open.

"Good luck, Red!" He pulled the door closed behind him.

"You're a bastard!" Her muffled yell came just as he reached the top of the stairs.

As a matter of fact, yes, he was.

CHAPTER FIFTEEN

Writing the kiss was almost worse than reliving the kiss. She had to write about hand placement, the sensation of his mouth, the feel of his skin, the slide of his mouth. By the time Margot was done with the last few chapters, she'd written two kissing scenes, was sweating profusely, and was desperate for a cold shower.

A really, really, cold, Bentley-free shower.

She closed down her computer and leaned back in her chair. Why had she let him kiss her a second time? She'd known it was coming; she'd seen the fire in his eyes and known she'd pushed him too far in their previous conversation. Maybe it was because the more run-ins she had with him, the more she wondered if there was something below the surface.

The lines between them were blurring in a quick and confusing way. Was he kissing her to prove a point? Or was he kissing her because he really did like her lips? However swollen one of them might be.

"Why?" She groaned out loud and then banged her head against the desk, once again reliving the searing kiss.

Maybe he just wanted to be her friend.

With added benefits.

Right. Like she'd agree to that. He still hadn't even apologized for abandoning her or even explained why. And honestly, she was afraid to ask.

Afraid that he would say something earth-shattering like, *You weren't worth it,* or *I was too busy.* Or, worse, *I didn't really care.*

His lips had been soft, his hands hot as they traveled over her body. She shivered.

Friends with benefits?

Really awesome, mind-numbing, tummy-clenching benefits?

"This is what men like him do, Margot," she whispered to herself. It was why he had the reputation that he did.

She eyed her computer.

And before she lost her nerve, she opened it up again and typed Bentley's name in the search engine. Her finger hovered over the Return button.

Did she really want an update on his escapades?

Yes. She did.

Because it would be sobering.

And revealing.

And a painful reminder of why people like Bentley Wellington were users, the type who didn't care about anyone but themselves.

The first story was from the auction, with a photo of him looking gorgeous in a tux, smiling for the cameras on the arm of her grandmother. It made her grin; he looked more pissed than anything.

How was it after only a few days with him she knew what type of smile was forced or real? That really couldn't be a good sign.

She kept scrolling through stories, some old, some new, all of them confirming her suspicions.

The stories of his glamorous lifestyle sucked her in, so much that an hour passed before her stomach reminded her she hadn't eaten anything since breakfast.

Just one more.

She clicked the third page.

And frowned.

BENTLEY WELLINGTON HOSPITALIZED FOR EXHAUSTION, read the headline.

Exhaustion?

She clicked on the article. It was vague. He had a towel over his head and was walking into a treatment center. The buzz in the article mentioned drugs and alcohol, but that didn't feel right.

Oh great. Now she knew his medical history based on the fact that it didn't feel right?

She kept reading.

And then felt her entire body go numb.

The date was the day after her parents' accident.

He'd been hospitalized?

Her eyes raked over the article until they fell on the name of the hospital that he'd been checked into.

With a gasp she shut her computer and placed her hands over her mouth as tears welled in her eyes.

They'd been in the exact same hospital.

And he'd still never thought, *Hey, I'm going to go hop in that elevator and see my best friend*?

Anger surged through her, and then sadness. The same choking sadness that threatened to overwhelm her all those years ago.

She reached for her computer again. There had to be an explanation. What was she now? A stalker? It was not like she was writing a book about hospitals, exhaustion, and reasons for abandonment.

With a groan she shook her head, stood, and went in search of food. Maybe after a full stomach she'd be able to think clearly; maybe then the hollow feeling would go away.

When she opened the door she nearly tripped over a giant basket. A note was taped to the outside.

One day we'll go on a real picnic, but for now, I thought you might be hungry. Eat me. It had a smiley face next to it.

She shivered. Yeah, she knew exactly what "eat me" meant.

Because that was just how his twisted mind worked.

Her smile fell.

She was getting attached to him all over again. Only this time they were alone in a huge house filled with her pain and his secrets.

He'd been hospitalized. In the mental wing of the same hospital she'd been in. He'd never done drugs in high school, and back then she'd known him better than anyone. And while she knew he was guilty of underage drinking, he'd never been a huge partyer. That came later.

It was staggering, thinking she knew everything about him, only to find out that maybe he'd kept her in the dark even back then.

With a shaky hand, she opened the basket to find it empty. Where the heck was all the food?

Something at the top of the stairs caught her attention.

A bag of Doritos?

With a smirk she picked it up, opened the bag, and walked down the stairs. On the middle landing there was a sandwich wrapped up in a Ziploc bag, and on the bottom of the stairs a waiting Bentley with a soda in hand.

"Let me guess." She eyed the soda, leery of his motives. "It worked on your dog so you thought it might work on me?"

"Stole the words right from my mouth." He winked and handed over the soda. "Also, my arm's cramping. I thought I heard you get up a while back and then nothing, no door opening, no yelling. I almost called 911, and then I remembered you're a vampire who prefers darkness to light, so I banked on you still being alive. Question: When you get hungry do you just lure wildlife into your room and stake it, or—"

She covered his mouth with the part of her hand not covered in glorious Doritos cheese. "Are you done?"

His eyes darted down to her fingers. Before she could pull back, Bentley had snatched her fingers and slid his tongue around the one covered with the most cheese. With a moan he closed his eyes, giving her a quick moment to freak out over the fact that if his tongue felt that good against her finger, what else was his mouth capable of? And why wasn't she pulling away?

"Delicious." His deep voice interrupted her vivid daydream about him licking her neck like a Popsicle. "Careful, Red, when you look at a man like that he's bound to get ideas."

"Like you need my help with your . . . ideas."

Heat spread through her and she had to grip the railing to keep from pressing herself against his chest.

"Soda?" he asked in a low voice.

She was parched and starving and had Doritos breath and was so confused she didn't know what to do.

Cringing, she took a huge gulp of Coke and eyed him over the aluminum can. "Why are you staring?"

"Your lip's a bit better." He pointed. "How does it feel?"

"Oh, I don't know, like I got stung by an angry bee whose home you destroyed."

"Bees live in hives."

"And flowers, apparently."

"Touché." His smooth voice really was addicting. Damn him for making her realize that.

Another shiver wracked her body.

"So do you want the rest of the food?" Bentley asked.

"The rest of the food?"

"A plethora of food."

"Big word."

"Big basket." He smirked down at the basket. "What do you say?"

"What's the point of this? The luring me out of my room with food?"

"The point," he repeated, "is to make sure you don't starve while enjoying a nice, friendly conversation about something besides the elephants in the room."

"Plural?"

Bentley nodded. "Your leg, my sexcapades, your grand-mother, my grandfather, your parents, hell, *my* parents—"

"I get it," she snapped. " 'Elephants' works."

He held out his hand. "Come on, let's go eat."

She didn't have a chance to protest, because it was Bent-ley, and he took what he wanted, which included her hand when she refused to give it to him. He led her into one of her two large living rooms, the one with the ninety-inch flat-screen TV and the bar. Except for the fact that it was decorated in bright pinks and whites, it was more man cave than anything.

A bottle of expensive whiskey sat on one of the coffee tables next to pita bread and hummus, ice, fresh fruit, and chocolate.

"You did all of this?"

"I'm a man of too many talents to count," he said in a

teasing tone, which upset her more than it should. He always teased, but she was noticing his teasing took on two very different tones—one was playful and fun, the other was distant.

She preferred playful over distant.

The distance reminded her he wasn't really there for *her*.

But for her grandmother.

For charity.

Bentley poured her a large shot of whiskey and pressed the thick glass into her hand. "Drink."

"It's three in the afternoon!"

He blinked. "So?"

"So it's...not five yet."

"Do you have a curfew still, too? Because I remember a few nights where I snuck you in at least five minutes before eleven."

"Shut up." She grinned at the memory and took a sip and nearly gagged. "That's way too strong."

"Thought you might say that." He took her Coke and poured some in the glass then handed it back to her. "So how's the book coming?"

She rolled her eyes. "You want to drink whiskey with me and ask about my book?"

"It's either that or the elephants, remember?"

Margot chugged more whiskey and shuddered.

"Good choice," he muttered under his breath.

"The kissing scene was good," she finally managed to squeak out. "Probably one of the best I've ever written."

"Margot." He leaned in so close she could smell the whiskey on his breath. "Are you saying I inspired you?"

"No. Because saying that would inflate your ego and it's hard enough being in the same room with you as it is." She shoved his chest playfully.

He retreated with an easy grin and picked up a grape,

popping it into his mouth before saying, "You only write historical romances."

Margot traced her fingers around the rim of the glass. "Have you been Googling me?" she asked. And immediately images from her own Google search of him flooded her brain. No. Elephants.

"I own a phone, it has Internet access; it took me three seconds." He shrugged as if stalking her wasn't a big deal. As if it didn't mean anything more than mild curiosity. "I bought one."

She spit out her whiskey. "You what?"

"Bought one of your books." And then he proceeded to quote, straight from one of them. "His flavor was unique, like leather and honey...the whiskey of his lips was—"

"Okay!" she yelled, interrupting him. "That was...what did you do, memorize one passage for the past three hours?"

"No. Actually, I read the entire book and then memorized it. I think you should have killed the duke, though. He was a complete bastard to Rosalyn. She forgave him way too easily." He drank more whiskey and then just kept on talking as though her mouth hadn't just dropped open in shock. "I mean, I get what you were trying to do with their relationship, create enough hate for it to turn into love, blah, blah, blah. It's a fine line, it always is, but you pushed him too far, almost made it so you couldn't redeem your own character. You basically wrote yourself into a corner, and it was painful watching you try to write your way out of it. But then, just when I thought you couldn't do it, you did. I liked it. I'm not saying I like the guy, but it was good."

When he quit talking, Margot responded in the only way a shut-in afraid of the world knew how.

She kissed him.

On the mouth.

And quickly pulled away. "Thank you."

Holy crap, what did she just do?

The silence was thick. Bentley's wavy dark hair was mussed, unkempt, as though he'd been running his hands through it. His eyes hooded as the rasp from his voice interrupted her internal meltdown. "Here's a thought. Feel free not to shoot it down right away."

"I'm listening." Her body still felt heavy and needy from the stupid kiss she'd just given him.

See! This was why she was a shut-in! Among numerous other reasons! You didn't just go around kissing houseguests on the mouth, especially ones who feel sorry for you and who abandoned you when you were at your worst! God, why was it so hard to keep hating him?

"Every time I read one of your books, I get a kiss." His eyes twinkled. "What do you say?"

"I say I have eighteen," she whispered as a laugh took hold.

"Give me twenty-four hours," he said immediately.

"A question for a question?" she asked.

His eyes were hesitant, but he nodded anyway.

"What does your grandfather have over you that's keeping you here for thirty full days?"

"That's easy. He threatened to send the mafia after me." Bentley shrugged. "But I've got friends in low places, so I think I could probably make it out alive."

"Be serious."

He lowered his gaze to a spot on the floor and then finally spoke. "If I said I was here out of the goodness of my own heart... would you believe me?"

"Nobody's that good. Besides, I talked to my grandmother. I know this was something she and your grandfather cooked up. Because they're *insane*."

He laughed, but there was no humor in the sound. "Well, what if I said I wish I was...that type of man, the type that would drop everything to help a friend he hasn't spoken to since she was sixteen. What would you say if I told you I wish I could go back in time, and be the friend you needed then, rather than be coerced into it now?"

A lump formed in Margot's throat. She tried to clear it away, but it was useless. "I'd say—" her voice thick with emotion, she locked eyes with him "—that I don't believe you."

Bentley cursed. "Margot, look, back then—"

"No." she interrupted; she wasn't ready for the truth.

His eyes searched hers. "What if I told you there was a reason?"

"Is there ever a good reason for abandoning your best friend in her time of need?" Her voice dropped as she tried desperately not to let any tears fall.

Bentley pinched the bridge of his nose. "Back then, I would have said yes."

"And now?" She just had to ask.

"No." He looked angry, his nostrils flared, his jaw clenched. "Now, I say it's a fucking excuse, and a poor one at that."

He shouldn't have said that.

It gave her hope.

Hope that she misunderstood the situation.

Hope that they could start fresh.

"Do you believe me?" He reached for her hand.

"Maybe." She found her voice.

He exhaled. "Then that's all that matters."

"Is it?"

"For now?" He reached for his glass. "It has to be."

CHAPTER SIXTEEN

He waited for Margot to call him out. It was something she would do, call bullshit when he deflected, but instead, she blushed.

Bentley would rather have been punched in the face.

Her blush meant he was getting to her.

It meant that part of her façade was cracking.

It also meant that in a few short weeks, he'd be gone, and she'd be hurt, because no matter how pretty she was, or how often her lips made his body ache—he couldn't go through it again, the thought of losing her.

She may not make it.

Dead.

Dead.

Dead.

Every single time she blinked in his direction he was reminded of their shared past. Stolen moments. Laughter. And like an idiot, he forgot about it whenever they were lost in conversation.

The hard part?

He meant every word.

And he really shouldn't have.

He shouldn't say those things and mean them.

Bentley wished he was that guy, the one that was deserving of the look she was giving him right that minute—but he wasn't the hero, he'd never been the hero.

He'd proved that when he left her.

He'd proved it when he lost his mind with grief and anger—when anxiety overtook common sense and caused him to lash out.

No, he wasn't a hero.

If she knew that the only reason he was there was for a job that he was no longer sure he even wanted? So he could get paid more money he didn't need? So he could finally gain approval from his family after all these years?

If she knew that she was his ticket to bigger and better things within the company, and that he'd had to be bribed to even spend time with her?

Then again, it wasn't like she didn't know he was there for a reason. How was being there for a job worse than being there because her grandmother paid for him at an auction?

Maybe it wasn't as bleak as he thought.

But that was what spending time with Margot did: It confused him; it reminded him that he'd snapped once and it all came back to her—their friendship, the relationship he'd always wanted, and the one he thought he'd lost.

"So." Margot popped a grape in her mouth. "You asked about my career and even read one of my books...but I'm pretty sure there isn't any book out there that reveals more about the great Bentley Wellington."

"Oh, so now I'm great?"

"Well, you fed me." She shrugged. "And offered whiskey."

"That's how I lure every woman into my bed. You've

been warned." He held up his hands in innocence as a deep shade of red stained her cheeks.

An uncomfortable silence stretched between them.

He coughed.

Seriously?

He was coughing to fill awkward moments now?

"No book," he said quickly. "But I'm pretty sure a quick Internet search will tell you anything you're dying to know."

Was it his imagination or did she look guilty?

"Really?" She averted her eyes. "So all the women...all the parties..."

Bentley tried to keep his grin in place, but it hurt to stretch out a smile he wasn't really feeling—especially since he didn't have a past he was proud of. And no matter the reasons behind his actions, it still didn't justify what he had done, not fully.

Suddenly itching to move, he crossed his legs and leaned back in the chair. "All the women," he repeated. "All the parties." With a nonchalant shrug, he took a sip of his whiskey and prayed it would magically be enough to get him drunk. "All of it's true."

"The senator's wife?"

He shrugged and took another sip.

"Married women?"

Another shrug.

"Bentley!" She threw her hands in the air. "Okay, at least answer this: Why would you sleep with a married woman?"

"I think the correct question would be: Why would a happily married woman sleep with me?"

She gaped and then narrowed her eyes. "So it's their fault?"

"Do you think I actually need to roam the streets to find someone willing to spread their thighs for me?"

Margot gasped.

"Oh, I'm sorry." He snorted. "Does my bluntness offend you?"

"No." Her nostrils flared as she crossed her arms and glared.

"They come to me." Why were they having this conversation? What was supposed to have been a nice way to lure her out of her cave had suddenly turned into the damn inquisition.

"But you could always say no."

He grinned into his glass. "You're cute, you know that, right?"

"Well, that's offensive," she mumbled.

Bentley grinned harder and set down his glass. "Riddle me this..." He eyed her up and down. "Why do people take risks in life? Why do they take chances knowing that they could get hurt or hurt someone else? Why the hell would someone base-jump off a cliff when they know that there's a fifty percent chance the chute won't open?"

Swallowing, she tucked a piece of red hair behind her ear. "For the thrill?"

"Because it feels good," he whispered. "So if a married woman wants me to fuck her brains out because her dumb-as-shit politician husband's been cheating on her for the last ten years? Then yeah, I'm probably going to go for it, especially if that same politician's known for being dirty and the only way to expose him is to splash his image across every newspaper in the United States." Bentley stood. "Was it wrong?" He made a face. "Probably." He leaned over her, his body casting a shadow across her cheeks. "Am I sorry? Absolutely not."

Her gaze darted like a scared deer's from his lips to his eyes. "I've never done anything bad."

His eyebrows rose. "Nothing?"

"Not after the accident."

"That's a pity."

"Why?"

"Being good all the time is boring as hell, Margot. Believe me, I watched my brother Brock try to live that life."

"So you took it upon yourself to be the yin to his yang?" she shot back.

Digging. Margot was digging.

He jerked back. "Don't pretend you know the man I am now just because we used to be best friends and I was obsessed with your hair."

She gasped.

"Sorry," he mumbled, hating himself for lashing out at her—again. "I didn't mean…" Shit. He ran his hands through his hair. How had the conversation gotten away from him so fast? "I'm not the same guy. I wish I could say I was, because maybe that would mean all this shit between us wouldn't exist. It was easy then…at least it felt like it. Movie nights on the weekends, sleepovers where I begged to jump into your bed only to get shut down every damn time…" He smiled at the memory. "My girlfriends always hated you, you know."

"Girlfriends, plural?"

Well, at least she was talking and not trying to strangle him for his asinine comment. "I typically dated two at once."

Margot rolled her eyes. "Screwing and dating are two different things, you know that, right?"

"One of them threatened to break up with me. *It's me or Margot.*" He could still hear her shrill voice as she stomped her foot and waited for him to make his decision.

Margot hung her head. "So that's why?"

"That's why what?"

"You left."

"Hell no." Bentley reached for her hand. "I told her to go screw herself and showed up at your house a few minutes later begging for food."

"You were always begging for food."

"I was growing." He teased. "Besides, you always had Doritos."

"And Coke," she finished.

"Sometimes, if I was really lucky you'd have donuts, too, but beggars can't be choosers."

Her smile fell.

Shit.

Her eyes narrowed in on him, all traces of teasing gone. "A question for a question, right?"

Dread pooled in his stomach. "Right."

She blinked up at him. "What kind of man are you, now? Really."

He offered her an easy grin, the same kind he gave his brothers when he wanted them to believe he was totally fine. The same grin he wore when his grandfather stomped all over his dreams. The same damn grin he'd been wearing his entire life, the phony one. "I'm like Fort Knox. Don't mistake my confessions as something they aren't. This—" he gestured between the two of them "—is just an indoor picnic between two old friends who are trying desperately to bury hatchets, elephants, and a shitload of sexual tension."

"Wow, and here I thought we were having a real moment with real progress." She rolled her eyes.

She saw too much. Cared too much. Wanted too much.

Margot stood and shoved past him. "You know…" Hands on hips, she turned and glared. "I don't think you're scared of letting people in. I think your fear is that once they get in, they'll realize there's nothing there. You're empty,

because you don't even know yourself, do you? Who is
Bentley Wellington? A playboy? A man who sleeps with
politicians' wives? Do you even know who you are anymore
besides what your family wants you to be?"

"Margot—"

"Who is Bentley Wellington?" she asked again.

And he had no answer.

Because she was right.

He didn't know.

And that was one of the scariest realizations of his life.

CHAPTER SEVENTEEN

Margot couldn't sleep.

Not after her fight, or whatever it was, with Bentley. He had to be the most confusing man she'd ever met, not that she had many people to compare him to, but still. One minute he was all easy smiles and chatty, the next dark, moody, and defensive.

It was irritating that she'd spent the better part of the night, the part where she should have been sleeping, searching through her high school memories of the best friend she used to adore.

He was still there.

But he was beneath so much emotional turmoil, she had to wonder what sort of traumatic thing happened to him to make him feel the need to go to such great lengths to pretend like everything was perfect—when it wasn't.

Did it have something to do with his whole "exhaustion" stint in the hospital?

Her heart dropped.

She shouldn't have said what she did.

She actually had no right to say those things to him, not anymore, but they had just come out. Was she that much of a homebody that she didn't even know how to have normal conversations with people anymore without getting nosy and asking personal questions?

She punched the pillow to her right.

And stared at the door.

Maybe he was still up.

Maybe she could just apologize.

Even though she wasn't sure it was entirely her fault that the conversation had floated into dangerous territory.

Mumbling to herself, she sat up and put on her prosthetic, then pulled her pajama pants down over the leg.

The house was blanketed in darkness.

Bentley's light was on.

The crack beneath the door glowed in the dark hallway.

She lifted her hand to knock when the door jerked open.

"You are literally the loudest walker I've ever heard." He crossed his arms over his naked, bronzed chest.

She sucked in a breath.

"You should probably close your mouth—don't want me to take that expression the wrong way—it's two in the morning."

She finally found her voice. "Meaning?"

"Meaning," he said, leaning against the door, "you could be down here for a booty call…"

She laughed.

His eyes narrowed. "I wasn't making a joke."

"Oh." She bit down on her lip and blurted out, "I'm sorry."

Bentley took a step backward, his eyes widening. "You're apologizing?"

She nodded.

"To me?"

Another nod.

"Why?"

"Because I was being nosy, and what I said was mean."

"Even if it was true?"

"Yes." Her voice cracked. "Even if it was true. Anyway..." She forced a smile. "I couldn't sleep so, hopefully, now I'll be able to."

"Oh, I get it, so you were down here apologizing because you couldn't sleep, so really, it's about you." He smirked.

"Ughhhh, why do you have to make it sound so selfish?" She walked into his room.

"Isn't it?"

"No!" Her shoulders slumped. "Sorry, apparently I'm the loudest walker ever and I can't even apologize right."

He grinned. "I'll give you a free pass this time." Bentley slid off his boxers and walked, completely naked, to his bed. "Can you get the light?"

Margot gaped after him.

"Margot?" He pulled the covers over his gorgeous body. "The light?"

"Y-yes, sure, I..." She did a slow circle. Where was the light again? Why did it need to be turned off? "I, um—"

"It's by the door."

She mentally slapped herself in the face. "I know."

"I know you know. I just wanted to remind you just in case the view of my dick was blocking the way."

She clenched her fists. "I really don't like you sometimes."

Margot could have sworn she heard him mutter, "Good," before she flicked the light off and made her way back upstairs.

It wasn't until she was tossing and turning, again, that she realized he'd done it on purpose.

To punish her.

Because visions of his naked body were the only thing she could concentrate on.

And when four a.m. came around, she gave up and went to her computer. At least now she had something to work with.

She smiled and started to type. *"His body glistened with sweat..."*

*   *   *

"It's really good," Bentley said.

Bentley? Why was he there? What was happening? An ache pounded in her temples, and she slowly blinked her eyes open.

"I mean, I don't know if I'm that big, but still...I think that she needs to scream a bit more, though."

Why was he talking?

The first thing she saw was her computer on the side of her desk. She'd fallen asleep against a stack of books.

And Bentley was standing over the computer.

Reading.

Coffee cup in hand.

Looking way too sexy for however early it was.

He winked at her. "Don't you think she should scream more? I don't think I've ever screwed a woman who didn't scream my name at least a dozen times."

"What?" she rasped. "What are you doing?"

"It's nine a.m. I was worried...I knocked, but you didn't answer, so I let myself in."

"Clearly."

"And started to read that dirty sex scene I must have inspired last night..." He grinned and took another sip of coffee. "I think the part where she has three orgasms is my favorite."

Groaning, she banged her head against the books and willed him to go away.

"Up you go." Bentley set down the coffee mug by her face and pulled her into his arms.

"What are you doing—?"

"Sleep." He dropped her onto the bed and pulled the comforter over her. "I'll check on you later. Oh, and Margot, if you needed more inspiration, all you needed to do was ask."

She chucked a pillow at his face.

He dodged it then turned to her, and his eyes drank her in. "You can laugh, you know, even smile a bit. I won't tell anyone."

She pressed her lips together to keep from smiling.

And then Bentley tossed the pillow back at her face.

She gasped. "Did you just hit me in the face with a pillow?"

"I was returning the favor." He chuckled and then moved over to the bed and straddled her. "Say thank you."

"You're annoying," she said breathlessly.

"But I kind of grow on you, right?"

"Like a fungus."

"Was that a compliment?"

"Did it sound like one?"

He nodded and then leaned down until she could have sworn she could hear her heart pounding in her chest. "I miss your laugh."

All the air whooshed out of her lungs. "What?"

"I want to hear you laugh again."

"I heard you the first time." She shook her head. "You can't... you can't say things like that to me."

"Funny." His eyes lingered on her mouth. "Because I just did."

Neither of them moved. Her breathing was way too loud. He probably thought she was hyperventilating. And maybe she was; her chest felt tight, and it was nearly impossible to suck in a full breath without drawing attention to herself. It had everything to do with how beautiful he was—and how he was looking at her.

The way she wrote about the hero looking at the love of his life in her books.

The way she wanted to be looked at.

Her leg throbbed.

She quickly shifted away and closed her eyes. "You're right... I should get some sleep."

"Okay." Soft lips met her forehead and then the bed dipped. The door clicked shut.

Margot exhaled as a single tear ran down her cheek.

It wasn't fair.

He wasn't playing fair.

Because he would end up hurting her without even realizing it—because she already knew she'd miss him when he left.

And he would leave.

Just like last time.

Only for some reason, she was terrified this would be worse.

In high school he'd broken off a piece of her heart.

If he left now? He just might take it all.

CHAPTER EIGHTEEN

Margot woke up from a much-needed three-hour nap—to absolute hell.

Her phone showed that she'd slept through two calls and numerous texts.

She recognized the numbers, but she needed to take at least ten deep breaths before listening to the two missed voice mails.

One from her agent.

The other from her editor.

Hands clammy, Margot dropped her phone onto the table and forced herself to take a few more deep breaths, then finally logged onto her e-mail to confirm what both her agent and editor had said in their messages.

Congrats, you've been nominated for another RITA!

Dinner.

Drinks.

In town for RWA.

Know you hate public appearances, but at least meet with your publisher. So exciting!

Margot's agent had, of course, thrown her under the bus and said that Margot would love to meet for dinner.

This was a complete nightmare.

The last time Margot was at a public dinner had been an absolute catastrophe. Her grandmother had begged Margot to let her take her out for her birthday.

Her fingernails dug into her palms while she tried to calm herself down. She could still remember the curious stares from people. It was normal to be curious, even she knew that. But what wasn't normal was the whispering, pointing, laughing.

She'd tried to ignore all of it, but her nerves got the better of her and she'd fallen.

God, she could still hear the noise of the silverware slamming against the floor. She'd been so insecure about the stares from people that she'd tripped and taken half the table down with her.

It was the last time she'd been in public, and after driving home in tears, she made her grandmother promise never to ask her to do it again.

That had been five years ago.

With a gulp she read the e-mail.

They had reservations at seven that night. "Bring your significant other!" the e-mail encouraged.

Right. Because she had one of those.

A plus one.

The problem was, anytime her agent assumed she had a boyfriend, Margot had always laughed it off or responded with a vague e-mail in hopes that the subject would be dropped.

So now, not only did she have to go out in public…

…but the expectation was that she'd have someone with her.

Hell.

Her mind drifted to the man downstairs.

She sighed. He'd hold it over her, or at least make her give him something in return. And the last thing she needed was to be in a position where he could take more of her heart.

With a groan, she slapped her hand against her clammy forehead and kept reading.

"It's good for you to meet your editor in person, gives them confidence in your work..." Blah, blah, blah.

The more she read, the more her stomach clenched with dread. It was going to be an absolute disaster.

And the worst part? She was actually tempted to ask Bentley. Not because she wanted him by her side—okay, so maybe that was part of it—but mainly because she was so terrified to go by herself that the thought had her dizzy.

Margot licked her dry lips. She could always cancel at the last minute, develop a stomach flu.

She pressed her fingers against the keys, then jerked back. A week ago she would have lied.

But today...something held her back.

Maybe it was the conversation she'd had with Bentley, where she'd done a stellar job of asking him if he even knew himself all the while feeling guilty for being the sort of person who knew themselves too well and kept hidden away out of fear.

She knew what people's reactions would be like—just like she knew what her reaction would be in public. For the most part, people were nice, but there was always that certain percentage that stared, that whispered. She broke out into a cold sweat thinking about it.

The problem was that he made her feel like a complete hypocrite and he hadn't even done anything! At least not yet.

How bad could it be? It had been years since she'd gone out to dinner, maybe it would be nice? A nice bottle of wine. Good food.

Maybe he'd hold the door open for her.

She would like that.

Maybe it was time, at least to go outside, drive more than a mile away from the house.

Live a normal life.

Her body shook as sweat started to trickle down her back. Just thinking about a normal life—going outside, driving—had her ready to have a nervous breakdown.

What the hell was she thinking? She had to decline.

And yet, the idea of staying in...

The idea of doing the same thing over and over again—living this insane life of repetition—was just as panic inducing as the thought of leaving the house.

Why was she even considering it?

She only had one answer.

Bentley.

Somehow without even trying he'd gotten to her, made her feel trapped in her own house.

Vampire!

She wasn't a vampire.

But she did have about five million takeout menus and an uncanny ability to one-click everything she needed on Amazon.

Because it was easier than the stares.

She gulped.

Maybe they had more in common than she thought.

Bentley might be a runner.

But Margot was a hider.

CHAPTER NINETEEN

He was in way over his head.

That was for damn sure.

Swimming laps had always been an almost spiritual experience to him: the quiet rhythm of his strokes, the easy way he glided through the water. It helped him think.

And think he did.

About Margot's hair.

Her kissable lips.

Those damned freckles.

Her smile.

He swam harder as confusion clouded his judgment of what was really going on between them. It was becoming too easy to slip back into the friend zone, but the thoughts that lingered in his head were anything but friendly. No, they were downright dirty, tempting, wicked. Those thoughts fucking hated the friend zone...he'd never wanted to be there in the first place.

Since the moment he first laid eyes on her.

And he sure as hell didn't want it now.

How had things spiraled so far out of his control? Showing up had been like his worst nightmare come to life, like opening a Pandora's box of memories that he'd nailed down on purpose out of fear of them getting out and ruining him.

He should have known this would happen.

In the week he'd been there, she'd grown on him—even if she was abrasive at least 90 percent of the time. It was refreshing. Challenging.

Damn it, she'd always been challenging.

His arms burned as he swam one more lap then stopped to catch his breath.

"I have a favor to ask you." Margot's voice was barely audible.

"Shit." He turned to face her. "How long have you been standing there?"

"Long enough to appreciate your back muscles." Her face was pale but at least she was smiling—even if the smile was more wobbly then secure.

"You sure about that? Because you look ready to puke into the pool."

She wrung her hands together, opened her mouth, shut it, and then put her hands on her hips.

"Yes." Bentley drew out the word and grinned. "I'll have sex with you."

"Hilarious." Her nostrils flared.

"Go ahead, take off your shirt. I'll wait."

Her cheeks burned bright red. "No! That's not what I—" She shook her head. "That's..."

"The way I see it—" he swam toward the edge of the pool, where she was wearing a damn path from her awkward pacing "—that's the only thing that would make you look so nervous you look like a ghost."

"Sex doesn't make me nervous," she snapped.

"Could have fooled me." He swatted playfully at the water and grinned up at her. "You know, since my nakedness always seems to...offend you."

"People wear clothes for a reason."

"Stupid reasons."

"Can we get back to the favor?"

"Of sex?"

"I do *not* want to have sex with you!"

He blinked and then rested his arms against the warm concrete. "I honestly think that's my first rejection. Hurts more than I thought it would."

Rolling her eyes, Margot let out a groan and pulled a chair across the concrete until she was about a foot away from him. "I...I have to go out...to leave the house. I need you to come with me."

Why the hell was she so nervous about leaving the house? Had she even left the house since he'd been here? Who grocery-shopped? Gassed her car? Did she even *have* a car?

"Okay." He swallowed back all his questions. "So where are we going?"

"Dinner."

"Margot, are you asking me out on a date?"

"No!" she said quickly. "It's only business."

"That's what they all say."

"I knew this was a bad idea." She moved to stand, lifting a shaky hand and pressing it to her temple.

"Wait," he called out. "I'm sorry, let's start over. This favor you want is a business...dinner?"

She gave a jerky nod.

"With you and...?"

"My publisher." Her body swayed. Shit, was she going to pass out? Over a business dinner?

"Sounds fun." He nodded. "Right?"

"So fun," she choked out drily.

"Margot?"

"Hmm?"

"When was the last time you went out to dinner?"

She didn't answer for a while, just stared down at him like a war was raging inside her head: Tell the truth or lie. He wanted her to be honest. And he wanted to help. God knew why.

Suppressing a groan, he waited.

Margot finally ground out, "Five years."

"In human years?" he asked.

"No. Dog years."

"Oh, well, that makes more sense."

Her lips twitched.

"Better not laugh, Margot. The last thing you want to do is give in and laugh just because I'm dying to hear it."

"If I laugh, will you come?"

"So now you want me to come?" God he'd missed her. The thought slipped past his mental barriers before he had the sense to stop it, and like a wave, more thoughts of them in bed together came rushing through his brain. "You're so demanding today."

"Ha ha." She spoke the words rather than laughing. "Good enough?"

"Eh, we can work on it later."

"Thanks, Bentley." Her eyes filled with tears. "Seriously, thank you."

"You used to call me Bent."

"I also used to call you jackass," she countered. "I'd take what I can get."

"This." He pressed his hands against the side of the pool and heaved himself up onto his elbows. "This is what I miss."

"Arguing with me?"

"Arguing, flirting, talking, joking...You asked me if I knew who I was." Why the hell was he speaking? "I think I lost a part of him—when I lost you."

Margot froze, her eyes darting between him and the pool. "But you didn't."

"I did," he whispered. He'd said enough. He was losing his mind, and for the first time in a really long time, the crazy that came along with it didn't bother him.

*   *   *

"Margot." Bentley knocked on her door. "Are you ready to go?"

"No!" she wailed from inside.

With a sigh, he tried the knob. It turned, so he pushed the door open and walked in.

"What the hell are you doing?" she screamed from her spot in the middle of the floor, holding a black scrap of a dress against her almost fully naked body.

He raked his eyes over her luscious form and barely managed not to groan out loud when a piece of the black fabric fell away from her right breast.

He'd seen a lot of women naked.

None of the women even compared to the smooth supple feast that was before him—like a fucking buffet of curves he couldn't wait to sample.

"Bentley!" She pointed to the door.

He braced his hands against the door frame. "I think I'll stay."

"You don't get a vote!" Her voice screeched and then tears welled in her eyes as she looked down at her prosthetic leg.

He followed her gaze. "Battle scar."

"What?" she exclaimed.

"It's not a wound. It's not a weakness. It's a battle scar... You warred. You came out on the other side. Don't ever look at your leg like that again in front of me." The harshness of his voice surprised even him, the anger he felt at the way she saw herself had him ready to rip something— anything—apart with his bare hands.

He had no idea where it was coming from, this insane need to protect her—even if it was from herself.

"Look at me," he commanded, taking a step toward her.

One more step and his body was hovering over her shaking form. "You're beautiful."

She wouldn't look at him. "I don't know what to wear."

"Go naked."

She giggled.

"We can match." He started removing his tie.

"No!" Her eyes went round as saucers as she half-leaped at him and grabbed his hands.

"Why not?" he teased. "Nobody would stare at your leg if I arrive with my cock out."

Another giggle, and then she burst out laughing.

He cupped her chin, flicking her bottom lip with his finger. "Don't get me wrong... a naked Margot..." He whistled. "But that laugh... I've stored that laugh in my memory—forever."

She kissed him.

He tugged her hard against him. "We're going to be late."

"I know," Margot whispered against his mouth. "I... I'm sorry, I don't know what came over me." She wriggled away.

"You can't just kiss a man and run away. I've read that story. She drops her shoe, he chases her, there's a pumpkin—and he has to go through hell to get her back."

"You have to have her in the first place in order to get her back." Her eyebrows rose in defiance.

"Who says I don't?"

"The girl."

"She's crazy, doesn't know her own heart or mind—but her body?" He pulled her back in close. "It hums..."

"You're a dangerous man, Bentley Wellington," she breathed. "A danger to women. Society—"

"Wear red," he said, surprising himself because the woman was half naked in his arms, and he was actually telling her to put clothes on. Another first. "Show off your legs."

"But—"

He pressed a finger to her mouth. "And no buts."

She gave him a shaky nod and whispered, "Give me five minutes."

"You have two." He kissed her again. "Or I'm coming back in and there won't be any dinner...at least with your publisher."

She blushed and looked away.

"I lied. I'm giving you one minute."

"Bentley!" She shoved him toward the door. "I can't move around that fast."

"That's too bad for your publisher. Oh look, I win again."

She shoved him out the door, and he heard the lock turn.

CHAPTER TWENTY

Margot had a car.

A car that worked.

A really nice car that sat in the garage gathering dust.

She never drove.

Ever.

She'd stopped driving. Only bad things happened when she drove—she had proven that to herself a long time ago. So when Bentley offered to drive she nearly sobbed with relief.

Except she hadn't exactly put two and two together: a sports car and Bentley Wellington.

Needless to say, he drove fast.

Way too fast.

"Hey, are you okay?" He grabbed her thigh.

"Watch the road." She gripped the leather seat with both hands, and sweat pooled at the base of her neck as they passed car after car. It had been two minutes, and already she was regretting the decision to go.

She'd thought about her leg.

About how the last outing had gone.

But she hadn't thought about the car ride.

"B-Bentley." She clenched her eyes shut. "Can you please slow down?"

"The speed limit's fifty; I'm going fifty-one and one half."

She opened one eye then the other. "You can't go in halves!"

"It sounds less like breaking the law."

"It's still too fast!" Tears welled in her eyes.

He looked at her, then back at the road, his jaw clenched, and for whatever insane reason, he hit the accelerator.

"*Stop the car!*" she wailed. "Bentley!"

"If I go ten miles over, twenty," he said in a calm voice, "what's going to happen?"

"*Bentley!*"

He slowly applied the brakes as they drove into town. "And now I'm going under the speed limit, while turtles pass us and grandmas flip me off. But one thing still remains the same."

She was going to strangle that smug grin right off his face!

"You can do everything right, and bad shit still happens. Or you can do everything wrong and walk away without so much as a scratch. Accidents. Happen."

"What are you trying to say?"

"I wasn't there." No. He wasn't. The reminder was jarring. "But I do know this...you didn't purposely injure yourself or kill your parents. Accidents happen. End of story."

He gripped the steering wheel so hard that she was surprised it was still attached.

"How much do I owe you for that therapy session?" she asked snidely. "I'm not stupid—"

"I didn't say you were stupid. Stupidity has nothing to do with it. You're smart, too smart. You overthink and over-analyze every possible situation, every possible outcome; you always have. You think if you can explain the why be-hind the accident then you'll finally be able to move on, but you'll never know why, or how." He pulled into a parking spot and turned off the engine. "I could have kissed you, you know."

"What?" What was he talking about? "While you were driving like a speed demon?"

"When you were sixteen." His voice was distant. "I could have kissed you that day, could have delayed you at least five minutes. God knows I wanted to. And then fucking Jen-nifer, who wasn't even supposed to show up for another hour, came up to us, and I hated how the girls treated you so I thought, well, I'll get Jennifer away from Margot now, and hang with her later."

"We made plans." Margot swallowed the lump in her throat. "To watch movies later."

"Yup." Bentley released the steering wheel then slammed his hand against it. "So really, it's my fault, Margot. All of it. If I hadn't been such a coward, had I kissed my best friend, like I'd wanted to do since the minute I set eyes on her, your parents wouldn't be dead, and you wouldn't be think-ing of yourself as a woman who had nothing to offer—when you've always had everything."

She opened her mouth and then closed it.

"We're going to be late." He jerked open the car door and slammed it behind him then kicked the front tire all while Margot had a minor nervous breakdown inside the car.

He'd wanted to kiss her.

He'd wanted *her*.

It hadn't been her imagination.

Tears filled her eyes.

Well, this was basically the worst timing in the world. Her publisher was going to think she was an emotional wreck.

When he came around to her side of the car, he opened the door, leaned down, and whispered in her ear, "We can talk later. I'm sorry, that was shitty timing."

"Supershitty."

"I like it when you curse."

And just like that, Margot was smiling again. Damn him!

"Be brave." He pressed a kiss to her mouth and looped her hand through his arm. "And kick some ass."

CHAPTER TWENTY-ONE

Bentley wrapped his arm protectively around Margot. He hoped that by smiling he'd deflect the attention away from her and her leg and onto him.

Not because he was ashamed of her.

No fucking way.

He knew how to divert attention, how to be the Bachelor Playboy everybody expected, and he was more than happy to step back into that role if it meant protecting Margot.

"Bentley Wellington." He ignored the woman who whispered his name under her breath, and then another feminine call rang out. What the hell was wrong with people? Couldn't they see he was on a date? He was used to the attention; people always said his name, women screamed it, men cursed it. That was his life.

"Bentley!" Finally, he turned and came face-to-face with the same girl who'd been in his bed nine days ago.

Sarah. No, Shelly. No,...shit!

She sighed and crossed her arms. "You still don't know my name, do you?"

They were standing in the lobby of the restaurant, near the bar. The woman's dark hair was curled and pulled into a low ponytail; her lush lips were red and Botoxed.

Not real, like Margot's.

As if reminding him of her presence, Margot clung to him.

It felt good.

"Margot, this is…" He arched an eyebrow at the woman in question, who rolled her eyes and held out her hand to Margot.

"Christine," she said through clenched teeth. "Nice to meet you, Margot." And then her venomous gaze turned to Bentley. "It's so nice to see Bentley supporting a handicap charity."

Whispers erupted around them while Margot stiffened at his side.

"Actually," he said in a low voice, "I'm picking up stray dogs for the shelter." He eyed her up and down with a sneer. "Say, you're a bitch. Want me to give them your number?"

"You're a bastard," she seethed.

"Thank you." He grinned and shoved past her with Margot in tow. He made a beeline to the maître d' and gave Margot's name.

"Right away, Mr. Wellington." Margot wasn't even acknowledged. Well, except for the pitying glance the man gave Margot when he saw her leg. Was this what it was like for her in public? People didn't want to look at her because they didn't want to stare, so she was just ignored?

Margot's palm grew more clammy by the second as they passed through the restaurant before finally stopping at a booth near the back. A gorgeous woman who looked to be in her fifties stood as they approached and greeted them with a smile.

"Margot!" She held out her hands and grabbed Margot before Bentley could utter a word of protest. She air-kissed Margot's cheeks, one after the other.

Jealousy sliced through him.

Great. He was jealous of Margot's publisher for kissing her cheek? Really? He needed a drink.

"And this is?" The lady turned her attention to Bentley.

He held out his hand. "The significant other."

Margot's eyes widened briefly before she pinched him in the side. He winked. Yeah, she looked ready to pass out into the breadbasket.

Well, that was comforting.

"You didn't tell me that your significant other was the notorious Bentley Wellington." The woman's eyes sparkled. "My, my, what other secrets are you keeping, Margot?"

Bentley laughed and answered for her. "I've been trying to find that out myself."

"Well." The woman clasped her hands together then reached for him. "I'm Lynn Harrison." She pumped his hand and then took a seat, directing her attention to Margot again. "I'm so glad we could finally meet in person after all these years. I decided at the last minute to fly into town for RWA, and I wanted to take you out to celebrate the nomination."

"RWA?" Bentley repeated, motioning for the waiter.

Lynn squared her shoulders as a proud smile spread over her face. "Romance Writers of America."

He laughed.

The women just stared at him.

"So that's really a thing." He nodded. "Nice."

"It's more than nice. Margot was nominated for another RITA this year." Lynn smiled brightly. "She's very talented."

"I know," Bentley agreed. "I've been reading her work."

He slid his hand down Margot's thigh. "I think my favorite so far was the Regency spy series."

"Mine, too." Lynn reached for the bread. "She truly understands what it's like to be in the mind of a man."

"Must be nice, being able to read men so well."

Margot flushed and reached for her water like she wasn't in the middle of an air-conditioned restaurant.

"So what's a RITA?" Bentley asked.

Lynn waved the waiter over. "It's one of the most prestigious awards you can get in our industry. Margot's been nominated several times, but I think this year's her year."

"I think"—Bentley caressed Margot's thigh—"I'd have to agree with you on that."

The waiter approached and took their drink order.

All in all, Bentley knew his job was to keep Lynn talking, to make sure Margot didn't fall into her food or pass out from the anxiety of being out in public, and to make certain they got home safely in one piece.

And he took his job very seriously.

So he peppered Lynn with questions about Margot's books while Margot reached for the steak knife at least a dozen times and pointed it in his direction.

They'd made it through dinner without any disaster striking, and dessert menus were placed on their table. "So." Lynn reached for a menu. "How did you two meet?"

"We were best friends in high school," Bentley answered honestly. "I basically stalked her until she agreed to hang out with me. The rest is history. Lynn, I can't even tell you how many times I used to walk by this woman and flex just so she'd notice me."

Margot gasped. "You never flexed!"

"Oh, I did." He nodded seriously. "You just never noticed. Apparently I can't compare to men in books." He winked at

Lynn. "But she finally opened the door"—he smirked "—and let me in."

"Kind of like picking up a stray dog," Margot added. "Wouldn't you say, Bentley?"

He choked on his whiskey. "Great example."

"I thought so."

Damn it, he felt her teasing smile in all the wrong places. When would it be considered appropriate to leave? Now?

"You guys are seriously adorable." Lynn sighed. "Really, I can't believe this isn't already all over the tabloids."

A smile froze on Bentley's face. "Excuse me?"

"America's richest playboy lands reclusive yet gorgeous romance author?" She shrugged and took a sip of her drink. "It seems like news to me."

Bentley swallowed. *Shit. Shit. Shit.* "We like to keep our private life private."

"Well, I hate to break it to you," Lynn said, pointing behind them, "but two camera crews pulled up halfway through our meal."

"Shit."

Margot pulled her hand away from Bentley. He felt the loss in his chest, like a hollow ache that refused to go away.

"Do you think there's a back door or something?" Margot asked in a low voice.

Lynn shook her head. "Honey, snap out of it. You've got a gorgeous man on your arm. Besides, you have a book release in a few weeks. This is good for sales. No offense." She smiled at Bentley. Somehow that didn't comfort him.

He felt used.

And pissed that the publisher would short-sell Margot's talent that way.

"Her book will sell with or without me," he finally said.

"Well." Lynn leaned back in her chair. "Her last book

didn't perform like it should have, so I'm glad you're here to help boost sales. Because, let's be honest…" She pulled out her phone and slid it across the table. "You aren't exactly known for being a one-woman man, ergo, it looks fantastic that you've finally settled down!"

Margot hadn't spoken a word.

She was white as a sheet.

"I think," Margot finally said in a small voice, "that we should call it a night."

Lynn was clearly clueless as to Margot's sudden change in mood. She started firing off more chatter about catching up later in the week. "I'll e-mail you more details Monday."

They hugged.

Margot was visibly shaking.

Bentley wrapped a protective arm around Margot's waist and led her toward the flashing lights and camera crews.

"You can do this," he said.

"I know," Margot answered.

"I was talking to myself."

She blinked up at him in shock.

He was used to being offended by the media. That was what they were paid to do: get under the target's skin, ask inappropriate questions, capture them at their worst.

But he still wasn't prepared for the reaction toward Margot.

"Is she your auction charity date?" someone asked.

"No." Bentley clenched his teeth together. Margot may have started off as his charity date, but charity wasn't part of it, not anymore. "It's a real date. With real food. And real conversation…you soul-sucking idiots."

Margot held his hand tighter and ducked her head against his chest.

God, he wanted to be worthy of the trust she was offering.

They were almost to the car.

Just a few more steps.

"Never took you for the kinda guy that was into kinky shit," a voice said amid laughter. "So, are you into disabled women now?"

Bentley froze.

Margot let out a little gasp.

"Get in the car." He opened her door and basically pushed her inside.

When he turned around the cameras were nearly blinding. "Who the fuck said that?"

Nobody spoke.

And then a man raised his hand. "Come on, Bentley, play nice. Just answer the damn question."

"Answer the question?" He laughed. "You got it, buddy." With a nod, he stalked toward the reporter and slammed his fist into the asshole's face. He got two good hits in before he was pulled away from the man.

"You son of a bitch!" the reporter wailed. "You broke my nose."

"You'll survive." Bentley lunged for him again but was held back by a few other paparazzi who'd been watching the exchange. "And if I ever hear you say anything about Margot again I'll fucking kill you. Do you understand?"

He didn't realize what he said until it was too late.

Until people gasped.

Until a small hand touched his back and the familiar scent of Margot invaded his scenes. She'd gotten out of the car and was trying to calm him down. "Bentley, come on."

"Apologize to her," he spat at the man. "Now."

"I'm sorry." His bloody smirk just made Bentley want to punch him again. "Sorry that a woman as beautiful as you is stuck with a womanizing bastard, a man who's had so many issues since his overdose that he feels the need to sleep with other men's wives in order to feel good about himself—"

"That's it." Bentley charged the man and pummeled his face with his fist. He still wasn't satisfied. He threw the man against the nearest car just as the sound of sirens filled the air.

CHAPTER TWENTY-TWO

This looks familiar," Brant said from his spot on the other side of the cell. His eyes were clear, not bloodshot, which was really the most shocking part for Bentley about seeing his brother. It was a Friday night. Brant never stayed in on a Friday night.

"Go to hell." Bentley crossed his arms.

"Looks like you're already there, brother."

"I've had better nights."

"No doubt." Brant grinned.

"How much?" Bentley hated to even ask.

Brant leaned casually against the bars. "Two million."

"Dollars?"

"No, he said to pay him in hugs."

"Fuck off."

Brant pushed away from the bars. "Lucky for you, the reporter has a gambling problem and an addiction to coke, so we offered him five hundred thousand to walk."

Bentley nodded. "He take it?"

"Probably high right now."

"Fuck." Bentley ran his hands through his hair. "The things he said...I don't know how the hell he knew any of it."

"Public record?" Brant offered. "And since when have you ever cared about your dirty laundry?"

Bentley frowned. "Right."

Since now.

Since Margot.

Since arriving at her house.

Since kissing.

Hell.

"You look like shit."

"Why are you here, again?"

"Someone had to post bail." Brant shrugged. "And Brock's too busy trying to keep Grandfather from cutting you off."

Like he could. But still, the fact that Grandfather was seriously pissed did not bode well.

"Because I defended a woman?"

"Because you didn't kill the man," Brant said seriously. "And because you went back for more when you should have just let it die."

Bentley shot to his feet. "He brought up the hospitalization." His blood boiled. "In front of Margot, and she doesn't know—"

"Fuck." Brant's face went white as a sheet. "We need to do damage control. The last thing we want is the media digging up shit from your past that doesn't even matter anymore. Worse yet, if the board gets wind of it and is reminded about your less than stellar ways, you're screwed. As of right now, that promotion—"

"Fuck the promotion!" Bentley yelled. "This is about my reputation. The last thing we need is to focus on my past drama when the board is starting to trust us again." When Margot was starting to trust him again, when things finally felt right. It pissed him off to admit his grandfather was right, but staying out of the limelight, spending time with her—it wasn't all bad. And yet the first time he made a public appearance with her, he not only got shoved back into the playboy box but he got arrested.

Brant's eyes narrowed. "What the hell's wrong with you? You've never cared about your job. Or the company."

"I grew a heart."

"Would a certain redhead have anything to do with that?" He smirked.

"Look, are you going to bail me out or not?"

"Not."

"Brant—"

"Relax, I just need to finish some paperwork. I came back here to make sure some bastard wasn't making you his sub."

"Thanks for your concern."

Brant saluted him with his middle finger. "I'm a good brother."

"Yes that's exactly what I thought when you came in here *six hours* after my arrest. What the hell took you so long? What did you do, walk?"

"Never mind what I was doing." He shifted on his feet, and a haunted look crossed his face before he nodded. "I'm going to finish up that paperwork."

"Right."

Bentley didn't taste freedom until another hour later, and by then it was almost three in the morning.

Margot wasn't answering her phone, so he still didn't know if she got home safely or if she was camped out in her car in the parking lot too scared to drive herself home.

"Stop." Brant sighed in an annoyed voice when he had picked up Bentley. "You've been thumping your phone against your leg for the past ten minutes."

"Sorry." Bentley checked the screen. No missed calls. No messages. "Damn it."

"What?"

"Nothing."

Brant whistled. "Clearly you're not suffering out here." He turned his Bugatti down the dirt road and crawled along at five mph. He had a thing about getting his car dirty, which meant Bentley would be better off walking backward.

With a blindfold on.

The light was on by the front door when they finally pulled up in front of Margot's house.

Was that a good sign?

Bad sign?

Brant turned off the car.

"Whoa, what are you doing?" Bentley didn't want Brant hanging around. He needed to apologize to Margot stat, and he preferred to do that without his womanizing twin in tow.

"What's it look like I'm doing?" Brant frowned and unbuckled his seat belt. "It's three a.m., man. I'm not driving back into the city. Your sorry ass is stuck with me. Hell, I'll sleep on the floor if I need to."

"Great," Bentley mumbled. "Just…don't stare at her leg, all right?"

Brant held up his hands.

"She's sensitive and—"

"Have you grown a vagina since I last saw you?"

"Shut the hell up!"

Brant let out a dark chuckle and got out of the car. Bentley had no choice but to follow as they made their way toward the front door.

Toward Margot.

Just as he shoved the key in the lock, the door flew open nearly taking him with it.

"You're okay!" Margot launched herself into his arms.

Warm lips pressed against his and then pulled away too soon.

"That's quite a welcome," Brant whispered under his breath. "For a *friend*."

Margot jerked away, nearly stumbling backward against one of the entryway tables. "Brant?"

"Red."

Her eyes narrowed. "Why does everyone remember that nickname?"

Brant reached for her hair and picked it up. "Gee, I'm not sure."

Bentley had never been so tempted to punch his brother in the face—just because he was touching her hair. Great. Another fight, just what he needed.

Margot smiled politely and stepped closer to Bentley. "I was worried."

Brant snickered. "It's not like he went off to war and barely made it out alive. He sucker punched a dude in the face. It won't be the last time that happens, either."

"Brant," Bentley said in a warning voice. "Could you just...go be anywhere but here? Right now?"

Brant rolled his eyes and sent a knowing look to Margot. "Are you going to nurse his wounds tonight or mine?"

A month ago Bentley would have laughed.

And might have been game.

They'd shared women before.

Now? He wanted to end his brother's life for even thinking about Margot that way.

"Okay, you're done here." Bentley grabbed his brother

roughly by the shoulders and shoved him toward the hall-way. "My room's the first on the left. You can take the one right across from it."

"Last chance." Brant completely ignored Bentley and eyed Margot up and down. He didn't even flinch when he saw her leg. For that matter, when Bentley had mentioned it, Brant hadn't even asked questions.

A prickling awareness trickled down Bentley's spine.

"Pass," she said in a bored tone that had Bentley doing mental backflips while his dick took a bow.

"You always did prefer him to me back in high school." He locked eyes with Bentley while still addressing Margot. "My warning still stands. Be careful, Red."

The hell?

Margot flushed and then jerkily folded and unfolded her arms.

What just happened?

Suddenly Brant's smile was back and he was making his way toward the bedroom only to stop and turn around. "Will I need earplugs?"

"Brant." Bentley's tone had a warning edge.

His brother smirked, then sauntered off.

"Always fun hanging out with sober Brant," Bentley said under his breath.

"You mean he's normally...not sober?"

Bentley exhaled. This really wasn't the time to get into his family drama or Brant's particular demons. "Sorry, he's...honestly, I don't know what the hell his problem is. Ever since the auction he's been like a different person."

"Trauma does that to people." She smiled.

"Did you just make a joke?"

"Depends." She scrunched up her nose. "Was it funny?"

"I laughed on the inside really hard. Promise." He pressed

a hand to his chest. "I'm just a bit distracted by...you."
Bentley reached for her hands. "How are you?"

"I'm not the one who spent half the night in jail."

"Eh, jail's not so bad. At least this time I didn't get felt up."

Her eyes widened.

"I'm kidding."

"Oh." Her smile was back. "The elephants are back,
aren't they?"

"Stampeding through the damn house," Bentley said in a
hoarse voice. "And in my head."

She broke eye contact and looked down. "How are
you...really?"

"I'm fine." *I need to tell you things I don't want to tell
you.*

"Okay," she whispered. Then she got up on her tiptoes
and kissed his cheek. "Tonight...you were my hero."

She might as well have knighted him.

"I'm not sure I've ever been anyone's hero, except for
Jennifer in eighth grade, but I think she was using me for my
math skills."

"You were my hero in high school...the only boy other
than Brant who even looked in my direction more than
once."

"Seven hundred and eighty nine," Bentley whispered.
"Give or take a few hundred."

Margot's eyes filled with tears. "What?"

"The number of times I caught myself staring at you. And
those are just the times I counted."

"Oh."

Bentley nodded, not really sure what else to say. There
was too much to choose from. And most of his options were
harsh reminders of all the baggage he carried and how it was
all directly related to her, without her even realizing it.

"So really." She took a deep breath and wiped at a few fallen tears. "You were more stalker than hero, is that what you're saying?"

Bentley choked out a laugh. "Yes, Margot, yes, all right?"

"Yes to stalking?"

"Yes to being obsessed."

Her eyes lit up before she again looked away and tucked some fallen hair behind her ears. "It's, um, it's late, I should..." She pointed toward the stairs.

She backed away. "Well, good night."

Shit, it was now or never. "About being hospitalized," he called after her. Like an idiot.

She tilted her head. "I didn't ask."

"I know, but—"

"You don't have to tell me—at least not after being in jail all night. There's always tomorrow," she finished. "Thanks again...now, go put your sword away and get some sleep."

She grimaced.

While he burst out laughing. "What's this about my sword?"

"Its three a.m. Don't." Margot held up a hand. "Just. Don't." A smile tugged at the corner of her lips.

"Aw, one laugh, Margot. I've had a rough night. Just one."

"No." She straightened her back.

"I'll pull out my sword and let you play with it."

"I'm never living that one down," she whispered, more to herself, and then nearly knocked the wind out of him by smiling so brightly he couldn't tear his eyes away. "Bentley?"

"Yes?"

"Tomorrow...we should do that picnic."

"It's a date."

She grinned harder.

"And if you're having trouble deciding what to wear, just go naked...that's the new rule. I don't want to stress you out with hard decisions." He made sure to draw out the word *hard*.

"Yeah, I'll totally keep that in mind." She rolled her eyes and made her way up the stairs.

CHAPTER TWENTY-THREE

The last time Margot had been that terrified was when she woke up in the hospital with her leg in a cast and a tell-all expression on the doctor's face that instantly worried her.

And now, she was worried for Bentley. Worried about the aftermath and what was said.

And she was selfishly worried about herself.

Her eyes were heavy with exhaustion as she lay in bed and replayed the night's events. Her mind was going at a million miles a minute, and her heart was still thumping against her chest like it was going to seize.

She should have admitted to Bentley that she already knew that he'd been hospitalized.

But it seemed like the wrong timing: *Oh, thanks for standing up for me and going to jail for the night over something that I already knew. By the way, did you know that there are over fifty websites dedicated to your hair and smile alone?*

Margot groaned and covered her face with a pillow, letting out a little scream as she tried to force her racing mind to slow the hell down.

He was a complete enigma.

What did she even know about this man staying with her? This man who had walked away from her when she'd needed him most?

Fact: Bentley always deflected with humor.

Fact: He was angry with his grandfather.

Fact: Clearly he was trying to prove himself, but to whom?

Fact: The auction was the only reason he was at her house.

Fact: Had he not been in the auction, would he have ever confessed all of those things to her? Would he have ever sought her out and apologized for abandoning her all those years go?

Fact: He didn't know that Brant knew about her leg.

And that, that was going to be a problem, because while Bentley hadn't made sure Margot was okay after the accident, Brant had.

She still remembered his dark, worried expression. She'd thought he was Bentley at first and reached for him, only to jerk back with surprise when she realized it was Brant.

Margot swallowed the ever-present lump in her throat and tried once again to focus her thoughts on the positive.

Like kissing.

Kissing Bentley.

Kissing Bentley and forgetting about everything auction related and focusing on...

...a picnic.

She could do a picnic.

Picnics were harmless, right? Children went on picnics, not sexy ex–best friends who tasted like sin and reeked of poor life choices.

Okay, that's unfair.

He smelled amazing, too.

What type of unjust God allowed men like Bentley to exist? He needed a flaw other than his abandonment, because no matter how hard she tried, it was getting more and more difficult to hold on to the anger.

And without the anger, she was in dangerous territory, wanting more than friendship and actually believing that he might want more, too.

Ugh. Kisses probably weren't included in the auction package.

Great. Now she was thinking about packages.

His package to be exact.

NyQuil. Sedation. Sheep.

"Damn it!" She thumped the pillow against the headboard around eight times and crossed her arms.

A soft knock sounded at her door. Jolting upright, she fixed her hair, tucking it behind her ears, before clearing her throat and offering a polite and oh-so-very-high-pitched "Yes?"

This was it.

The doorknob slowly twisted as light flickered in from the hall.

Bentley.

Kissing.

Bedroom.

"Brant?" She didn't mean to sound disappointed.

"Curb your enthusiasm," Brant said in a low voice as he let himself into her room, shut the door behind him, and approached her bed.

"Um…what are you doing?" She pulled the sheets tighter against her body and waited.

Brant's clear blue eyes flickered from the bed to her face before he let out a sigh and sat near her feet. "He doesn't know."

"Doesn't know?" she repeated.

"He doesn't know that I visited you in the hospital...he, uh..." Brant swore. "Look, here's the thing. I was going to pretend to be him, that's all you need to know. If he could have physically been there, he would have, and then it was just..." He fell back against the mattress. "You have a frighteningly low ceiling."

"Brant?"

"Seriously, it's like an attic ceiling."

"Brant." She said it a little more urgently. "Why are you really in here?"

"Why indeed," he repeated. His gaze didn't waver from the ceiling as he put his hands behind his head and yawned. Where Bentley was charismatic, Brant was a bit predatory, and a whole lot of intense. "You know, Red, I just didn't want it to blindside you. Bentley and I don't talk about the accident. Ever."

"Because he feels guilty that he didn't come to see me in the hospital?"

"I wasn't talking about *your* accident," he whispered and then slowly rose to his feet. "Try to get some sleep. If you have any hope of surviving a picnic with Bentley tomorrow, you'll need it."

"Eavesdropper."

His smile was almost sad as he bent over and kissed her on the forehead. "It's good to see you again."

"You, too."

"Brant?" she called out once he reached the door. "His accident..." She hated asking this. Hated it. "Was it—"

"I've said enough. Go to sleep." The door clicked shut.

Great, now her mind was reeling.

She was never going to get any sleep tonight.

CHAPTER TWENTY-FOUR

He's not coming with us?" Margot secretly hoped that Brant wasn't joining their picnic, but she didn't want to be rude by suggesting he not come along. But something about Brant was different. Startlingly different from when she'd seen him last. Yes, he was an adult now, they all were, but he seemed...heavy. Was that the right word?

And it wasn't like she was in any position to be psycho-analyzing anyone.

Brant laid his lean body across the couch, stretched his arms over his head, and then sent her a lazy smile. The TV was on ESPN, and two empty beer bottles littered the coffee table.

"Nope." Bentley turned her toward the door. "He's basically in a catatonic state at this point. Basketball's on. You could probably do a striptease in front of him and he'd still ask you to move."

"That only happened once!" Brant called out. "And it was the championship game!"

Bentley smirked. "She broke his TV."

Brant turned around from his spot on the couch. "You kids have fun. Wear a condom—I'm not ready to be an uncle yet."

Margot's cheeks heated. Brant winked, probably knowing he was making her uncomfortable. He'd always been that way, though, very unapologetic about how he acted. She quickly grabbed the picnic basket to distract herself and waited for Bentley to open the door. She'd slathered on sunscreen, and at the last minute she'd tossed on a hat to cover her face. She tanned pretty well for a redhead, but she didn't want to take any chances.

The minute she stepped out of the house, she froze. The warm wind tickled her bare arms and legs.

Maybe she shouldn't have worn denim cutoffs and a tank top?

"You ready for this?" Bentley tossed on his sunglasses, took the picnic basket from her, and then took her hand.

She squeezed. "Totally."

How many times had she taken this exact trail with her parents? And how many times had she begged them to let her go by herself so she could read by the stream?

"I..." She choked back the memories and gave herself a few seconds of silence to gather her thoughts. How much to share? How much to say? "I used to go on picnics with my parents all the time."

"I didn't know that." They started down a trail that led by the pool and farther down across the field that connected the horse stables to the tennis courts.

"Well, I'm not exactly an open book."

"No," Bentley teased. "You don't say?"

They walked in silence for a while, accompanied by the rustle of the breeze through the leaves overhead and the crunch of gravel under their feet. When they topped a small hill, Bentley looked over at her, his eyes clear, searching, and maybe just a bit sad.

"I think I'm lost."

"We're on the trail, your house is that way." He pointed over her head. "The stream is—"

"Not geographically!" She smacked him in the chest. "But with what's going on between us...I don't think I understand."

Bentley set the basket down and interlinked their fingers, pulling her against his body. "I was always horrible at the tell part of Show and Tell..." His gorgeous grin was wreaking havoc on her ability to string together a thought other than *Kiss me*. "I want you."

He wanted her? What, like he'd wanted the other girls he had slept with?

"Wow, I fully expected at least a smile. I must really be a dick." He ducked his head toward her neck and slowly kissed his way to her ear, his lips grazing her skin. "This." His kisses were causing a tingling sensation to build in her body, but it was wrong. All wrong. "I want this."

Insecurity slammed into her like a bucket of ice water.

No he didn't.

She was just available.

And when she gave in—which she would because she'd always been in love with him—he would leave. And never look back.

And she knew she couldn't handle him walking out of her life twice.

With a sigh, she untangled herself. "We should go set up our blanket."

He turned around and put his hands on his hips, then hung his head. "All right."

She didn't miss the part where he adjusted his pants. Or

kicked the dirt in front of him, missing a boulder by an inch before he stopped at the stream and dropped the basket again.

The nerves returned as she watched his mini temper tantrum. She opened her mouth to suggest they return home when she tripped over a branch. All at once she was flying through the air, headfirst down the hill. She cried in terror as the ground rose up to meet her.

"Margot!" Bentley called.

Her hands stung from trying to break her fall and her prosthetic was twisted awkwardly beneath her.

Groaning, she rolled over and looked back along the trail just as Bentley reached her. Her prosthetic lay caught on a large branch that had fallen across the trail.

The thing had come clear off.

Shame built up inside her chest until all she could do was stare at the ground as tears filled her eyes.

"Hey!" Bentley was on his knees in front of her, his hands cupping her cheeks. "Are you hurt?" He didn't wait for her to answer, just started rubbing his hands all over her arms and left leg, and then, he hesitated.

There it was.

He was disgusted by her leg.

His eyes were locked on her leg. Her bad leg, the one that was half of what it should be.

"Let me see," he whispered.

"No!"

"Margot." He slid his hand up her bare thigh, his fingertips grazing the fray of her shorts. "Please."

"Can't we just have our picnic?" she begged, tears filling her eyes again. "I don't want to...I just..." She blinked as he started massaging her leg, digging his palm into her muscles. It felt good. Too good. She hadn't realized how sore that leg was from all the walking she'd been doing.

He stopped moving his hand and stood. "I can do that."

She'd been expecting him to fight her on it, so she was surprised when he grabbed her prosthetic, and allowed her privacy to put it back on as he left her to lay out the picnic.

And for some reason, she was disappointed he hadn't pushed her to let him help her. Which was crazy, right?

She got to her feet and made her way over to Bentley. He was already unscrewing the wine they'd packed and popping cheese in his mouth while a duck and her little ducklings made their way over. He completely ignored Margot and started feeding the duck breadcrumbs.

She'd either pissed him off or hurt him.

"Am I boring you?" she asked, and tried to keep the hitch out of her voice as she continued. "Wasn't my Olympic tumble amusing enough? Or do you expect more from your charity dates?" Great. Now she was being a bitch.

"You're more than that." His eyes locked on her. "You're someone I can't keep out of my mind." A sad and lonely expression crossed his face. "You're someone I want to spend time with, not because of the auction, but because you make me want to try to be better than the person I really am." He scowled down at the blanket. "And I know I left you. I know that. I know I'm an asshole, but having you back, even for just a few weeks, has been— everything. I have my friend back, at least part of her— and no, I don't mean your missing leg."

She scowled, and he tentatively reached out and placed his hand on her arm. "Please, let me finish. This is hard for me, too." She nodded and he continued. "I just meant I have part of you, the part that slips through when you forget to stay pissed at me, and I miss it. I miss us. I miss my best friend. My *only* friend. A friend I want to kiss. A friend I've always wanted to kiss. A friend I want to share things with, even though most of the time she yells at me and slams doors—which probably says something about my masochistic personality, since I keep coming back for more." He stood. "Friends share things..." He dropped to his knees in front of her, moving both hands up her legs until he stopped where her prosthetic met her leg. "You show true friends the ugly—and trust them enough to turn it into something beautiful."

Margot didn't know what to say.

"I-I don't have any friends, either," she finally stuttered.

"So you aren't counting me?"

She grinned. "Okay, fine. I have one."

"Oh, tell me about this friend," he whispered, sliding his hands up her legs and then slowly pushing her back against the cool grass.

"He's kind of a prick," she teased.

"Sounds like he needs a strong woman to keep him in line. May I recommend spanking as a punishment?"

"You may..." she breathed, as he kissed one cheek and then the other.

"What else?"

"He's too good-looking. I think he needs to get roughed up."

"Is that an offer?"

"Do you want it to be?"

"Margot, I'd let you rough me up any day..." His lips met hers briefly before he pulled back. "I think I'm kind of jealous of this guy."

"Oh, you should be."

His eyebrows rose.

"I mean, he is your brother, so..." She lifted one shoulder and smiled.

"That's it," he hissed, and started tickling her until she was crying tears of laughter. "Thank God."

"Wh-what?" She caught her breath.

"I needed that today."

"Huh?"

"Your laughter." He sat up and faced her; his expression darkened. "Being reminded of our past...it's not my most favorite topic. Your laughter makes it better. Funny, I'm so used to being the guy that makes everything better, it's kind of nice to be on the other end of it."

"Yeah." She ducked her head, but he tilted her chin back up and brushed a kiss across her bottom lip before pulling back and holding the wine bottle between them.

"Wine." He nodded. "You drink the wine—and I'll just drink you."

"Where do you come up with this stuff?"

"This?" He pointed between them. "Oh, I read this really great romance author, maybe you've heard of her? Writes these crazy sex scenes, though they may be too explicit for your eyes. But they may help you with your new friend; I've heard he's amazing in bed."

"Yeah? Lots of screaming?"

"So much screaming," he replied playfully, tilting his head back. "But I think my screaming days are over."

"Huh?"

"I think I'd much rather settle for a really, really, really loud sigh." He trailed a finger down the front of her T-shirt. "Followed by a few breathless moans." His finger dipped into the V-shaped neckline as his hand spread across her right breast. "Maybe even a few *Don't stop, Bentley, you're a sex god, Bentley, yes, Bentley*s."

She could hear her own heartbeat in her ear. "I think I can manage that."

Wait?

Was this happening?

Did she just agree to have sex with him?

Did he just ask?

"Oh, you'll manage," he growled, capturing her mouth with his just as a loud voice rang through the air.

"Stupid Thunder lost! I bet ten grand on that game."

Margot's body jolted at the sound of Brant's voice. What was he doing down there? And how much had he seen?

"Oh good, there's still cheese left." He plopped down next to them and started eating, as if he hadn't just interrupted what Margot had been convinced was about to be the most mind-blowing sex, ever.

"I heard there's a storm coming in. Looks like I'll have to stay an extra day," Brant said, pouring himself a glass of wine. His eyes were glassy, and she wondered how much he'd already had to drink.

"The hell." Bentley pulled away from Margot and blinked at Brant. "Absolutely not."

"Afraid so." Brant tugged on his sunglasses and sat right next to Margot then lazily put his arm around her shoulders. "Once you go twin you never go back—"

Bentley punched him in the face.

Margot gasped.

"Fuck!" Blood drenched Brant's hands as he held them up against his nose. "What the hell, man? I was joking!"

"And it was funny, too," Bentley said drily.

"You're so easy . . ." Brant slurred his words a bit as blood ran down his chin. "Grandfather sends you here for a weekend, dangles that VP of marketing job in front of you if stay a whole month." He looked genuinely disgusted. "And then what? You're just going to leave her again."

Margot froze.

Bentley lunged for his brother again.

Brant tilted his chin toward him. "Do it, I dare you."

"You're drunk." Bentley clenched his hands into fists. "And you don't know what the hell you're talking about."

"I know exactly what I'm talking about, and from the crestfallen look on Margot's face—you still haven't even told her why you stayed longer than the weekend!"

"P-promotion?" Margot repeated in an angry voice.

"No." Bentley pointed at her. "It's not like that. He's wasted. And angry. This is more about him then it is about us."

"It's exactly like that." Brant rolled his eyes. "What? He didn't tell you about the promotion?"

"One that I don't even know if I want!" Bentley yelled, jumping to his feet. "Margot, we talked about this. I don't even know if that's what I want anymore!"

"Then why did you come down here?" Brant crossed his arms. "Oh..." He looked down at the ground and laughed. "Right, because Grandfather offered you a job and because you've been dying for a way to impress him." Brant jerked to his feet. "But sure, have a great fake picnic, because we all know how this story's going to end. Bentley's going to walk away—like he always does. And break your heart—"

"What the hell is wrong with you, man?" Bentley was genuinely confused while Margot looked ready to burst into tears.

Margot stood on wobbly legs and marched over to Bentley then slapped him in the face. "So what? All the kissing? The compliments? Was that part of it? Do you get a bonus if you fuck me?"

Brant whistled.

"You stay out of this!" She jabbed her finger in his chest. "I don't know what's happened to you but you're... you're a complete jackass. You need to go back to the house and sober up. This, this is not the Brant I remember."

Brant's expression fell as guilt washed over his face.

"That's right," Bentley agreed.

"And you!" She returned to Bentley. "I trusted you, you said we were friends—"

"We *are* friends!" He threw his hands in the air.

"I kiss all my friends like that. Like every day. *Oh hi, Bill, how's it going?*" Brant added. "*Your tongue feels different, did you get work done?*"

"Brant!" they yelled in unison, and he held his hands up.

"I can't even look at you." Margot pushed past him. "I did it again! I ignored my gut, I ignored the little voice in my head that told me you were using me, and you were! All that talk about being friends again, about wanting to see the ugly, well, here it is. I hate you." Her voice wobbled at the end, like her mouth had trouble forming the sentence. Because even though she wanted to still hate him, even though she was so angry she couldn't even see through her tears…

…a part of her still wanted him to deny it all.

To say he loved her.

To say Brant was so drunk that he was making up stories.

But he said nothing.

He might be a runner.

But she was a hider.

So she did what she did best.

She walked back to the house, head held high, took the stairs one at a time, hid in the darkness of her room, and tried to put all those walls back up around her heart, only to find out they were in pieces just like the rest of her.

He'd wrecked her.

CHAPTER TWENTY-FIVE

Thanks, man." Sarcasm dripped from his words. It was hard not to punch his brother in the face again. "Next time you get drunk can you maybe focus on ruining your own life rather than mine?"

Brant chugged another bottle of water and popped two aspirin. "I had too much to drink, looked out the window, saw you doing exactly what you always do...kiss the right side, kiss the left." Brant smirked at his bottled water like he was lost in his own thoughts. "Treating her like every other girl I'd ever seen you screw. And I just...I'm sorry. I lost it. I like her."

"No shit."

"No, I really, really like her."

"Try liking her a little less."

Brant scowled. "She deserves better than you. Better than me."

Bentley groaned into his hands. "Trust me, I know that."

"And I know you're still hiding shit from her. You're not being fair to her, Bent. You're either all in, or you're nothing."

"Seriously? Is this your pep talk right now? From the man who literally can't even date a woman who wears red lipstick."

Brant froze, his swallow visible as he took a deep breath and then licked his lips. "That's different."

"Good one."

"Thanks," Brant said drily. "Look at it from my side. For all I know you're just going to freak out again and run away and then what? Margot's already lost a leg, and you. Don't do it twice, man."

"Is that your apology?" Bentley asked.

"Yup." Brant finally took his shot. "Look, whenever a girl clings to you for too long, I'm always the one who steps in, pisses her off, gives you that clean break, hurting her on your behalf so you can fill your bed with someone new. What I just did with Margot was no different, except since you punched me in the face, I'm gathering it's a hell of a lot different."

Bentley glanced around the room, mindlessly looking at the gourmet stainless-steel appliances and the way the light cast a glow across the mahogany dining room set. Had he really been that guy? The one that had his twin take care of his dirty work? He rubbed his hands over his face and let out a sigh. "Things with her are delicate ... her accident, my past." He shook his head. "She's not trusting, and I'm not helping matters."

"Well." Brant leaned back against the countertop. "Your reputation does precede you."

"So?" Bentley shrugged. "I can't change?"

"In a little under two weeks? You're going to change your playboy ways and play nice with your ex–best friend? The amputee? Is that what you're saying?"

"Don't fucking call her that." Bentley's jaw ticked.

Brant just grinned. "What are you going to do? Punch me again?"

Bentley lunged, gripping Brant by the shirt and shoving him away from the counter and against the wall. "Maybe."

Brant's eyes widened. "So what is it? Are you that desperate for a taste of her, or is it the real thing?"

"It's not about sex." Bentley's teeth snapped together.

Brant's gaze zeroed in on Bentley. "You fuck." His voice was so cold. "It's what you do. It's what *I* do. It's what we've always done."

"Funny, because I remember a time where you used to go to bed at nine every night and make love to your wife— before you walked."

Brant let out a hoarse gasp and then charged Bentley, shoving him back against the granite counter. His fists pounded into Bentley's kidneys as though he'd been practicing in the boxing ring for the past few months.

"Son of a bitch!" Bentley roared, shoving his twin away and getting a good punch in before Brant pulled him into a headlock.

"Don't ever mention her again." Brant tightened his hold. "Ever."

Bentley slammed his elbow into his brother's side and gasped for air as he punched him in the stomach. "The hell I won't. Nobody ever talks about it. Just like nobody ever talks about Brock carrying the fucking world on his shoulders when Mom and Dad died, just like nobody ever talks about my overdose, just like nobody talks about *her*!"

Brant froze, his eyes locked on Bentley. "Don't."

"Why?" Bentley rubbed his sore jaw. "It doesn't help, you know, keeping secrets, pretending that everything's fine... and we both know it sure as hell doesn't go away no matter how many thighs you fall between. How much you drink—"

"You go away for two weeks and now you're giving me the same lecture Brock did before I left." Brant grabbed a towel and held it to his face. "What's happening to you?"

Bentley shrugged, even though he knew exactly what was happening to him. He was falling for someone, someone who deserved everything good in life, and he wasn't sure he could give Margot those things.

"She's different," he finally said. "She doesn't want my money, she looks ready to slap me every time I try to kiss her, and she's...she has no idea how beautiful she is, how talented." Bentley sighed. "She makes me laugh."

"Well then, clearly you should marry her," Brant said in a deadpan voice. "Let me know how that goes when she ends up hating your guts for not being strong enough to withstand the hells of being in a relationship—for failing."

"Is that what happened? You weren't strong enough? You failed?"

Brant's eyes took on a haunted appearance. "Sometimes love...just isn't. It morphs into something you don't recognize, just like your own damn reflection." He stared off into the distance and then drummed his fingertips against the table. "You know, you could always seduce the hell out of her and then apologize for all the shit you've been keeping from her once you think you're on more even ground. It's always easier asking for forgiveness than permission, you know?"

Bentley blinked at his brother; the man was actually serious. "How the hell do you get so much ass?"

"Eh, it's a gift." Brant grinned, breaking the tension.

God, he was surrounded with ghosts and elephants everywhere he looked. Brant's anger, Brock's indifference, his grandfather's controlling ways.

Everywhere Bentley looked he saw paths that were drawn out for him, lines that he wasn't allowed to step outside, at least not if he wanted to be a good grandson.

What if he didn't take the job?

What would his grandfather think of him then?

"I think Grandfather's really trying. In his own warped way, he's trying to make up for being so distant from us during our childhood...I think." Brant sighed. "That's probably why he's taken on the role of matchmaker. With the help of Nadine Titus, God help us."

"Scariest sentence I've ever heard come out of your mouth." Bentley leaned across the granite countertop and placed his head on his arms, stretching out his back while he tried to think of what to do next.

They fell into silence.

Still no sound from upstairs, which meant she was beyond angry. If she was mildly irritated, she'd have been slamming doors or she'd have come downstairs and faced him.

Which meant she was probably hurt.

Which pissed him off more.

Things were going great until Brant had opened his giant mouth.

"I should go talk to her," Bentley finally said, but didn't move.

Brant's eyebrows rose. "Cool. You guys have telepathy nailed down or what?"

"Shut up."

"You still haven't moved."

"My hand twitched."

"Oh, sorry. I didn't see the hand twitch, because obviously that means you're about to sprint up the stairs and bang down a door." He grabbed a bottle and poured himself a generous shot of whiskey, then offered more to Bentley.

Bentley shook his head, hating that he wasn't just worried about Margot but Brant's drinking habits and the dark circles under his eyes. "I'm just...prepping my speech."

Brant burst out in a mocking laugh. "Yeah, I call bullshit. You just don't want her to yell at you."

"She always yells. Hell, I'll take yelling over tears."

Brant nodded in understanding. "You know, I'm tired. I think I'm going to go to bed. I'll leave first thing in the morning." He peered down into his glass. "I'll, uh, be sure not to start off the day with mimosas so I can drive."

His tone was light.

But Bentley knew his brother. He was allowing his past to eat him alive, and it had only gotten progressively worse since the auction.

"Why did you really stay, Brant? The truth. You could have easily driven back this morning—hell, you could have driven back tonight had you not decided to get bat shit crazy drunk and try to destroy my life."

"Exaggerate much?"

Bentley stared while Brant lowered a shaky hand to his side and exhaled. "Grandfather. Nadine," Brant said quickly. "I'm next. I need another day. Days. To get my shit together. You walked in blind." Bentley winced at his brother's poor choice of words and hated that Brant paled only to force a fake smile and half-assed shrug. "I have a plan. No chance in hell I'm letting Grandfather play the fairy fucking god-mother in my life. I'm happy. Single. And rich. I don't need to deal with drama from the past."

Bullshit. Brant wasn't happy. He hadn't been happy for four fucking years, but it wasn't Bentley's place to remind him of his unhappiness. Clearly Brant was aware of it. And things had only been getting progressively worse. Apparently, you can only run for so long before the past catches up, or you simply collapse from the exhaustion of constantly looking behind you to make sure you've escaped.

Brant and his ex-wife had been college sweethearts. Married after Brant's last year of college. They'd been in love. It was hard to be in the same room as them.

And then suddenly...

They were enemies.

Their fights were legendary.

There were few things that had the potential to come between two people as in love as they were.

Money and loss.

And the loss they'd experienced had been the stuff of nightmares; even Bentley didn't know all the details. One day Brant was married, the next he was divorced and a shell of the man he used to be. He went from wanting everything that used to give Bentley hives to drinking and seducing half of Phoenix. It changed his brother for the worse, and Bentley had taken it upon himself to try harder, to party with Brant, to make him laugh, to help him through the pain, live life like it owed them something—because maybe Bentley thought that life did owe at least Brant something for taking so much from him and leaving him so altered.

The divorce had nearly killed Brant.

Sighing, he said good night to his brother and glanced up at the ceiling, like he could magically see through the plaster and wood and see Margot pacing back and forth.

He needed to apologize.

But most of all, he wanted that moment back. The moment where she looked at him like the impossible was possible. Like he really was more than just a stranger living in her house for a few days because her grandmother was just as insane as his grandfather.

She'd looked at him and seen *him*—and now, his greatest fear, was that when he opened the door, that look would be gone, replaced with distrust.

"Shit." He slammed his hand on the table again before slowly making his way up the stairway.

CHAPTER TWENTY-SIX

Margot was too angry to cry.

And too heartbroken to do anything but sit in her darkened room and listen for more sounds from below.

Was he going to apologize?

Leave?

Or just continue yelling at his brother until he went hoarse? As it was, they were making so much noise it was impossible not to wince every time it sounded like a face was getting slammed into a nice granite countertop.

Their voices rose. Bentley yelled, Brant yelled louder, and her breath hitched when the accusations and cursing reached her burning ears.

Every punch.

Every curse.

Every scream of pain.

Was like a vise to her heart.

It seemed everyone had their secrets, and while Margot sat there and felt sorry for herself, and allowed insecurity to take over every piece of logic she possessed, she wondered if she hadn't run away in angry tears because she'd expected it all along.

She'd set him up for failure.

Because she couldn't handle the fact that maybe, just maybe, it was okay to forgive, it was okay to forget, it was okay to move on from your past.

Move on from your demons.

And, it seemed, she wasn't the only one who had them—she just wished that Bentley would come clean. She needed to hear what she already suspected even if it hurt.

Because not knowing? Assuming the worst? Was almost as painful as she imagined hearing the words *I just didn't care* or *I left because I never felt anything for you* would be.

She'd decided in that moment to try to rid herself of all the anger she had toward him once and for all. To be his friend. And to let him walk away. No more secrets. No more lies. They would be friends. And hopefully, he'd still stay in touch.

But no more kissing.

None.

That made it too difficult to be his friend when she wanted so much more—when he dangled the carrot in front of her like he was capable of actually giving it.

Other than calling her grandmother and yelling, she really didn't have any other solution. What the hell had her grandmother been thinking? Sending Bentley hadn't done anything but cause more confusion and pain—and if she were being completely honest with herself—longing. She wanted to be worthy of him; she wanted them to fix each other like her characters did in her novels. Wasn't that how it always worked?

But she knew the answer to that. The stories she was writing were pure fantasy. Reality just didn't work that way. Not for her, at least.

Besides, they'd already proved that they fought more than they got along. What kind of relationship hell would they be embarking on if he did in fact mean all the things he'd said?

She'd kill him before the week was over.

Sighing, she leaned her head against the window and looked out at the garden. If someone had told her a few weeks ago that Bentley Wellington would be at her house taking her on picnics and massaging her injured leg, she would have burst out laughing and then probably cried herself to sleep with bitter longing.

But now that she'd had this time with him, she had to wonder if any of it was real.

Could she even trust him after finding out that he'd been staying with her for a freaking promotion?

Anger surged all over again before she quickly squashed it back down. Margot felt used, but at the same time it was her expectation, right? She always knew that he was here because he was forced to be, but with each kiss, her doubts faded into blissful ignorance and hope that the playboy wanted her.

That he was here for reasons neither of them could control, that he wanted more than her friendship—more than sex—that he wanted the us, the team of Bentley and Margot back, with the bonus of something much more special.

Something she'd been pining for since she was sixteen.

Her heart clenched in her chest. God, this was bad. Because she liked him.

She more than liked him.

And that was the problem.

People like Bentley had an uncanny ability to use your

feelings against you, to make you forget all of the bad every time they did something good.

Like pick flowers.

Kiss her tears away.

And massage half a leg.

She groaned, sucking in her tears.

Whatever happened...would happen. Beyond that, she really had no control. And maybe she never had.

*   *   *

The first shock—her door was open.

The second?

So were the blinds.

"This is new," he said, stepping over the threshold.

Margot was sitting by the window. Her prosthetic wasn't on, and that was a jarring sight, not because he was disgusted but because it made him so damn angry.

Angry that she blamed herself.

Angry that she wasn't living her life when she had every reason to.

And angry that people would look at her and see what she was missing rather than what she had.

And maybe, just maybe, angry at himself that he hadn't been there all along to tell her how worthy—how *beautiful* she really was.

"I liked our picnic," Margot said without looking at him. "But Brant I'm not so sure about anymore."

"He tends to grow on people."

"He's changed." When she finally turned to him, he could see her cheeks were stained with tears. "So...if you can stand me for thirty days you get a fancy new job?"

"The marketing position," he repeated, buying himself

some time. "Honestly, the position has more to do with this insane desire I have to do something that gives me more of a purpose. I like marketing. I do. But there are other things I'd rather—" He stopped himself. The last thing she needed was for him to dump all of his stupid dreams on her lap and ask her to hold his hand while he gave her a sob story about how nobody ever took him seriously or believed in him.

Hell. He was in deep.

Because her look said it all.

Trust me.

And he wanted to.

But something held him back—and that something always held him back when life got confusing. Trust had to be earned, and the only person he really trusted had the uncanny ability to piss him off without even trying.

Her clear green eyes drank him in. "Anything else you want to tell me?"

The story of his past welled up inside him like a giant fire-breathing dragon: *Tell her you didn't abandon her, not on purpose. Tell her you're afraid you'll lose her again.*

Tell her!

"No," he lied, hating himself for it. But the past was the past, right? It didn't matter now; all that mattered was that she knew how much he cared for her. His thoughts lingered around the list in his pocket, the one that sparked his interest all over again, the one that forced him to see her on a daily basis rather than hide out in the house. *Well done, Nadine Titus, well done*, because without his need to cross off things on that list, he probably wouldn't have tried as hard, and he would have missed out on Margot.

"Nothing else. Well, I mean, besides the whole staying here for thirty days in order to secure the marketing position. My insane grandfather offered it to me for the weekend, then basically pulled a *Oh just kidding, stay thirty days and the job is yours; stay the weekend and you have to fight for it."*

"So." She sighed. Her shoulders slumped forward. "Rather than fight for a job you want, against people more qualified, you agreed to stay thirty days with me?" Her eyes lost focus a bit as she looked anywhere but at his face. "So it took an actual threat to keep you here and a charity donation of ten grand to get you here in the first place?"

"Shit." He rubbed his eyes with the backs of his hands. "When you put it like that, it sounds really bad."

"So bad," she agreed with a small smile. God, she was pretty even when she was miserable.

"I missed being outside," she confessed, changing the subject. "You were right about that... so at least one good thing came out of this, right? I saw sunlight. Lay down in the grass. Got felt up by a millionaire playboy who's probably going to forget my name the minute he leaves."

"That's not true," he rasped, and he meant it.

"The feeling-up part? It's completely true." Her voice dropped to a low whisper. "I can still feel your hands on me."

He felt his chest tighten. She was trying to joke it off. Joke *him* off. He needed her to believe he was serious. "Margot, I need you to believe me. I would never forget you or just leave and never look back."

"Don't make promises you can't keep." She gave him a sad smile. "Can you get me my prosthetic? I may have tossed it across the room."

"And here I thought temper tantrums were my specialty." Bentley stood and walked over to the prosthetic, then picked it up and brought it to her. "This can't be comfortable."

She rubbed her leg again. "Believe me, it's not."

Margot's family was loaded. Why not go into the city and

get fitted for something that worked better for her? An idea formed. "How long have you had this?"

"Too long." She grimaced as she adjusted the prosthetic.

Confused, he watched her stand and walk right past him.

"Where are you going?" he asked.

Margot looked down at her clothes and scrunched up her nose. "I was thinking it would be a good idea to shower."

"Oh."

Hell, things were awkward.

Bentley was almost tempted to cough out, *Want help?*

But she was already in the adjoining bathroom shutting the door before the words could tumble out of his mouth. The unmistakable snick of the lock being set was like a punch to the gut.

He stared at the closed door, listening to the muffled hiss of the water and watching as shadows moved across the floor. He wanted to pick the lock and watch as she peeled the clothes from her body. Just thinking about it had him hard.

What the hell was he doing standing outside her bathroom like a complete loser who'd never seen a naked woman before?

He wiped his face again with his hands and did a little semicircle.

Fucking Brant.

This was all his fault. If he hadn't gotten drunk and then pissed, Bentley and Margot would have already been in bed, or at least at a point where they were finally friends. She'd even agreed to it, damn it!

He waited a few more minutes and then slowly started making his way out of the room. Maybe he should just cut his losses, walk away.

His heart jolted at the thought. The idea of going back into Phoenix left a bad taste in his mouth. It also made him angry enough to search out Brant and punch him in his perfect face again.

He stopped and braced himself against the door frame as his eyes fell to the picture of her parents, the one with him in the background. He picked it up and stared at his teenage self.

Part of him felt like he was still that boy, just waiting for someone to discover that he was terrified on the inside—of failure, of never living up to expectations, of the anxiety that constantly banged around in his mind.

Always waiting for the other shoe to drop.

With Margot, he'd gone from a guy just trying to make it through to someone who looked forward to waking up in the morning just so he could make her smile.

And now he'd turned into his old lovesick teenage self, obsessed with her hair, and the way her green eyes locked on him—like he was the only one in the room—even though that was kind of a given, since it was just the two of them.

He'd gotten a significant part of his past back.

The best part.

He'd gotten Margot.

The choice loomed over him.

Stay and fight for a woman he was coming to care for.

Or walk out the door, ignore his feelings, and walk away, like she expected him to do.

He set the picture down and turned back around.

He found himself waiting by the door.

For something.

Hell.

He moved toward the bathroom, rested his head against the door, and listened as water continued to spray, probably all over her now-naked body. Suppressing a groan, he pulled out his phone and looked up doctors who specialized in prosthetic fittings and sent a text to one of his grandfather's assistants to get in touch.

It was the least he could do.

A parting gift if she rejected him.

Margot was basically ignoring him, allowing him an out. And there he was, still staring at a damn door while his body strained to touch hers.

The shower shut off.

Bentley grabbed a chair and sat in front of the door.

When it jerked open, she was covered in the smallest towel he'd ever seen. If she bent over it would basically be like Christmas morning.

His lips curved into a smile. "Nice legs."

"Cute line, but you've used it before."

"Because it's true." He reached for her. "Margot, I'm not going anywhere."

She eyed him wearily as a sad expression crossed her features. "Maybe not now, but you will."

"That's not fair."

"Life isn't fair!" she snapped.

"I thought you were dead!" Bentley shouted.

Margot blanched. "What?"

"Dead. Not living. Not breathing. My best friend. Fucking dead!" Now that the words were out he couldn't stop them. "Brant came to tell me what had happened. When he said your name and accident, I lost my shit." His chest heaved as he ran his hands through his hair. "I just... reacted. I destroyed half of the club lobby, was taken away in handcuffs, and when I finally got home, I thought for sure the reason Brant and everyone else refused to look at me was because my best friend in the whole world was gone. Fucking gone." His voice broke and he stopped to take a huge, heaving breath.

"Bentley. You don't need to do this." Margot laid her hand on his arm. Her hand was small, fragile. Damn it. She deserved to know.

"No. You deserve to hear this. You need to know who I am." He ran his hand through his hair and continued. "I seriously thought you were dead. And it didn't make any sense. How could God have taken you and left me? So I took pills, too many pills. I just wanted it to stop. The thinking. The anxiety. The guilt."

"My God, Bentley. I . . . I had no idea." She looked ghostly pale, and he wondered if he should continue. But no, he had to. He had to finish this.

"I'm surprised anyone even cared what I was doing that day, I'd been such a fucking asshole. Crazed out of my mind. But Brant cared. He came looking for me, and when he found my door locked he knew. He just . . . knew. He broke down the door, found me passed out on the bathroom floor, and called the ambulance." Chest heaving, Bentley could only stare at the floor. He didn't want to see the look she must have in her eyes.

"Weak," he whispered hoarsely. "You made me weak. And every time I see you, I wonder, will it happen again? Because you, you're the game changer, the one who makes me question everything, the one who makes me want to be better, the one I almost lost—the one I am so damn terrified of losing again."

A tear slid down her cheek followed by another.

"They put me in rehab for exhaustion," he continued. "In the same fucking hospital as you. I wanted to see you once I learned you hadn't died. But they wouldn't let me. They wouldn't even let me speak of you. They locked me up in my room, and when I was finally released I convinced myself you were better off without me. But it wasn't true." He felt his control snapping. "I was just too fucking scared that seeing you would bring me back to that dark place again. But I'm not scared anymore, Margot. I want to be your friend, a really good, mind-blowing friend."

"My friend." She swallowed convulsively, her eyes squinting as she sucked in a breath.

"My version of friendship involves multiple orgasms," he said seriously.

Margot's lips twitched as tears stained her cheeks.

"Let me in," he begged. "Let me see all of you, too."

"I can't," she whispered, lip trembling.

He pulled her into his arms, and their foreheads touched. "Live dangerously."

Margot's green eyes searched his as a panicked expression crossed her features. "What if all I want is sex?"

It felt like he'd just been punched in the stomach.

Two weeks ago, he would have offered a smug grin and ripped the towel away from her body. He would have thanked the sex gods for a woman who didn't want commitment and worshipped her with adoration.

And now?

He just felt sick.

"What if I want more?" he whispered, eyes searching hers for the smallest sign that there was more than just a physical attraction.

"Then I say no." She swallowed and looked away.

"Okay." He lied. To her. To himself. "Just sex." Because he knew with Margot it was going to be more, and he was going to regret it, regret allowing her in when she kept him at a distance. But even as his brain screamed at him to stop and think, his hands continued to move until he grasped the edge of her towel with his fingertips and slowly freed it from her body.

Body shaking, she quickly covered her breasts.

He moved her hands away, replaced them with his own. "You said just sex."

Frowning, she gave her head a shake. "I know, but—"

"Sex involves being naked." Her breasts were heavy in his hands.

Her breath came out in a whoosh, and then Margot's entire face transformed in a smile as she whispered, "That feels good."

"I aim to please."

Her lips parted and he captured them in a searing kiss.

"Just friends, right?" Margot gasped, as he rained more kisses down her neck.

"Sure." His mouth whispered against her skin. "Just friends."

CHAPTER TWENTY-SEVEN

Bentley's eyes traveled over her naked, trembling body. He gripped her face with one hand and pressed a heated kiss to her mouth followed by another and another across her eyelids. Then with an aching slowness, like the world had been put on pause, he knelt in front of her and kissed her scars.

Tears clogged in her throat.

A week ago, she would have been horrified, angry, embarrassed. She still felt some of the anger boiling at the surface, the intense need to shove him away and make a run for it out of the sheer terror that he was going to finally realize how broken she was.

But instead, she gripped his shoulders and kept her eyes closed as his lips moved across the marred skin.

Bentley Wellington was kissing her ugly.

The worst and most deformed part of her.

The part even she had trouble looking at—and his lips were tender, coaxing.

"You're beautiful," he whispered against her wet skin. "So beautiful."

He stood abruptly and picked her up in his arms, carrying her over to the bed before he opened the curtains even wider.

"What are you doing?" she asked while he went to the door and locked it.

"I'll be damned if I'm going to miss any inch of you because you have a tendency to live in a cave."

"Oh." Heat flooded her body.

He licked his lips and then she blurted, "I haven't—"

"What?" He cupped her breasts again and she was shocked to hear herself moan a little. His hands felt amazing, rough, against her soft skin.

"I'm..." What was she saying, again? His palms slid down her ribs and she released a little cry before she found words again. "I don't do this."

"I would hope not." His hands moved to her hips.

And that was when she panicked.

"I write about sex."

"I know."

"I don't exactly...have it."

He stopped kissing her. "Have what?"

"It."

Bentley frowned.

"Sex!" Her cheeks burned.

His hands froze on her hips. "I'm sorry. Are you saying you write about dirty sex but you've never had it?"

Oh God. Embarrassment washed over her. She tried to reach for the covers, but he pinned her hands down at her sides.

"Margot?"

"Yes," she squeaked out.

You'd think she'd just given Bentley a gold medal in the Olympics. "I think..." His grin grew. "This may go down as the best day of my life."

"Huh?" His fingers dug into her arms, and it felt good.

"First, you have nobody to compare me to, so that takes all the pressure off. Second," he said as he tapped her nose with his finger, "I get to go painfully slow and most women just want to be f—" He coughed. "Most women I'm with want—" He shook his head. "You know what?" He stood and marched over to her computer. "We're going to act one out."

Margot's jaw dropped. "Act what out?"

He turned toward her with a grin that had her thighs clenching and her heart slamming against her chest. "A scene, Miss Romance Writer."

"Oh no no no no no, that's a horrible idea!" She covered her breasts with her hands and then realized she'd just left herself even more naked, and she slid her right hand down to cover herself up.

Bentley peeked at her over his shoulder and let out a groan. "Touch yourself and it's going to be game over."

"I'm covering myself."

"I really wish you wouldn't cover my second and third favorite parts of you."

She moved her hands and leaned up on her elbows, her mind a blur of questions. "What's the first part?"

"Your leg." When she flinched, he added, "The one that has the pretty scars."

And in that moment, Margot fell not just a little in love with Bentley Wellington but a lot, more than she knew what to do with as her throat went dry.

His favorite part of her—was her least favorite part of herself. How did that work? The part he wanted to kiss and see the most was the part that held her shame, her regrets, her mistakes.

"This one!" Bentley said, triumphantly waving her last novel in the air.

"How did you find one so fast?" She cleared the tears from her throat.

"Easy." He shrugged. "I just grabbed one of the millions of books on your bookcase with naked chesty men and looked for the word *cock*. Imagine my surprise when I saw it at least twelve times in the first chapter. Dirty girl." He winked.

Margot gasped. "There's no way I used cock that many times."

"And yet"—he sauntered lazily toward her, lifting his shirt over his head—"you did."

"I—" She gulped. Why did he have to be so fit? So distractingly beautiful that she wasn't sure if she should stare or talk or kiss him or—

"The duke takes the servant girl two ways."

"I'm blushing, aren't I?" she murmured, covering her burning face with her hands.

The bed dipped under Bentley's weight as he whispered in her ear, "You match your hair."

She shivered.

He placed a kiss on her shoulder. "I promise I'll take care of you."

Slowly she pulled her hands away from her face. "I know."

But how was she supposed to take care of him? It wasn't the same as writing out a scene, where she could pause, delete, rewrite.

This was real life.

All thoughts of what was about to happen rushed to the surface of her mind as Bentley took greedy possession of her mouth.

His hands roamed all over her body, from her breasts to the ache between her thighs.

As her legs entangled with his, she could feel how turned on he was, and a small part of her wanted to cheer. At least her leg hadn't disgusted him so much he wasn't even able to get aroused around her.

"The duke seduces her slowly." Bentley spoke softly, sliding his hand down her side. She sucked in a breath when his fingers danced along her hipbone, and he gave her a teasing smile. "I think you'll like this slow."

She gulped.

And tried to calm down as he moved his hand along the curve of her ass and then moved lower on the bed, tilting her hips up to him.

Crap. She couldn't remember the scene!

What did the duke do?

He breathed against the innermost part of her thigh.

Oh, hell.

She knew exactly what the duke did.

After all, he was a rake, he didn't play by the rules; he was—"Bentley!"

"Red?" He whispered her name, following it with his tongue like he was sealing it inside her.

She tried clamping her legs together, but he made a groan of pleasure and she dug her hands into his shoulders and then finally allowed herself to relax and get lost in the feeling of his mouth on her.

She'd always been in control with her stories, her characters, and now? It was like she'd just given Bentley free rein of the pen.

And her words.

Her fantasies.

It was exhilarating.

It was terrifying.

"Come on, Red," Bentley coaxed, then sucked again.

She panted out his name as he licked.

"Where's my loud sigh?" he asked. Then he replaced his mouth with his hands and sent a shock of pleasure through her that had her legs shaking. "I need to try harder," he added. She was still riding a cloud of bliss when he palmed her and then held her good leg over his shoulder.

And then, Bentley Wellington drank her.

With a scream she reached for him.

He evaded her reach.

And kept his torturous mouth in place.

"That's better." He chuckled darkly, heat and power radiating from him. "I think the duke gave her two orgasms this way. Should we try for three? I don't like the idea of some old British guy doing better." And then his head was gone again.

"Bentley!" She said his name like a curse. "I can't think straight."

"You shouldn't be thinking at all. If you're thinking, I'm doing a shit job."

CHAPTER TWENTY-EIGHT

Bentley was hanging on by a thread. He wasn't used to being patient. He also wasn't used to doing much work—which really didn't speak highly of the type of guy he'd turned into. One who gave women direction and expected them to suck him off and say *Thank you* afterward, like he'd done them a favor.

He sucked in a greedy breath as his eyes feasted on Margot's naked body. Her chest rose and fell as her gaze locked on his stomach and then drifted lower. Her lips pressed together and then parted.

Bentley could have stared at her all day.

The way she watched him wasn't just with curiosity—it was straight-up lust mixed in with something else he couldn't quite put his finger on.

Maybe because most women wanted only one thing.

But Margot? She was the type of girl who unapologetically asked for it all, and refused to give back the pieces.

Tamping down the intense need to claim her, Bentley

moved to the bed and loomed over her. His lips grazed the soft skin below her belly button, then moved up her body until he fused his mouth with hers. Her hips were made for him, her curves; every inch of her body pressed against his was perfection. He wanted sex, no doubt about it, but sex with her? He imagined it would wreck him in the best way.

Sex with her more than once.

Would probably destroy them both.

Then again, he'd never been the type to play it safe.

He gripped her hips and pulled her to a sitting position. "I'm going to do a rewrite."

"What makes you think you're good enough to write a scene?"

"I should probably show you." He drew out a languid kiss from her and then parted her legs with his knee. Then, as if he didn't like that angle enough, he gripped her by the ass and pulled her onto his lap, leaning back so that she was straddling him.

Margot let out a breathy sigh as he guided her into a slow rhythm. Every sliding thrust brought him closer to the brink—he'd always had trouble keeping himself from getting it over with, finishing, and leaving the woman pissed that he didn't spend time worshipping her form head to toe. With Margot? He wanted to lick every inch, explore every crevice, build a shrine to everything he saw.

Bentley kissed her nose. "Are you doing okay?"

She looked shocked that he cared.

"Y-yes." Margot tangled her hands behind his head. "But..."

"But?" His stomach dropped. Was she not enjoying this as much as he was?

"I hate the rewrite." She grinned, then captured his lips with hers.

Her kiss was the knife that cut the thread he'd been hanging from. With a growl, he picked her up off his lap and pressed a feverish kiss to her mouth as he slowly ran his hand down her hip. Then somehow he managed to get her onto her back as he plunged into her again, deeper, harder, faster than he'd intended.

A sense of crazed urgency took over. He couldn't stop, he didn't want to stop, he wanted more of her, he wanted to feel her every day just like this.

Margot squeezed her eyes shut. "This. This isn't. This is better. I must write horrible sex scenes if this is what it's really like. This—"

"Was that a good this or a bad this?" When had Bentley ever worked so hard to please a woman in bed? Sweat collected on his skin and hers.

"Good this." She pressed a hand against his chest. "Kiss me again."

Her full lips trembled beneath his as he rocked into her, their bodies moving together perfectly—her shallow breaths had him clenching his teeth and praying for control.

And then her body clenched around him.

And he lost his damn mind.

He didn't even realize he was yelling her name until it was over.

He ignored the fact that his body felt like he'd just participated in a marathon, and the funny feeling in his chest when she found her release and cried out his name.

He ignored it all.

Because he knew it wasn't normal.

Not any of it.

Having sex had never been like this for him.

"I thought," she panted, "you were over the screaming and wanted panting and deep sighs?"

"Clearly I was mistaken," he joked, still looming over her, his large body pressed against hers in a comfortable way that made him want to stay put for a little longer. "How do you feel?" And why did that question make him feel like he was a virgin asking if he'd performed okay?

"I feel like I want my own duke," she said in a deadpan voice.

"I used to do theatre."

"Liar."

"Okay, so I thought about doing theatre, but give me a few minutes and I'll sew a costume."

"You sew?"

"No." He grinned. "But how hard can it be?"

She sobered, and averted her eyes. "Bentley?"

"Yeah?"

"Thank you."

A grin tugged the corners of his mouth. "For?"

Margot's face turned bright red. "Thank you for...that."

"You know, for a dirty author you don't really say the sexy words very well, do you?"

"It's easier to write them."

"I'll let you in on a little secret..." His lips grazed her ear. "It's better to act them out."

"I know." She let out a happy sigh. "So, how many times did I say *cock* again?"

"Hundreds. Why? What's going on in that pretty little head of yours?"

"Nothing," she said quickly. "And yet so many things. Our friendship. This. Hell, I just said this again. What does it mean? Can we do it again? Why the hell am I suddenly obsessed with the duke's cock? I just thought—"

"Relax." He pulled away from her. "I was thinking the same thing."

"You were?" She perked up.

"Absolutely." He nodded seriously. "Act out the scenes, make sure that they're physically possible. Take one for the team. Delete all the crazy duke references. And replace them with Bentley."

"Oh, sorry, I meant, I should probably go through and delete half the *cock*s." A taunting smile followed.

"That sounds painful. I'm oddly offended."

"It's not your cock," she pointed out.

"You'd be sad if you deleted my cock, admit it."

She giggled and then burst out laughing. God, he loved her laugh. "I'm not sure who would be more sad, me or you."

"Very funny." He grabbed her by the arms and then straddled her again.

"You know…" She trailed a finger down his chest, and he sucked in a breath. "You lived up to the hype."

It was like getting punched in the face.

Was that all this was to her?

She was trying him out for her stories? For the hype? Seriously?

He recoiled and masked his expression, and then Bentley Wellington defaulted into what was familiar, into what he knew best. He pasted a fake smile on his face and shrugged. "There's more where that came from." His words sounded normal, clear, teasing, nonchalant, but his heart cracked a bit.

Because it was the first time he'd actually had an emotional connection during sex.

Only to wonder if it was completely one-sided, and then left in the dark as to what to do next.

Was it sex? Or more?

And suddenly, he transformed into every single chick he'd ever screwed, wondering, overanalyzing.

Karma.

Sucked like a bitch.

CHAPTER TWENTY-NINE

Bentley was being too quiet.

And his fake smile was back.

She had no one to blame but herself. But what did she expect? That he'd stay with her after the month was over? Want to be with her? It was laughable.

Sure, he might like her enough to sleep with her—but he said it himself, he did what he did to push the anxiety away, to escape.

Why was she working so hard to convince herself that she was a distraction to him? When it could be so much more.

Then again. She could be nothing to him. A way to pass time. To scratch an itch. To heal from the trauma of his past.

And then she'd be his nothing.

Oddly enough, the thought didn't have her dry-heaving all over the bedroom floor or even tearing up—because he'd given her a gift.

Not just sex.

But confidence that maybe, just maybe, one day someone might look at her like he did and tell her she deserved to be loved.

That was when the tears came.

"Okay!" Bentley charged into the room with a tray of food and two bottles of wine. "You literally have no healthy food. Only snacks, snacks, and more snacks. I thought I found peanuts—they were covered in chocolate."

Margot gasped and snatched the candy from him. "I've been looking for those!" She ripped them open and popped a handful into her mouth. "What?"

He gave her a look of disbelief. "You just stole my food."

"My house." She chomped down on the nuts. "My food."

"Whatever happened to sharing?" He jerked the candy from her hands. "Does that mean that since I claimed you first, you're mine? Like the food?"

She gulped. "That's completely different."

"Really? Because the way I see it, I searched, plundered, and planted—" he grinned as she covered her face with her hands "—my flag."

Air whooshed out of her mouth. "Your flag?"

"I would have said *cock*." He grinned. "But you keep deleting those, so I'm on high alert where that word's concerned."

She burst out laughing.

He held out his hand. "Come here."

"Where are we going?" She tugged his shirt tighter around her and crossed her arms.

He led her down the stairs and toward the front door. "We are going for a walk."

"We are?"

"Yup." He held the door open. "Brant just texted that he

took off, and I have about five minutes to kill before I do more—" his eyes roamed over her "—planting?"

"Is that what we're calling it now?" She cringed.

"Only because it makes you blush here." He cupped her neck with one hand. "And here." He slid the other hand down her backside.

"My ass blushes?"

"I don't know, should I check?" he teased, as she gently shoved him away.

Bentley was in just his jeans; his abs were on full display, as was his bronzed and muscled back. It hurt to look at him too long.

The outside air hit her skin, causing a shiver to wrack her body. She wasn't cold; it was more the fact that her skin felt sensitive, even to the air.

Bentley smiled down at her. "Are you okay?"

She didn't trust her voice, so she nodded, even though she wasn't okay. Nothing about taking a walk postsex with a man like Bentley Wellington was okay, especially since she woke up a virgin and was now...with the guy she'd always wanted to be with. Whenever she thought about sex or wrote about it, it had always, irritatingly, been Bentley's face she'd seen. And she'd hated herself for it.

Now? She realized her fantasy wasn't even close to the reality of what it felt like to be in his arms.

Her breath hitched when he leaned down and placed a kiss on the top of her head. "You got quiet."

"I was thinking."

He made a face. "I must be shit in bed if you're actually able to still do that."

"What?" She elbowed him playfully in the side. "Is that a side effect from being naked with you? The loss of all co-herent thought?"

"Damn well should be," he grumbled as he wrapped an arm around her waist and tugged her against him. Then a bright smile lit up his face as he went down on bended knee.

"Please tell me you aren't proposing."

"I'm offended that you look like you're ready to pass out."

Margot's eyes narrowed. "Bentley—"

"Go on a date with me."

"A date?" she repeated. Her body hummed with excitement, and then shame.

Because the last time she was on a date it hadn't gone well. Not at all.

Embarrassment washed over her. "No, I, um, I don't think—"

"You really need a break from thinking so much." He stood. "Fine, I'll just have to get you naked again so you stop analyzing every damn thing I say."

Just the thought of being naked with him again—being that vulnerable—had her ready to break out into a cold sweat.

"Yes," Margot found herself blurting. "I mean, sure, that would be fun. A date."

"Fun?" He shoved his hands in his pockets. "Is that why you're making a face like you just drank rotten milk? Because you're so excited about the fun we're about to have on our date?"

She crossed her arms so he wouldn't see the shaking in her hands. "I don't...date."

"I know." He reached for her. "That's why I got down on one knee. I figured I should make it special for you...since it's technically going to be our first date."

"Even though we've already had sex?"

"I never claimed to be a gentleman," he whispered huskily.

"I don't think I asked for one," she retorted, shocking herself and probably him, too, if the surprised expression on his face was any indicator.

"Good." A smile tugged the corners of his lips. "Because I'm pretty sure I would be complete shit at it." God, he was hot when he didn't have a shirt on. The man didn't need clothes. Ever. "But I think I can at least manage to open the door for you."

"Be still my heart," she said drily, as he slowly eyed her up and down. "What?"

"Sorry. I'm still thinking about it."

"*It?*"

"You. Naked. Multiple orgasms. All of *it*."

Her throat went completely dry.

"I'll probably be thinking about it later, too, during our date, after our date, but don't worry," he said quickly. "It's just sex, right?"

She gulped. "R-right."

She could have sworn she saw more hurt than humor in his hazel eyes, and when he turned around to open the door, his hands were clenched in tight fists.

But that would be impossible.

Laughable even.

That a guy like the one she was unabashedly lusting after—would want more than her body.

Guys like Bentley never asked for a girl's heart—even though they ended up with them regardless.

She was way past being able to protect herself from him—and the thought was terrifying.

Margot sighed and tried to focus on the positive.

A date.

She was going on a date.

"Be ready in fifteen," Bentley said, interrupting her thoughts, then softly kissed her on the cheek.

Margot nodded and felt like she was floating as she made her way back inside the house. For the first time in years, she was looking forward to getting in a car.

Because Bentley Wellington was by her side.

CHAPTER THIRTY

The minute Margot got into the car Bentley wanted to make up an excuse—any excuse, that would keep them in bed.

For the rest of the day.

Week.

Year.

The rest of his life.

One.

It was one time, with the woman he'd always wanted, and now he couldn't stop thinking about all of the short little gasps and moans she made when he entered her, or how she gripped his biceps in awe as he kissed down her neck.

Hell, it was going to be a long day. Already his brain was mapping out all the different ways he was going to take her—and although he knew she probably wouldn't turn him down, he wanted her to want him.

Basically, in the short span of a few weeks, he'd turned into a chick.

There was no other explanation for the overanalyzing and

constant state of worry he'd been in since she gave him "the look" and basically admitted she was just using him for sex.

When it was so much more.

Which meant he had to laugh it off so she wouldn't see how much it had both pissed him off and hurt his feelings.

Fifteen minutes ago he was ready to talk to her about it, and then he chickened out and asked her on a date instead.

He was dating her so he could get her to like him...and then what? They'd ride off into the sunset together? Great. Awesome. Good job, Bentley.

Good plan.

"Hell," he muttered.

"What?" Margot's excited green eyes blinked back at him as she clutched her seat belt with her hands.

"Nothing." He forced a smile and then hit the accelerator.

"Bentley?"

"Hmm?" It was hard to keep the car on the road when she was licking her lower lip like that, especially now that he knew what she tasted like.

He held his groan in when she leaned forward, and the material from her loose tank top pooled near her breasts, flashing him, blinding him, nearly killing him.

"Thanks for getting me out of the house." She was pale when she said it, like she meant the words, but her body wasn't completely on board with the entire idea.

He tore his gaze away from her and focused on the drive into the city. "You're welcome."

They rode in comfortable silence all the way into town. Well, as comfortable as was possible since his dick tried to rise to the occasion every time she moved, exposing a bit of skin or sending her perfume wafting toward him.

Bentley grinned when he pulled into the parking lot of the go-kart lot. "Ready?"

"Where are we?" She frowned, looking up at the sign. "Go-kart racing?"

"Affirmative." He turned off the car and opened his door. "When was the last time you drove *anything*?"

Her lips drew into a straight line as she scowled over at him. "I don't see how that's any of your business."

"Prickly." He grinned over at her, then got out of the car and made his way over to her side. She was still sitting in the car, arms crossed, face full of fear, seat belt on.

He opened the door. "Unbuckle your seat belt, Margot, we're going for a ride."

She snorted out a laugh. "Is that what you tell all the girls?"

"What other girls?" he countered as he closed the door again. "Because I'm only looking at one. I'm on a date with one girl. The only girl. Some may say I'm with the girl that got away."

Her breath hitched and a blush stained her cheeks. "I was in a hospital bed. Kinda hard to get away from that." Voice wobbly, her eyes filled with tears.

"Fuck." With shaky hands he reached for her face and kissed her—hard. "I'm sorry, so damn sorry." He wiped the moisture from her cheeks.

"Me too," she said.

"What?" His chest tightened. "Why are you sorry?"

"The phone works both ways, right?" She lifted a shoulder in a halfhearted shrug. "I let my hurt and anger destroy a good friendship. Don't act like I didn't have a part in this. I just...you were so you and I was so me."

"I'm not following."

Their foreheads touched as she kept talking, running her hands up and down his chest, making it hard to focus on anything but the way her fingers felt against him. "We never made sense, you and me. I was the painfully shy, awkward bookworm, and you were the most popular guy in school. I let my fears, my insecurities, convince me that you'd only been using me, that you'd never actually been my friend. That someone like me could never have deserved you as a friend."

"Margot." Bentley cupped her face, his thumbs brushing her lips as they parted on contact. "Listen to me very closely…" Her half-lidded expression was almost his undoing, so beautiful. She was gorgeous. "I was terrified of you in high school. You were so smart and so pretty that most of the guys in our class were afraid to even talk to you." She frowned. "And as far as deserving me? Hell, Margot, I could spend the rest of my life trying to deserve you and still fall short."

"That's not—"

"Shh." He kissed her sweet mouth. "Let's make a deal."

She chewed her lower lip. "I'm listening."

"Let's go on a date."

"Um, we *are* on a date."

"Let me finish."

"Sorry."

"You interrupt a lot, you know that?"

She smirked. "I do not!"

"Margot," he warned with a smile.

"Fine. Go."

"Oh wow, now you're demanding," he teased. "Let's go on our date and let this be about us. Margot and Bentley now…not the past, no elephants, no regret…and see where that takes us."

She didn't say anything.

He waited.

"Margot?"

"Oh, I wasn't sure you were done, I didn't want to interrupt you again," she added with a teasing smile that had his heart bursting with—*something*. Shit. He was in too deep.

"Cute."

"I thought I was pretty."

"Fishing for compliments now? What have I done to you?"

She swallowed and glanced away. "Maybe you just made a broken woman"—she looked back at him—"a little bit more secure."

"Life made." He kissed her. He couldn't help it.

She wrapped her arms around his neck as she pressed her body against his.

Bentley hissed out a breath when she took his bottom lip between his teeth and slid her hand slowly down his chest. Her hands kept moving, pausing to flick open the button of his jeans before reaching around to his ass.

"Did you just squeeze my ass?" he asked against her mouth.

She laughed. "I've always wanted to do that."

"Squeeze a guy's ass or *my* ass?"

"Both," she admitted. "I have this one scene where—"

"Margot." He pulled away and then kissed her again, and again, before finally breaking away. "Are we acting out a 'sexy times in a carriage' scene?"

"No." She slid her hand inside his jeans and gripped him. Bentley saw stars. "I'm writing my own." Her hand moved.

"Damn good chapter." His mouth found hers again as she pumped her hand. Bentley swallowed kiss after kiss, imagining her mouth in place of her hand.

If he didn't stop her, they were going to get arrested in the parking lot, and he was going to have to explain to the officer why he couldn't walk—or think—or get out of the car.

"Margot—" He jerked his mouth away from her. "If we don't stop—"

"You're interrupting," she whispered with a wicked expression on her face. He reached for her hand but stopped.

It felt so good.

Too good.

"Just like that." Hell, she was killing him. "Margot—"

He roared out her name, gripping the steering wheel with his left hand while he reached for her with his right, grabbing her hair instead of her body by accident.

His orgasm hit him so hard for a second he thought he was going to pass out. He was afraid to look down.

Only to see Margot had already thought of everything.

"Huh." They both stared at his lap. "Starbucks cup, huh?"

"It was that or my purse."

He burst out laughing and then kissed her again, because he couldn't help it, because he wanted to. Because the last time he'd gotten a hand job like that had been never.

Because he already knew he was in love with her.

He just needed her to catch up.

"We write really well together." He buttoned his jeans back up and adjusted himself as best he could, trying to think of anything that would help alleviate the sudden ache he had to press her against the car seat and devour her.

"You did okay." She winked.

"I like you."

She gulped and wrung her hands together, whispering, "I like you, too."

"Ready for our date?"

She looked out the window and gasped. "Go-karts?"

"Go-karts."

"We just did—" she pointed to him "—*that* . . . in a go-kart parking lot?"

"Family fun for everyone." Bentley nodded seriously then cracked a smile. "Let's go."

They both got out of the car and made their way across the parking lot.

She pressed a shaky hand between her breasts. "I know this sounds ridiculous, but what if I crash?"

Her face was so crestfallen he wanted to pull her into his arms and protect her, from everything. It hadn't occurred to him a go-kart might scare her; it wasn't even a car. "Look." He nodded toward the track. "You think that you'll actually get hurt? I'm pretty sure that kid who keeps driving around in circles is only six. The other one just ran straight into a wall and bounced back like a beach ball. You'll be fine."

She nodded. Twice. Her eyes scanned the cars as they whipped around the corners and ran into each other and every other object in their way.

Bentley excused himself and went over to the main counter to pay for their cars.

"Hey," he said to the teen with braces at the counter. "Can we get two cars for the next hour?"

The kid grunted and handed him two keys and two helmets. "Try not to run over the cones."

Bentley fought the urge to roll his eyes and point back at his sports car parked outside. Cones? He was going to be completely fine.

Margot, on the other hand...

"I'll let my date know." He knocked his knuckles against the counter and turned to leave when the guy called out to him.

"Dude, you brought your date here? To race go-karts?"

Bentley frowned. "Yeah, why not?"

"Most people are under the age of twelve." The kid rolled his eyes. "Doesn't exactly scream romance." He scrunched up his nose. "Then again, you *are* old..."

"Listen up, punk." Oh God, he sounded like his grandfather. "You're probably too young to understand this, but the best kinds of dates are the ones where you get blood pumping. Blood pumping to all the right places causes a woman to get excited, and when she's excited, she's—" Holy shit, why was he giving scoring advice to a high school kid? "You know what? Never mind."

The kid's wide-eyed look was almost comical. "No, I want to hear this. When they get excited, what?"

Thankfully, Margot came up behind Bentley just then and reached for his hand. "Everything okay?"

"Holy shit, you're hot." The kid eyed her up and down, and his cheeks took on a pink hue as he licked his lips and focused in on Margot's chest.

Yeah, Bentley was going to land in jail again.

Only this time for punching a minor.

"You look intense." Margot frowned up at Bentley. "What's going on?"

"Sorry, ma'am." The kid flashed her a smile. Back the hell off, kid. "Your boyfriend was just telling me how to get a woman excited."

Bentley groaned.

Margot smacked him in the chest. "Was he, now?"

The kid nodded enthusiastically. "It's why he brought you here."

"Listen, punk." Bentley pointed at him. Oh good, he'd used the word *punk* again. Fantastic.

"Thank you!" Margot said quickly to the kid and grabbed a helmet from Bentley's hand. "For, uh, the rental." She jerked Bentley away even as the kid checked out her ass and gave Bentley a thumbs-up.

"Leave it," Margot said under her breath, then burst out laughing once they were out of earshot.

Bentley's blood was still boiling, and rage clouded his vision. And he had no idea why. He pointed at him. "That kid was disrespectful." Yes. Those words. They just came out of his mouth. The hell?

"That *kid's* maybe seventeen. Of course he's disrespectful." Margot rolled her eyes. "As I recall, you were worse at that age." She eyed him up and down. "You may be even worse now."

"Do *not* compare me to that punk!"

"'Punk'?" She giggled.

"I've apparently turned into my grandfather," Bentley said, mostly to himself. "If I wake up tomorrow with gray hair and my pants pulled up to here"—he pointed high on his waist—"just do me a favor and pull the trigger."

"Stop being so dramatic." She put on her helmet. "How do I look?"

"Good enough to eat. Oh wait, I already did that." Bentley pulled her roughly into his arms.

She stiffened and then looked up at him with fear in her eyes. "I don't want to drive."

"I know."

"No, I really don't want to drive. The thought of it makes me sick."

"Margot, I say this as a *friend*..." He nodded toward the track. "If you don't get your ass out there and teach that kid a lesson, we can't have sex tonight."

"There are so many things wrong with that sentence," she muttered.

"Just think." He tapped her helmet. "Beast mode."

"I'm not racing a six-year-old!'"

Bentley pulled the helmet over his head and shrugged. "If you don't, who will?" He tossed her the key to her go-kart.

She rolled her eyes. "You're insane, you know that, right?"

"Margot." His lips teased the outer corner of her ear. "Our sex life depends on you."

She giggled and walked over to her car, then got in, but not before the same six-year-old rounded the corner, slowed down, and said, "Hey, baby, wanna race?"

"That little shit!" Bentley turned the key to start his engine just as Margot threw her head back and laughed. Damn, she was beautiful.

His jeans tightened as an ache to have her built inside him, which was really unfortunate, since he was surrounded by children and sitting in a too-small go-kart that was littered with popcorn and bubblegum.

Margot started her go-kart, and she and the little jackass were racing at ten miles an hour, away from him, laughing.

Unbelievable. He'd just been taken down by a first-grader.

Cursing, Bentley jammed his key to the right again. The engine finally started with a snarl and a puff of white smoke. He hit the accelerator and then managed to nearly take out the parked go-kart in front of him. He turned quickly and the go-kart started going backward.

"Out of my way, loser!" The first-grader was moving toward him so slowly he wasn't sure if it was an optical illusion. Margot followed, clearly allowing the kid to beat her, and motioned for him to move out of the way.

"I'm trying!" he shouted through clenched teeth.

"If you can't drive get out off the track!" the high school guy shouted from his little booth.

"Fun date!" Margot passed him by and waved.

He hit the accelerator again and turned the go-kart to chase after Margot.

The go-kart jerked forward and then stopped, only to jerk forward again.

"What the hell is wrong with my car!" he shouted.

"No cursing!" The high schooler pointed to a sign that had all of the rules listed, including no cursing, no destroying cars, no fighting. The hell with that! What kind of racetrack was this?

"So," Margot called to the kid she was racing as they made their way back toward Bentley. "How old are you?"

"Today's my birthday. I turn six!" He nodded proudly. "Want to be my girlfriend?"

Margot laughed. "Of course."

Bentley glared and started after them. "She's taken, Romeo!"

"My name's Jay!" The kid glared back at him and then shared a smile with Margot. "My mom says not to talk to strangers, but you're not a stranger anymore." He sighed. "He's mean."

Bentley turned around just in time to see the kid pointing at him.

"Oh, he's not mean," Margot said. "He just doesn't like losing."

Jay giggled. "Yeah and he's losing bad!" he yelled out. "Loser, loser, loser." For a good five minutes.

And that was how the rest of the date went.

Bentley followed them closely while the little man flirted circles around him.

And Margot drove the entire time.

How was it possible that he didn't even get the girl—and it was still the best date of his life?

He parked his go-kart and hopped out to go rescue Margot from the snot-faced Casanova in training.

"Jay, it's been a pleasure." Margot held out her hand to the little guy once they both stepped out of their cars. Bentley waited a few feet away. "Have a happy birthday!"

"You're a good driver, Mar Mar."

Bentley rolled his eyes. Nicknames? They had nicknames?

"Well, I had a good teacher." She winked.

The kid's chest puffed out. "Let's do this again sometime."

He walked off and grabbed a juice box from one of the tables. Then he turned and gave Bentley an evil glare.

"So your new boyfriend's kind of a bully," Bentley said when Margot rejoined him.

Margot sighed and gave Jay a longing glance. "Yeah, but he really gets me."

"Between you and me, I think he'd probably choose pizza over you, but to each his own." Bentley pointed to the birthday boy, who was in fact devouring a huge slice of cheese pizza, getting more of it on his face than in his mouth. A guy who looked like the kid's grandparent brought over napkins and some bottled water.

Margot burst out laughing. "He's adorable."

"I can be adorable," Bentley grumbled.

"You—" Margot trailed her finger down his chest "—can't even drive a go-kart." She pulled her hand away. "Plus Jay's going to be an astronaut."

"Damn it, Jay!" Bentley put on his sunglasses. "I can't compete."

"You can't win them all. It's not you." Margot put a hand on his shoulders. "It's me."

She looked so free, so beautiful, that he couldn't help it anymore. He lifted her into the air and swung her around, then let her slide down his body. When her feet were on the ground, he pressed a kiss to her parted lips.

"What was that for?" she asked breathlessly.

"For being beautiful," he answered truthfully. "And for driving a car for one whole hour."

"Thank you." She kissed him again and again.

Bentley groaned as their bodies pressed against one another. It was hard as hell not slipping his hands under her shirt or just taking her against the car.

"Anytime you want to thank me," he said in a husky voice, "I'm here."

With a laugh, she stepped back. "You're a good friend."

"Best friend." He accentuated the *best* part. "Right?"

"The best I've ever had," she whispered.

And suddenly, the fear was back.

That same choking feeling he'd had when he thought she'd died—it was back, reminding him it could happen again. Logically, he knew it was his anxiety speaking, but it was hard to control the choking sensation wrapping around his throat as he imagined a world with her no longer in it.

And just like that, his world went dark again.

And he was afraid.

So damn afraid that maybe, just maybe, his anxiety never went away, he'd just been keeping it in check with the art of distraction. But Margot wasn't a distraction—she was the trigger.

Bentley inwardly cursed as he opened her door. "Let's grab some takeout? I bet all that flirting made you hungry."

Margot kissed him one more time before getting in the car.

His body felt numb, hollow, as he walked around to the driver's side and pretended that his chest wasn't aching.

Hell, this was what he did, right?

He pretended he wasn't anxious.

Pretended he didn't care about anything but screwing.

He'd been pretending all his life.

CHAPTER THIRTY-ONE

Bentley was oddly silent after they picked up their Chinese takeout. One minute they were laughing and having fun on their date—kissing, even. And the next minute he looked like someone had just run over his favorite pet.

"Are you okay?" she finally asked, throat dry.

Darkness had already fallen around the valley, sending tremors of apprehension along her spine as they drove back to the house. The roads were winding, and it wasn't like there were a lot of lights lining them.

She needed to focus on something else—badly.

"Great. Why?" Bentley's jaw twitched, as if he'd been clenching his teeth.

"You just seem upset." She brought her focus back to the road. "That's all."

"And if I was upset..." Bentley's voice trailed off. "What would you do to make me feel better?"

He didn't sound like he was teasing.

He sounded serious.

"Talk to you," she finally answered. "I'd talk to you and

try to help you." It sounded stupid to her own ears. She'd talk to him? Like talking had ever helped her.

The only thing that helped was the very man who seemed hell bent on ripping the steering wheel from the dash.

Bentley's eyes flashed as he slowly drew out the word. "Talk."

"Yes, we'd talk." The air in the car was charged—though she had no idea why, or what had shifted between them. "Don't you *talk* with all of your friends?"

"Friends, friends, friends." Each time he said the word his voice rose. "I don't know what the hell you want from me right now." He ran his free hand through his hair.

Her eyes widened in shock as her pulse hammered in her chest. What had just happened? "I-I'm sorry, I thought we had fun today."

"We did." He swore. "Sorry, I'm just…" He exhaled roughly. "I'm tired. That's all. I'm not angry at you."

He was lying again.

The weird tension made her feel sick to her stomach, and confused.

"Margot, I have to tell you something and—" He squinted into the darkness, his jaw clenched.

Margot glanced up. "And?"

Bentley pulled over to the side of the road as the car kicked up dirt and gravel. "Stay here."

"What's wrong?" Panic welled in her chest. "Bentley?"

"It's okay, just stay in the car," he ordered, slamming the door after him.

He moved toward a small object on the side of the road. "Please don't let him be mauled by a bear," she said to herself.

Did they have bears in Arizona?

She was being ridiculous.

Bentley kneeled down; his back was illuminated by the headlights, but his body completely blocked whatever he was doing. When he moved again it looked like he was picking something up.

He turned toward her.

A mangy, rat-looking thing was resting in his arms as Bentley quickly ran to the car and opened the back door. "He's hurt."

"Who's hurt?" She wrinkled her nose at the sudden sour, earthy odor.

"The dog." With gentleness that made Margot's heart hurt, Bentley spread his hands over the dog's body and sighed. "I think he got hit."

It was on the tip of her tongue to ask why he was rescuing the dog, not that she didn't care, but he didn't even know the dog and he wasn't responsible. Who just rescued a stray dog?

Correction, what was Bentley Wellington doing rescuing a stray dog?

"We need to find a vet clinic that's open," Bentley said almost to himself, as he continued running his hand over the dog's matted fur. She couldn't tell if it was dirt and gravel making the fur brown or if the dog really was that color.

"I'll look it up on my phone," Margot offered.

It took a few minutes but she finally located a clinic that was open 24/7, and the on-call vet said he'd be waiting for them.

"Do you—do you want me to sit in the back with him?" Margot asked once Bentley got back into the driver's seat.

He nodded. "Yeah, that would be good. He's probably scared and in a lot of pain."

"Okay." She quickly unbuckled her seat belt and got in the backseat, careful not to get too close to the dog just in case it got agitated enough to bite her hand off. It wasn't that she didn't like animals—she'd just never had a pet before.

Bentley didn't count.

She smiled at her own joke.

"Something funny?" Bentley asked as he turned the car around and headed back into town.

"Nothing." Margot ran a hand along the dog's wet fur. "Do you think he's going to be okay?"

"I felt a broken rib or two," Bentley said, surprising her. "And his nose is dry, his breathing labored—"

"How do you know all of that?"

Bentley was back to clenching his jaw shut. Finally, he whispered in a hoarse voice, "Don't worry. He'll be fine."

Margot frowned down at the poor animal. "Bentley, I think . . . his back leg is twisted funny."

Bentley didn't say anything.

"Did you hear me?"

"It's broken," he said after a long pause. "Let's just wait until we see the vet."

Memories of metal crunching metal came flooding to the surface. The poor dog.

"It's going to be okay, buddy." Tears welled in her eyes. It was almost impossible to keep them back once they started burning. Why was she crying over a broken dog?

The dog snapped at her hand.

She jerked it away.

Stunned.

Not because it almost bit her, but because it suddenly hit her—Bentley was right. She'd been acting like a hurt puppy, an abused dog. She was crying because she saw herself in the dirty, mangy mess sitting next to her.

*   *   *

I'm sorry," the vet said after examining the dog. "There's nothing I can do for the leg."

Margot gasped. "But he needs his leg!"

Bentley was quiet and then pulled the doctor aside, leaving Margot with the dog. She refused to leave his side.

The black Lab puppy kept whimpering and he looked terrified even if he was sedated. A muzzle covered his snout, and his eyes locked with Margot's. A pang sliced through her chest.

"It's going to be fine," she whispered, running a hand across his back.

"Thanks, Doctor." Bentley shook the man's hand and returned to Margot. "You ready?"

"No!" She shook her head. "You can't just save him and then abandon him, Bentley!"

He smiled down at her. "I couldn't agree more."

"But…" Okay, he was confusing her. "You asked if I was ready?"

"To eat cold Chinese food." Bentley's hand found hers. "The vet is going to operate—he needs to amputate at the dog's hip."

Margot was frozen in place. "Will he be okay?"

"He should be great."

"I'll pay for it." Margot swallowed the thickness in her throat.

"No need." Bentley squeezed her hand. "I'm taking care of it."

"You?" The word was out before she could stop it, and her shocked expression didn't help. Did she still think so little of him? That he wouldn't go out of his way to do something kind for an animal?

"That hurts." Bentley looked down, breaking eye contact.

She choked back a sob. "I'm sorry."

"I know you are." He finally looked back at her. "But that doesn't change the fact that you think so little of me . . . when I think the world of you."

And then he walked away.

CHAPTER THIRTY-TWO

The cold Chinese food tasted like salt and sandpaper in his mouth and sat like a rock in his stomach.

Margot's words had hurt.

And he was pissed off that he'd let himself get hurt.

First the anxiety and now this. This horrible feeling that he had somehow fallen for Margot—but she still thought of him as the playboy who arrived on her doorstep—when he wanted to be so much more to her.

He was doing everything in his power to try to prove to her he was for real, and at every turn she fought him or unintentionally brought his past up. At least he hoped it was unintentional—maybe she did it to keep her guard up. She had no clue of the hell he was going through, the anxiety that she caused—and he was still there, he was still standing, willing to battle his demons for her.

Aggravated, he started to pace.

Margot had gone to grab coffee, leaving him alone in the silence with his dark thoughts. The last thing he wanted was to go home in a week without her.

But what was his other option?

Ask her to come with him? And hope that thirty days was enough for her to take a leap—when she still struggled riding in a damn car and was terrified to even go on a date? Right, that was going to go over well. *Hey, Margot, want to move in with me?*

He scowled at his reflection in the window.

"Hey!" Margot exhaled a laborious breath. "I just saw the doctor. He said Scar made it through the surgery! And he's recovering!"

Bentley tilted his head. "Scar?"

Margot blushed. "I named him."

"I see that."

"Because he's going to have—"

"—a scar," Bentley finished. "Just like you."

Tears welled in her eyes. God, he was an idiot, he didn't even think about how this was affecting Margot.

"I'm sorry," they both blurted in unison.

"Ladies first." He took a step toward her outstretched hand.

Briefly, she closed her eyes then opened them. "I'm sorry that I'm a judgmental bitch."

Bentley barked out a laugh. "Okay, not what I was expecting, but I'll take it."

Her lips trembled, and then she wailed, "I'm a dog!"

"Okay, really not where I thought you were going."

Margot laughed through her tears and stepped into his embrace. "I'm just like Scar. I bite at people and snap and growl and, and—" She hiccupped.

"Hey now, some men may like your bite."

She sniffled. "Such an optimist."

"Go ahead, I don't mind." He gave her access to his neck and laughed while she pinched him in the side. "Seriously, I'll take one for the team. I'll even let you scratch me."

"Leave it to you to make it sexual."

"Well, I'm a man, so there's that."

Margot cupped his face with both of her hands. "You're a good man, Bentley Wellington."

Emotion clogged his throat. Sadly, it was the first time anyone had ever spoken those words to him—and looked like they meant it. "You think so?"

"I know so. And I'm sorry that it took you getting forced into paid slave labor for you to see that about yourself."

"I always knew I was awesome."

She rolled her eyes. "Seriously, Bentley, you're incredible."

Guilt gnawed at him. "I use women and drinking as a distraction in order not to have an anxiety attack about the girl I walked away from and nearly killed myself over. What's so great about that?"

"You were young. You went through a traumatic event."

"And you didn't?"

She reached for his hand. "Brant said something...when he was here."

"Brant said a lot of things while he was here."

"About that day in the hospital."

Bentley froze. "Oh?"

"I wasn't supposed to say anything."

"Okay..."

"He was going to pretend to be you...since they wouldn't let you out of the room. Of course, I knew it wasn't you the minute he walked in the door because...I know you. I do." Tears filled her eyes. "I know the way it feels to hold your hand. I know the sound of your laugh—it hasn't changed after all these years. I know you, Bentley. You're stronger than you think."

"I would take it back if I could. I tell myself this all the time, and yet now all I keep thinking about is, what if? What if something happens to her again? I've done a good job of keeping the anxiety away...the marketing position was the next step in my plan, prove myself to my grandfather, stop dicking around, and then, *boom*." He shook his head. "I'm forced to face the trigger—the catalyst—my past—my Margot."

Tears filled her eyes. "*Your* Margot?"

"Mine."

She stepped into his arms and rested her head against his strong chest while he wrapped her in a hug.

"How come nobody at school knew about what happened with you? I mean, had I not dug a few days ago I would have never known."

Bentley tensed. "Dug?"

"The Google search mentioned it, but that's all. I didn't know any details."

"You were stalking me?" His voice was raspy.

She pulled away from him, prepared to apologize again, defend herself, but he was smiling down at her, the biggest grin on earth plastered all over his handsome face. "Any naked pictures saved to your desktop, dirty girl?"

"Eh, I have the real thing, so no."

"You do."

Her heart leaped.

"Have me," he finished. "You have all of me."

"Good, now answer my question."

Bentley sighed. "A Wellington doesn't show weakness. They also do what they're damn well told to do. My grandfather, well, let's just say my biggest fear wasn't letting him down—it was turning into my brother Brock, his carbon copy. And then it turned into this intense need to be noticed for something other than being a twin. When you're a twin you're constantly fighting for your individuality while at the same time basically protecting the other half of your heart and soul. With Brant..." He shrugged as his throat went dry. God, he hadn't ever really confessed any of this before. "With Brant," he tried again, "I felt like it was my job to make sure he was happy. It was my job to keep the brothers together through thick and thin—and then when I finally found something that I wanted to do for me..." His voice cracked. "I was rejected, laughed at."

"What was for you?" Her eyes searched his.

"You're going to laugh."

Margot reached out and touched his hand. "Promise I won't."

He took a deep breath and blurted, "I wanted to be a veterinarian. I had a dog when I was little, he got a tumor and died, and I don't know, I just—I didn't realize how much I loved animals until college."

Margot didn't say anything, her eyes filled with tears.

"Margot?"

She opened her mouth as tears streamed down her face.

"Margot, what's wrong?"

"I'm your dog!" She hid her face in his chest while he burst out laughing. "It's not funny, you jackass!"

"Actually..." He gently pulled her back and tilted her chin upward, capturing her lips in a salty kiss. "It's hilarious. You aren't my dog. I was kidding when I said all of those things. I was being my normal jackass self."

"It doesn't make it untrue, though." She sniffled. Her green eyes flashed with insecurity. "I'm like the broken dog you want to fix—and what happens when I'm all fixed?"

"Are you asking what happens when you go outside like a normal person? Or what happens when you start driving a car that isn't made for a first-grader?"

She gave him a nod.

"Nothing." They touched foreheads. "Nothing happens, nothing changes, it's still you and me, and honestly, Margot, I'm getting pretty tired of you constantly looking at yourself as broken."

Her breath hitched.

"You were never broken to me. Only to yourself."

A knock sounded at the door, and the veterinary tech poked her head inside. "Would you guys like to see your dog?"

"Oh my gosh!" Margot's eyes widened. "We have a dog together."

"Um, congratulations?" the tech offered.

"And my grandfather says I can't commit." Bentley winked at her. "I call bullshit."

Margot elbowed him. "Baby steps."

CHAPTER THIRTY-THREE

How the hell had he gotten himself into this situation? Bentley kept his grin in check while Scar slept on Margot's lap the entire way home. He'd been surprised they didn't need to keep Scar overnight, but the vet was confident that Scar needed human kindness more than he needed observation at the clinic.

A white-and-pink bandage was wrapped around the dog's leg. They had a bag full of pills for the poor guy, and since he had no collar, the vet let them keep the one they'd put on him at the clinic.

"We have a dog," Bentley said aloud. "Holy shit."

"Told you," Margot whispered. "Probably not exactly what my grandmother meant when she instructed me to stick a needle through the condoms, but it may placate her for now."

Bentley turned the car down the long driveway. "Again, that's why you bring your own condoms."

Her face fell.

Damn it. The last thing he wanted to do was remind her

of the sins of his past and make her even more dedicated to pushing him away.

"Right, but what if the girl in question searches your stuff, finds the packets, and then sticks a needle in them?"

"The girl's sure going to a lot of work to carry my child—maybe she deserves to, if she's willing to rifle through all of my things. But I'm pretty sure she'd have to get me drunk, since I keep my condoms in my wallet, ergo, she'd have to steal my wallet, and why the hell are we talking about this right now?"

Margot grinned. "Because we adopted a dog. A child is the next logical step."

"According to our grandparents? Yes. But let's just try to keep the dog alive for now, and then we can talk condom breaking."

Her smile dipped at the corners. He hated that he noticed something so small, but there it was. "You can't keep a pet alive?"

"Of course I can."

His eyes locked on the corner of her mouth, where he wanted to lick. Damn it. He was in for a rough night. "Let's maybe focus on making sure he's comfortable tonight."

"Sounds good." She blew air out through her lips.

It wasn't awkward.

They were talking about kids.

Had slept together once.

And were forced to live together for a few weeks.

And they were talking about kids.

Again, how did he get himself into this situation? Where walking into the house at three a.m. with an injured dog and a beautiful woman seemed like the best night of his life?

No drugs involved, no sex, no all-night orgies. Just Margot and Scar.

A small bag of vet-approved dog food.

And a bag of doggy pills.

Sighing, he started carrying the dog up the stairs when Margot's arm shot out across his. "What are you doing?"

"Um." Bentley was too tired to really think. "Taking the dog to your room? I thought you may want to sleep with him, in case he wakes up and gets scared." Damn dog! What about him? What if he woke up and got scared? Or horny? Same thing!

Margot slid her hand down his arm and gave him a little tug down the hall. "I thought maybe we could all stay with you. Together."

His heart shouldn't have reacted the way it did.

Slamming against his chest so savagely that he had no choice but to suck in a breath and pray she didn't see the excitement pasted all over his stupid-ass face.

It was what he wanted.

Needed.

Not the dog.

Just Margot.

All of her.

"Yeah," he finally managed to croak out. "That would be nice." Hell, it would be a lot more than nice, but bursting out into song and dance would probably scare the shit out of her.

"Good." They walked side by side into his room. Margot grabbed a blanket from the bed and placed it on the floor in a little makeshift bed for Scar and then glanced up with hopeful eyes at Bentley.

"You think he'll be okay?"

"Yeah." He leaned down, gently laying Scar on the pillow Margot had put in the middle of his bed. "This is probably the best night of the dog's life. A gorgeous woman petting him? I know I'd fake death for that."

"Well." She stood. "I don't think you need to go to those kinds of extremes."

"No?" He moved to his feet and reached out to tip her chin toward him. "What makes you think that?"

"Because..." Her clear green eyes were hypnotic in the way they locked onto him, with so much trust, trust he hadn't done a damn thing to deserve.

He wasn't sure who moved first.

But suddenly their mouths were colliding, devouring one another.

He loved this new, aggressive side of her.

With a jerky movement, she had his jeans at his feet. He kicked them off and nearly ripped her shirt from her body as she licked the side of his neck.

Margot collapsed against him and then pulled away, her cheeks red. "I, uh, I should probably..." She pointed down at her leg.

Bentley's chest warmed as his heart thudded loudly. "You want me to help you take it off?"

She gave him a mute nod, then with jerky movements walked over to the bed and sat, her eyes downcast as Bentley kneeled in front of her and examined the prosthetic.

"Here." Fingers trembling, she showed him how to unfasten the leg.

Emotion clogged his throat at the trust she was giving him. She was baring all—it wasn't just sex.

No matter what she believed or what the hell she said.

It was more.

"Beautiful," he murmured between kisses as he pulled her into his arms. "You're so damn beautiful."

"So are you." Her voice shook as she ran her hands down his naked chest, her fingers tickling his skin as she hooked her hands around his neck and pulled him in for a searing kiss.

"Mmm." He gently set her back in the bed and with one arm lifted her closer to the headboard. "I love you like this."

Hell. Did he just say…?

Margot froze and then pried her lips from his. "Like what?"

"Naked," he teased, kissing her again. "Writhing beneath me." Another kiss on her neck as he slid his hand between her thighs. "And without your prosthetic—just you."

"Are you saying that you like me better without my leg?"

He nuzzled her neck. "I like you best when it's just you, battle wounds and all."

"You can't say things like that to me and expect me not to fall in love with you."

"I just did." Their mouths joined in a frenzied rush as his hand explored her body, bringing her pleasure as she moved against him.

He moved his hand from her thighs to her hips, cupping her ass, pulling her closer while she grabbed him and whimpered, "I need you."

"Not as much as I need you." It was the truth. Another true thing he released out into the universe. Just another piece of himself that he'd given her willingly. Holding back was no longer an option.

He entered her with one fluid motion.

Margot gasped against his mouth.

"You feel so good." Bentley groaned as a feeling of completion washed over him.

It wasn't sex.

It would never be just sex ever again as long as he was with Margot.

"You do, too." She cried out when he increased his movements, only to slide his hand down her injured leg and press his fingertips against the scars.

Tears welled in her eyes.

"All of you," he whispered against her mouth. "I want all of you."

But she didn't answer.

Instead, she closed her eyes and found her release, leaving Bentley without an answer and wondering...if the silence *was* his answer.

CHAPTER THIRTY-FOUR

Margot checked on Scar throughout the night. He was sleeping okay, but he woke up a few times whimpering. She knew that feeling well—sometimes the pain still woke her up even though she didn't have a leg anymore. Phantom pain was a very real thing, something that even painkillers couldn't take away.

She'd woken up to an empty bed, and for a minute she panicked, thinking that Bentley had left her in the middle of the night—and even though she knew it was ridiculous, it was still a concern that flitted through her mind.

Time was going by too fast.

Soon their little whatever-it-was would be over.

Would he return to his glamorous lifestyle only to leave her alone in this giant house? Would he ask her to go with him? Where did they go from here? And why was she such a chicken? She needed to just ask. They were friends first and foremost, right?

When she'd hopped out of bed and grabbed her prosthetic, she'd seen a flicker of movement to her left.

Bentley.

He was on the floor with Scar, spooning the dog.

A smile curved around her lips.

This. This was the man who broke hearts all over the world—slept with other men's wives—partied until the early hours of the morning only to repeat the process the next night.

It was unfair.

Unfair that he let the world see only the playboy millionaire rather than the man who would rescue a dog he didn't even know, pay for the dog's surgery, and then sleep with him in the middle of the night.

Or the man who would kiss a woman's amputated leg and dare to call her scars beautiful.

Tears welled in her eyes.

She wasn't just falling for him—she was in love with him.

Damn it.

That wasn't supposed to happen.

She'd known it was risky, letting a man like Bentley Wellington into her life again—but she never realized how deep he'd root himself.

Or how much it would hurt when he did.

With one last glance at the man and beast on the floor, she slipped on her sock and fastened her prosthetic, then walked down the hall to make coffee.

To her utter surprise, Brant was already at the breakfast bar drinking coffee and reading the newspaper. He'd kept to himself since the big blowout with Bentley, and she'd wondered last night if he'd headed back to Phoenix. Apparently not.

"People love you," Brant said from behind his paper before lowering it and lifting his coffee to his lips. "You and Bentley together, that is."

"Huh?" Margot had completely forgotten about all the reporters out at dinner the other night.

Reality came crashing down when her eyes fell to the lead story: MILLIONAIRE FORCED TO DATE AMPUTEE FOR CHARITY AUCTION.

Her heart clenched. "What does it say?"

"You can't read?" Brant teased.

Rolling her eyes, she took a deep breath and went over to the coffeepot. "Why don't you just summarize?"

"You're in love." Brant sighed. "At least that's what this article says, since brother dearest basically went to jail for you."

Margot chewed her lower lip. "So?"

"So..." Brant shrugged. "I just thought you should know. Oh, and also, stocks are soaring."

"Your stocks?"

"*Our* stocks. Titus Enterprises, Wellington, McCleery."

"Nice," she croaked. "My grandmother hasn't even called me back. I'm still trying to figure out if she bid on him to cheer me up or if she was hoping something like this would happen."

"Eh, who knows?" Brant stood and grabbed his keys. "And who the fuck cares?"

Margot frowned. "What do you mean?"

"You like him." Brant crossed his arms. "Right?"

"Yes." Heat suffused her cheeks.

"Relax, I'm not going to go tell him you actually have feelings for him that have nothing to do with his six-pack or his bank account."

Margot scowled. "It's not like he doesn't know anyway."

Brant was silent and then said, "You'd be surprised how dense Bentley can be."

"Thanks, man." Bentley yawned and walked in with Scar in his arms.

"Uh?" Brant pointed at Scar. "You guys try to run over a dog last night?"

"No." Bentley placed Scar on the floor. "He got hit and we saved him."

Brant eyed the dog and then Margot. "He's missing a leg."

Bentley smacked Brant in the back of the head.

"So am I," Margot said in an irritated voice.

"But your tits more than make up for the missing leg." Brant winked. "Hell, your face alone—"

Bentley clenched his fists.

Brant choked out a laugh. "Damn, you guys really did play right into their matchmaking hands. It's about damn time the best friends are reunited." He patted Bentley on the back. "I'm going back to the city. You kids have fun...and Margot, remember what I said."

"Don't." Bentley shook his head. "Don't remember anything this idiot says."

Brant shrugged. "Fine, don't remember that I said Bentley is the best brother anyone could ever ask for—or that he's loyal to a fault—that he'd rather sacrifice his own happiness in order to put a smile on someone else's face. And definitely don't remember that he is quite literally the glue that holds our family together. Yeah, forget it all, all right, Margot?"

With that, Brant left the kitchen.

Bentley's face was completely pale. Eyes wide, mouth open. She wasn't sure if he was going into shock or if he was just stunned into silence.

"He's right, you know." Margot finally spoke. "You are all of those things."

Bentley's eyes fell to the newspaper. He read in silence and scowled. "Maybe to you, maybe to him, but to them"—he drummed his fingertips against the paper and shoved it away—"I'm a sex-crazed player seducing the panties off a romance novelist who just happens to be heiress to a multi-million-dollar whiskey fortune."

"So?" She shrugged. "You've never cared what they said before. Why start now?"

He leaned against the counter. "I didn't care before, because I never had anyone I cared about other than my family. But now...I guess, I don't want to let you down."

"Bentley..." Things were moving too fast. He was supposed to be leaving soon. What if she opened herself up to him fully? What if she told him she loved him? And he left again? She wouldn't survive it. "You know I..." This was it, it was the perfect moment. So of course she chickened out. Again. "...care about you."

His head jerked up. "You *care*?" His lips twisted into a mean smile. "Great, Margot, just, fucking great."

"Bentley—"

"Get ready," he snapped over his shoulder. "We have to take Scar to town."

He left without a backward glance.

Scar glanced up at her and whimpered.

Bentley still didn't get it. He still didn't understand how it felt. To have everything and lose it all within the same breath.

Although maybe he did.

He had lost her or thought he had. So maybe she wasn't playing fair, but she was still so terrified this was all just a really nice dream, a fantasy, and at the end of the thirty days, he'd say something like *It's been real* and take off.

Stay.

Just stay.

She cared. And for her? That was huge. Because she'd spent the better part of her life trying *not* to care for anyone or anything.

Because it hurt too much when they were gone.

CHAPTER THIRTY-FIVE

Bentley's jaw was going to probably fall off with how much he clenched it throughout the day. First when he was riding in the car with Margot, next when the vet stared at Margot's chest for way longer than necessary, and now, as they roamed Petco for everything Scar would need, and he realized that while Scar seemed to be a permanent fixture in her life, he wasn't.

She *cared*.

Great.

Because he cared about things like spinach and coffee, and checking his e-mail and making sure he brushed his teeth.

She fucking *cared*?

Really?

He was in love with her and she cared!

God, he hated that word.

His damn jaw ached as he followed Margot through the aisles.

"Okay." Margot halted abruptly. "What's wrong with you?"

"Nothing," he snapped. "We should probably get Scar a leash. You're going to want to take him on walks."

"Me?" She frowned.

"Who else would walk him?"

"His owner?" Margot blinked. "You?"

"Me?" he replied. "Margot, Scar's your dog."

Her mouth dropped open. "But I've never had a dog before! I don't even know how to put a collar on him!"

"Buckle it." Bentley had to fight to keep from smiling. *Angry. Stay angry.*

"But—" Margot put her hands on her hips and stared down at Scar, who was sitting in the cart like a king in his new bed. "But what if I kill him?"

A little kid walked by at that exact moment and gasped.

"No," Bentley said, holding out his hands. "She doesn't mean she would kill the dog."

The kid paled and ran off.

"Good job, Margot."

She scowled. "Well! You can't just thrust this on me! I mean, you're the one who wanted to be a vet!"

"True," Bentley said slowly. "But I can't have dogs in my apartment." Total lie. He wanted to give her a gift, damn it! A gift that would encourage her to go outside, a gift that would make sure that she wasn't lonely.

"Just take the damn dog and say thank you, Margot," he whispered harshly. "It will be good for you."

Her eyes filled with tears. "You mean when you leave, right? That's it? You're going to leave me a damn dog? Do you think that makes it easier?"

"I don't know." He pulled her close. "After all, you just care... why would I stay when you care? Hell! Is it just sex to you? What the fuck is even going on?"

He wasn't even aware they had an audience until a throat cleared to his left.

When he looked around he saw at least ten people were watching their exchange; several of them had phones aimed in their direction.

He hated technology sometimes.

"We should go," Margot whispered, linking her arm with his. He took it gladly; they needed a united front.

It took ten minutes for hell to break loose.

And fifteen minutes for his grandfather to call him and demand they figure out a way to get the press to print a retraction.

Within twenty minutes, Wellington, Inc., stocks were climbing.

His grandfather changed his mind about the retraction.

The Google alerts wouldn't stop popping up.

Oddly enough, they had nothing to do with the fact that Bentley and Margot were at Petco with their new dog.

And everything to do with the juicy piece of information that Bentley Wellington, heir to one of the biggest family dynasties in the world, was leaving the family company because he decided he wanted to be a vet.

*   *   *

It wasn't that big a deal. Or it shouldn't have been a big deal, but the minute the press latched on to something, it exploded.

The press that followed was relentless—covering everything from his actual job performance surveys, to the promotions he'd had in the past, and finally to the open position for marketing VP that was rumored to be his if he wanted it.

The focus had gone from the possible acquisition of Mc-Cleery Whiskey to Titus Enterprises's involvement—which of course brought up interesting gossip about the auction.

Did Prudence McCleery plan for her granddaughter to fall for the playboy? Were Titus Enterprises and Wellington, Inc., finally merging?

And worse?

The press linked his suicide attempt and his trip to rehab with his grandfather forcing him into the family business instead of allowing him to go to veterinary school.

It was a partial truth.

But it had been Bentley's choice to take the pills—it wasn't like his grandfather had shoved them down his throat. He'd thought his best friend was dead. He'd been heartbroken. Angry. Much like he was now...

The minute Bentley and Margot got back to her house, he locked himself in his room and lay down on the bed.

Exhausted.

Depressed.

And done with just...everything.

The press was that bored and hungry. And Bentley Wellington had always been like a feast to them. He eventually turned his phone off after speculation hit at least three entertainment sites that his playboy behavior was another cry for help.

People blamed his grandfather.

They blamed him.

They blamed America's school system.

But, lucky for his family, the stocks kept soaring.

Margot's face was splashed on the TV right along with his—her parents' accident once again breaking news for everyone to see. Pictures of the car, pictures of her parents, of her.

So while Bentley suffered alone—

He knew she was suffering more.

Because of him, she was being forced to relive one of the worst moments in her entire life.

Cursing, he pinched the bridge of his nose and stared up at the ceiling.

He'd made a mess of things.

Not on purpose.

But wasn't that what he did?

He messed up.

A knock sounded at his door.

He didn't answer it.

Another knock.

The handle jiggled. Thank God he'd locked the door.

He closed his eyes.

And then something hard slammed against the door.

He jerked up. "The hell?"

Barking commenced.

And then something hit his door again.

He ran over to the door and jerked it open just in time for Margot's body to come flying into his, sending them both to the ground, followed by a drugged-up Scar, who pounced on top of Margot.

Margot breathed out a sigh of relief and hugged his neck. "You turned off your phone, you bastard!"

Bentley huffed. "I think you may have ruptured my spleen."

"I'm sorry."

"At the very least my liver's bruised."

"That's from alcohol, not me," Margot grumbled, then moved off him, unfortunately. "I was so worried!"

"That I'd fallen asleep?" Bentley groaned, moving to a sitting position.

"No." A tear spilled over onto her cheek. "I just, I was watching the news—"

"Margot." He hissed out her name. "The last thing you need to be doing is reliving your parents' accident through gory pictures and assholes who like to feed off other people's pain."

She frowned. "I was talking about what they're doing to you."

"Let them fillet me alive." Bentley shrugged. "I've had worse."

"No." She wiped her tears. "I just, I didn't want you to go to that place...I didn't...You said I was a trigger and I said I cared because I'm a chicken and you scare me"

Bentley frowned as his heart hammered against his chest. "You are a chicken."

"I know," she wailed. "And it's my fault, I didn't want you to get sad or anxious, and it's all my fault."

"Come here," he said gruffly, pulling her onto his lap. "I'm fine, see?" He ran his hands down her arms. "Well, other than the bruising. What were you trying to do, anyway?"

"Break down your door."

He barked out a laugh. "Clearly it was working."

"I was close!"

"Very." He nodded. And then let out a loud sigh, touching his forehead to hers. "I'm sorry."

"For what?"

"For being a dick today. I just..." *Damn it.* "Margot, I really like you."

"I like you, too."

"I don't want to leave," he admitted.

Her breath hitched. "Do you mean that?"

"No, I'm lying to get you into bed, oh wait..." He

flashed her a playful grin. "We can figure something out, right?"

She nodded as more tears ran down her cheeks. "Are you saying you don't care about the marketing position or—"

He kissed her forcefully across the mouth and pulled back. "You. I care about you."

Scar barked from his spot on the floor.

"And Scar," Bentley added. "But he's a close second."

Another bark.

"So he's our dog?" Margot looked at him with hopeful eyes.

"Yeah." Bentley tucked her hair behind her ears as Scar tried to make his way over to them. He was just learning to walk on three legs; if only they had a prosthetic for dogs, one that fit.

Damn it!

He'd almost forgotten about the appointment he made for Margot!

"I have a surprise for you." He kissed her chin. "A huge surprise."

"Another animal?"

"Well, I do have an ass…"

"What?"

"Long story short. I won him in a bet." He winked. "He stays at the family ranch, though, with Brock—I think the asses are attached to each other."

"That sentence." She made a face.

"Yeah, not my best." He chuckled. "Come on." He checked his watch. "I need you to get ready for company."

"Company?"

He smiled. "Yup."

Margot didn't look so sure, but she nodded anyway. "Actually…" She cleared her throat. "I've been putting off writing for a few days. I haven't been in the mood. I should probably just check my e-mail and get some stuff done, so why don't you come get me once company's here?"

"Sounds great." He said smoothly as she shyly rose up on her tiptoes and kissed him on the cheek. "Nope."

"Sorry." She reared back.

"Don't be." He pulled her closer. "But I have to taste you. Knowing that your lips just tasted my skin and that I was left just dreaming of yours? Not fair."

He captured her mouth in one last kiss before turning her around and gently pushing her toward the door.

CHAPTER THIRTY-SIX

Margot walked on air the entire way up the stairs and into her room. He liked her.

Rolling her eyes at the fact that she was giddy because he confessed he liked her, she was painfully aware she was acting like a girl with her first crush.

A smile teased her lips. Did it really matter? He had been her first crush—and now? Now he yelled at her and said he loved her.

And he called her beautiful.

Kissed her scars.

Gave her a dog.

Her smile widened. Yeah, okay, she had a reason to smile, she really did. The smile only grew as she sat down at her computer and started firing off the next scene in her book.

Before she knew what was happening, thirty minutes had passed and she still hadn't really prepared for company in any way.

With a grimace she glanced down at her jeans and loose

T-shirt. She needed to at least put on something that didn't have wrinkles.

Yawning, she stood and stretched, only to have her e-mail alert ping.

"Crap." She hadn't checked her e-mail in at least two days, which was completely unlike her.

She had several messages from readers, which was normal, and a few from her editor, most of them about her deadline, business, cover art, the usual.

Normally she was better about answering her e-mails, but Bentley had been a distraction—a very welcome one.

The newest e-mail had an exclamation point in the subject line, and when Margot clicked on it, there was a link to a news article.

Margot had no desire to click the link. She knew what it most likely said, and the last thing she wanted was for her day to take a hit after having such a good morning.

Below the link was a message.

Keep dating him. Sales are incredible! We are looking at a second print run for The Duke*! See attached.*

Margot refused to click on the attached Excel spreadsheet with her sales numbers on it.

A sick feeling built in her stomach. She hadn't gone out with him in public to be seen. God, it was hard to even be in public let alone use it as a way to sell books! Did her editor have any idea how much anxiety she'd had during that dinner? Or the hell that she'd gone through afterward?

Writing had been about passion for Margot, not sales.

Being a writer was doing what she loved—and being able to escape reality for a while.

"Margot!" Bentley called from downstairs. "Ten minutes!"

"Crap!" She ran around her desk and into the bathroom to put on a bit of mascara.

*   *   *

Bentley stared up the stairway, waiting for an answer. "Margot?"

Nothing.

"Women." Scar whined as if voicing his agreement. The doorbell rang. Shit, he was early.

"Dr. Jones!" Bentley held open the door and ushered the aging man in. The doctor had silver-speckled hair and fashionable black glasses, and though he was a bit on the short side he made up for it with his firm handshake. "Welcome!"

"Happy to be here." Dr. Jones grinned. "This is a beautiful house you have." His gaze lowered to a whining Scar, who was still sitting in the middle of the floor, his amputated leg bandaged up. "And who's this little fellow?"

"Scar." Bentley grinned with pride, though he had no freaking idea why. It wasn't his house.

But it could be, a voice inside him whispered.

"I'll just go get Margot." He quickly dismissed the thought and took the stairs two at a time. "Make yourself comfortable!" he called behind him, sweeping into Margot's room.

"Hmm." It was empty.

"Margot?" he called again.

"Just a minute!" Her muffled voice came from the bathroom. "My hair was a wreck, you didn't even tell me! And I looked homeless!"

Bentley stifled a laugh. "You looked beautiful."

"You just want to get laid!"

"True!" He laughed.

"Ahh!"

"Everything okay in there?" He approached slowly, waiting for the door to open, but it stayed closed. "Margot?"

"Yup! Give me two minutes!"

"Great." Why was it that every time he was near her he wanted—*needed*—to touch her? Kiss her? His body felt the wrongness of not following through with what it wanted as he turned on his heel and walked back toward the door, only to knock over a stack of papers on her desk. "Shit."

"You okay?" she called.

"Yup." He put the papers back in order best he could and placed them neatly by the computer.

A grin tugged the corner of his lips. Had Margot been writing dirty scenes again?

The computer wasn't in lock mode yet. But there wasn't a document open, just an e-mail and...

He froze.

Disbelief washed over him as he read the e-mail over again.

No. She wouldn't.

Margot wouldn't use him that way.

Wouldn't she? Doubt whispered.

Because hadn't every woman in his life wanted a piece of something? Fame? Fortune? Status?

Rejection settled like a rock in his stomach right along with anxiety and a heavy dose of anger.

"Bentley?" The door to the bathroom swung open, and he jerked back and faced her. It hurt like hell to keep the smile on his face when all he wanted to do was run over to her, shake her, and ask if it was true.

And pray she'd roll her eyes and tell him to stop being so dramatic.

"Yeah?" His voice didn't sound right, he knew that, and so did she. Her eyes went from him to the computer then back to him.

"Were you...snooping?"

"No," he lied. "I just knocked over this stack of papers." He tapped the stack in question. "You ready?"

"Sure." Her eyes narrowed once again. He held out his hand, even though he was dying to say something.

Dr. Jones was waiting in the hall, rubbing Scar's fat belly while the dog grunted with appreciation.

"Well, he's not going to be a very good guard dog, is he?" Margot laughed.

Dr. Jones looked up. "That's what you have this young man for."

Bentley almost groaned out loud when Margot said, "You're absolutely right." She stepped forward and held out her hand. "I'm Margot, and you are?"

"Dr. Steven Jones." He pumped her hand. "I'm—"

"I know who you are." Margot stumbled back, her face going pale. "I, uh, I think that—"

"Margot." Bentley caught her before she tripped backward on the stairs. "He's here to fit you for a new prosthetic, a more athletic one that moves with your body." He cringed at the horrified look on her face. "Surprise?"

"Y-you." Margot shook her head. "You went behind my back?"

"What?" Bentley released her like he'd been burned. "Are you serious right now? I thought it would be nice!"

"No!" She jutted a finger at his chest. "You thought it would make me look more normal by your side, admit it!"

"What are you talking about?" Bentley ran his fingers through his hair. "You said your old prosthetic made your leg sore. Fuck what people think. It's about how *you* feel."

"Oh, that's rich, coming from you." She rolled her eyes and held out her hand. "Look at yourself! Your entire life is about your image! You just want me to fit the part!" She gasped and put a hand over her mouth and mumbled. "I'm sorry, I didn't mean it."

"Yeah, you did," Bentley croaked out. "By the way, how are book sales, Margot? Soaring?"

She paled.

"Should I come back?" Dr. Jones was already moving toward the door.

"No," Bentley said at the same time Margot said, "Yes."

"Maybe there's a better time." Dr. Jones's hand was already on the door when Bentley pressed his hand against the wood frame to keep it from opening.

"You read my e-mail." Margot lifted her chin. "My *private* e-mail."

"I read your texts, too, and watch you sleep like a real stalker." Bentley rolled his eyes. "I glanced at your computer. It was on."

She gulped, not meeting his eyes. What the hell? She wasn't even denying it? Insecurity came over him—was she really just like everyone else? Using him? And why the hell did he suddenly care? He waited. Waited for her denial. Instead she kept her eyes downcast.

"Is it true?" Anger surged inside him. "Are you fucking me for sales?"

Dr. Jones gasped. "This really doesn't seem like something I should be—"

"Stay!" Bentley demanded in a booming voice. "And you"—he turned to Margot—"is it true? Is that what this is? You like me? You *care*? Or is this all some twisted game? Get the playboy to fall for you and suddenly you get your own theme park named after you?"

Margot flinched. "If you truly think that low of me—you don't know me at all."

Bentley swore.

Dr. Jones cleared his throat.

"Fit her leg." Bentley clenched his teeth together. "I'm leaving."

He heard Margot's protests and slammed the door behind him as he stomped down the dirt road and then took a right toward one of the old trails. Anger made him hot inside, like he was ready to explode.

She didn't deny it.

He was willing to do anything for her.

And she didn't deny it.

God, it hurt.

Worse than his grandfather's rejection. Worse than his parents' death—damn it—her words hurt.

But what did he expect?

That she'd fall in love with him? Because he had a change of heart? Because he had a nice face and money?

He was being unfair, he was jumping to conclusions, but the fact that she was acting like every other woman in his life when everything he'd shared with her had been so different—burned.

What the hell was he doing?

He was willing to stay—willing to turn down the VP position—willing to fight for her even though every time he thought about losing her he got physically sick.

For once he wasn't walking away.

So why did it feel like he already had?

CHAPTER THIRTY-SEVEN

Margot felt like she was going to throw up during most of the fitting, but Dr. Jones was so kind, so gentle.

Eventually, Scar hobbled over to her side and licked her hand.

Fear.

Fear made people do stupid things.

Fear made people push others away.

She clenched her eyes shut to keep the tears from falling onto her cheeks. She'd purposely hurt Bentley out of fear and anger. And he was perfect, like, literally, the most perfect guy on the planet.

Who arranged something like this for someone else as a surprise?

A surprise was flowers.

A surprise for Bentley would be taking her someplace fancy and giving her expensive jewelry.

But no, he'd given her a leg that fit.

Tears spilled onto her cheeks.

"Did I hurt you?" Dr. Jones's concerned look only made her feel like more of a bitch.

"No." She sniffled. "I just, I was mean to him. That's all."

He quickly wrote down some numbers on his notepad. "In my experience, we tend to push away those we love the most for fear that the other shoe is going to one day drop, and they'll see us for what we really are. Weak. Scared. Insecure."

"Sure you aren't a shrink?" she joked through her tears.

"No." He stood. "Thank God."

He held out his hand and helped her to her feet. "He was right, you know. Your current prosthetic was fitted a long time ago. Your body's changed since then, causing you to put pressure on bone instead of what's left of your muscles. I imagine once you have your new prosthetic, you'll be able to run a marathon, if that's your wish."

"A marathon?" she repeated, eyes wide. "Are you serious?"

"If that's what you want." His smile was so kind she wanted to keep crying. He had a presence about him. Well, he *was* world renowned. Bentley didn't do things in half measures. He'd literally gotten one of the best doctors in the world to make a freaking house call.

She groaned into her hands. She didn't deserve him.

"It will get better. New love is always...rocky." The doctor patted her shoulder.

"Oh no, we aren't...I mean..." Her throat clogged. She loved him. Loved him so much it hurt.

"If you say so." He winked. "I'll be in touch."

He left.

She stood in the silence of her dark house hating herself, hating the walls that had been her prison, the blinds that had made it easy for her to hide.

Hating herself for allowing it to happen.

She took a deep breath and faced the door. "Well, Scar, if

I don't come back, send out a search party." She needed to apologize.

The door suddenly swung open. Bentley sauntered in, a look of indifference crossing his features. She backed up against the banister. "Bentley, I'm sorry."

"Me too. No more secrets, Margot. No more games. Which means..." He dug his hand into his pocket only to come up with a folded piece of paper.

With shaking hands, she took the paper and unfolded it.

"One compliment a day? A picnic? What the hell is this?" Horror washed over her as she read through the list of assignments he'd been given. "Bentley!"

"I love you now. I do. But yes, I was pressured into making nice with you, all right? I was given suggestions on how to get through to you. Maybe this makes us even. You were using me to get ahead in business—and I wasn't completely honest about my intentions in the beginning. But here I am." He shrugged. "I'm being honest now. I'm standing here now. Yes, I had to stay thirty days, but do you really think I would have stayed if a part of me didn't want to?"

"I don't know," she said honestly. "I just know that this...this changes things."

"How?" He reached for her. "How the hell does this change that I love you?"

Her eyes filled with tears. "You were doing a job."

"It wasn't a job."

"I can't trust you," she continued. "What else are you hiding?"

"Wow." He shook his head. "Really? Are you really doing this right now? Making excuses, pushing me away?"

"I just think—" She licked her lips and held out her hand to keep him from touching her—hugging her. "You're going to return to the real world and forget about me. It's not even like any of these things were your ideas, you did it"—she sucked in a breath—"you did it because you had no other choice."

"There's always a choice." He breezed past her toward his room. "Unbelievable."

"Where are you going?"

"I'm doing what you expect me to do, Margot. What you *want* me to do. What you won't even admit out loud. I'm leaving."

"But—"

The door slammed.

With tear-filled eyes she read through the list, her stomach dropping more and more as realization dawned.

So that was why.

None of it had been real.

The compliments. The flowers. The outings.

He'd done it for himself.

Not her.

Oh God! She covered her mouth as a sob escaped between her lips. She'd slept with him! Hot tears ran down her cheeks. He'd seen her scars! He'd called her beautiful.

Memories assaulted her over and over again until she had to lean against the wall. She was going to puke.

Just when she thought she was going to pass out, Bentley returned with his suitcase, stomping by her.

"You sick bastard!" Margot balled up the paper and threw it at him. "How dare you take advantage of me like that? You used me!"

Bentley froze and turned, his eyes flashing. "I *used* you?" Nostrils flared. "*I* used *you*? That's rich, you know that, right?"

"I would never—"

"Yeah, but you did, Margot, you did." He sneered. "Not

only did you use me to sell your little romance books—but you used my body for sex...isn't that what you said? 'It's just sex.' So basically, I was like a paid whore, isn't that right?"

"You have no right to be upset!" she yelled. "You had a fucking list! Pay me compliments? Get me to go outside? What was the plan? Get me so deliriously happy"—her voice cracked as more tears escaped—"then sleep with me and leave? It's like I was the test job before you got the real thing!" Throat clogged, she looked down at the piece of paper. And shook her head.

"It doesn't matter anymore," Bentley said in a hoarse voice. "I tried. It doesn't matter if it was real or not, because you never had any intentions of leaving with me, did you? Of moving to the city? On making this more than it was? I tell you I love you and you're still pushing me away, still making excuses."

Margot refused to give him the words that would mend what had been broken. She didn't trust him. And he didn't trust her.

"And that right there." Bentley shook his head. "The silence, the stubbornness. You can blame me all you want. Blame the list. Blame our grandparents. But all you have to blame is yourself. You know, I always thought I'd be the one that was afraid of commitment. But I guess the joke's on me. You'll never trust me enough to be what you need—I'll always be the guy you fucked in order to stop being sad. And you'll always be the girl I wanted too much to have."

The door slammed behind him.

Margot slid to the floor and sobbed.

CHAPTER THIRTY-EIGHT

It was the right thing to do.

The right thing to do.

Bentley tipped back the expensive Black Label whiskey and winced as it burned down his throat.

He was well on his way to being drunk.

And it wasn't doing anything except giving him heart-burn.

"Damn it!" He slammed his fist against the table and groaned as he hung his head in his hands, his throat clogged. He refused to acknowledge the sadness, the utter despair.

He'd done the right thing.

He'd left her.

And shown her the stupid list. Because it was the only way to push her away. She was angry—good, she'd get over it.

But he was heartbroken.

Because every single time he tried to do something that showed her how he felt—she reacted.

Out of fear.

Mistrust.

And he couldn't fight it—wasn't sure he knew how—so he released her. Wasn't that what you did when you loved someone? You let them go?

He did the right thing.

The door opened and closed, footsteps sounded, keys slid across the counter by Bentley's hand, and then a chair pulled out. "You look like hell."

"What are you doing here?" Bentley reached for the bottle again, but it was pulled away from him and lifted to his brother's mouth. "And since when do you ever drink whiskey straight?"

"Plan a wedding with our grandfather involved, and you'll understand. Hell, if I could be perpetually drunk and still function as a human being, I'd be absolutely thrilled."

Bentley turned his head toward his eldest brother. The mature one. The sober and serious one.

Brock always wore a scowl. He barked. He yelled.

But Brock ever since being engaged to Jane?

He was an entirely different man, always smiling, laughing. Bentley's chest tightened. Brock was like their father.

With a curse, Bentley jerked the bottle away from Brock and took another long swallow.

"It won't help, you know," Brock added in his deep voice.

"Shut the hell up," Bentley muttered.

"It's okay to feel sad." Brock just had to keep talking, didn't he? "Sadness helps you deal. And that's something you suck at…dealing with feelings. You'd rather just grin and bear it—and then when you can't take it anymore, you break down."

"Go. Away," Bentley said through clenched teeth.

"It's why you ended up in the hospital," Brock continued.

"It's why you stay up all night partying with Brant—not only to watch over him but to drink away all of the feelings until you're numb."

Bentley was quiet, mainly because Brock was right and arguing would only get him in a shouting match.

"All I'm saying is, it's *okay*."

"It won't ever be okay. Trust me." Bentley gripped the bottle with his right hand as visions of Margot's smile haunted him. She would never trust him—not completely. First she needed to be brave enough to trust herself, to love herself.

To believe that he really, truly loved her.

Oh God, the joke was so completely on him. He went from never wanting to settle down to imagining a life with a woman who clearly didn't trust him enough and most likely never would.

"The job's yours," Brock said after a few seconds of tense silence. "Grandfather made the announcement the minute you got home."

Bentley scowled. "I didn't even finish the list."

"It was never about the list."

"What?" Bentley finally met Brock's gaze. "What the hell do you mean it was never about the list?"

"Come on." Brock rolled his eyes. "I thought you were smarter than that. Grandfather wasn't seeing if you could accomplish the tasks. He knew you could—you're Bentley Wellington." He made little air quotes, which made Bentley want to punch him. "It was more about you following in- structions, taking orders, getting the impossible accom- plished, and honestly, he gave you the impossible. Did you know the last time Margot was out to dinner was right after college? It's been years. The woman doesn't grocery-shop. She refuses to go into her own garden, and doesn't even get her own mail. It's delivered. To say she's a shut-in would be putting it mildly."

"Don't talk about her that way," Bentley snapped, and rage surged through him as he grabbed his fist to keep from punching his brother in the face. He missed her. This feeling, this was what loneliness was like: empty, dark—hopeless.

"My point," Brock said slowly, ignoring his glare, "is that you tried to accomplish the impossible, which is exactly what we need if you're going to be VP of marketing."

Bentley sneered. "Oh great, now I get to work more hours in a job I hate." That completely slipped out before he could stop it. What the hell did he care if Brock was aware of just how much he didn't want the job?

With a grin, Brock stood. "I'm just the messenger. But Bentley?"

"What?"

"You could always march right up to Grandfather's office and tell him where to shove it."

Bentley smiled at the thought.

"Yeah." Brock knocked his knuckles against the table. "That's what I thought. You know I'm not planning on dying anytime soon, so the CEO position isn't going anywhere...and even if it did, you'd probably rather jump off a building than take it. Which leaves you with VP of marketing." He shrugged. "Or word on the street."

Bentley groaned. "Don't ever say that sentence again."

"Follow your dreams. Even if people tell you they're stupid. Life is too short to be doing something you hate—when you could be doing something you were born to do."

Bentley swallowed as a knot formed in his throat. "Thanks."

Brock wasn't the emotional type, so it was semishocking when he frowned and then awkwardly patted Bentley on the back, only to pull him into a full hug and whisper gruffly, "He's proud of you."

Bentley stiffened. "No, he's not."

"He just wants you to be happy," Brock said, pulling away and staring Bentley down with his piercing, green-eyed gaze. "We all do."

"So he sent me to Margot because he knew she was exactly what I needed? Bullshit."

"Of course not." Brock shrugged and started moving away. "He sent you to Margot because you were what she needed, not the other way around. That was just a happy co-incidence."

Guilt slammed into Bentley's chest as the scene unfolded before him, the scene where he threw their fragile relationship back in her face.

Out of fear.

Fear that she would never trust him.

Fear that she would never accept him for who he really was.

Hell, he claimed he left for her.

And yet again, he'd proven how selfish he could really be—he'd done it for himself. Just like he did everything else in his miserable life.

"You okay?" Brock stopped at the door and turned.

"Where is he, again?" Bentley choked out. "Where's Grandfather?"

"His office, he's in a meeting with—"

"I have to go." Bentley grabbed his keys and breezed past him.

"Oh no, you don't." Brock grabbed him by the arm. "I'll drive you."

"Thanks," Bentley choked out. "For—"

"Don't," Brock said in a low voice. "As far as Brant's

concerned, I punched you in the throat and we got drunk."
He leveled him with an amused glare. "There was no hug."

Bentley held up his hands. "Hug? What hug? Hey, you
did tear up though."

"Bastard." Brock chuckled as they made their way toward
the elevator. "You're not going to take the job, are you?"

"That's just the thing, Brock. I don't think I'm VP material." Saying it out loud was easier than he thought. In fact, it
felt like a giant weight had just been lifted off his shoulders.

"You don't say?" Brock mumbled, and a suspicious smile
formed across his lips.

It only took minutes to get to the downtown offices. All
too soon, Bentley was standing in front of his grandfather's
solid oak office doors. When he was little, he used to trace
the engravings with his fingers. He repeated it, his adult
hand much bigger, almost completely unable to fit the intri-
cate designs in the wood.

The familiar smell of spice and cigars floated through the
air. How many times had he been summoned to his grandfather's office?

And how many times had he actually gone in on his own?
This was a first.

Without knocking, Bentley opened both doors and strode
in. "Grandfather, I—"

Words died on his lips as Margot's grandmother leveled
him with a glare that would probably make a lesser man shit
himself.

Nadine Titus sat near the conference table and gave him
a little wave and blew a kiss in his direction.

Dealing with his grandfather was hard enough.

But any sort of engagement with Nadine Titus—well, it
was like working with a three-letter agency that liked to test
new ways to torture people and yet keep them alive.

This whole situation had started with her.

Funny how that was where it should end as well.

"Mrs. McCleery," he said smoothly, taking his attention away from Nadine. "A pleasure to see you."

"Hmm." She glared at him. "I can't say the same."

Nadine chuckled loudly, while Grandfather barked out a laugh. "Now, Prudence, I—"

"Don't you 'Now, Prudence' me!" she said, seething. "Your bastard of a grandson broke her heart!"

"Prudence—"

Bentley crossed his arms. "Let her finish."

"You!" She jutted a finger into the air. "You seduced her, you made her fall for you, and for what reason? For your own amusement! That wasn't part of the deal! And you showed her the damn list!" The more she talked, the louder her voice got until Bentley was tempted to cover his ears until her lips stopped moving.

"You're right," he said smoothly.

Silenced, she gaped and then looked from him to his grandfather.

Bentley cleared his throat and then stared his grandfather down. "And I quit."

His grandfather was silent and then a smile spread across his face. "Well, that's new. You're quitting before you even take the job?"

"I'm not happy."

"I know." Grandfather nodded. "You haven't been happy ever since the day I crushed your dreams and made you feel like less of a man, and for that, I'll never forgive myself."

"What the hell are you talking about?" Bentley growled.

Grandfather's eyes closed briefly before he bit back a curse. "Prudence, give us some privacy?"

She didn't look happy about leaving, and she made sure

Bentley knew exactly how unhappy she was when she nearly took him down with her bony elbow as she shoved past him.

"Forgive her temper." Grandfather chuckled and waved Nadine over. "We grandparents can get very protective of those we love."

Bentley nodded.

"I failed you," Grandfather said softly, as Nadine came behind him and placed a hand on his shoulder. "And I didn't even remember I had, until I saw the news, until my damned memory clicked and then..." He shook his head. "You were never quite the same after that day, were you, Bentley?"

"What day?" He played dumb. For once he wanted to hear the old man out.

"You told me you wanted to be a veterinarian, and I laughed at you. After all, you'd never taken anything seriously in your life, why start then? I brushed you off, and then forced you into an unhappy life, forced you to work at a job you hated. But I think what was worse is that you took the emotional baggage of this entire family and decided it was your job to be the comic relief, your job to make sure everyone was okay—I broke you, then encouraged you to take on a role in this family that just helped you mask the pain."

"Grandfather—"

"Let me finish." Grandfather sighed, clutching Nadine's hand as she locked eyes with Bentley. "Margot may be broken on the outside, but you were broken on the inside, and I played a larger role in that than I've ever wanted to admit."

Bentley pulled out a chair. "As much power as you have over me—over all of us—I still had a choice. And I chose not to make you upset. I was a coward. You blame yourself for breaking me. But I blame myself for always doing what's easy."

Grandfather stared down at his desk, his massive hands balled into fists. "So, I guess the question is, what do you do now?"

Bentley found himself smiling. "I think this is the part where I tell you to shove the job up your ass and go rescue the damsel in distress."

"Something tells me you just wouldn't have been a great fit for Wellington, Inc." Grandfather winked.

"Yeah, well, I was already planning on purposefully breaking the copy machines on my floor." Bentley grinned.

Grandfather let out a low chuckle. "And after you rescue the damsel?"

"That's none of your damn business."

Grandfather let out a hearty laugh. "No, I guess it isn't." He cleared his throat and locked eyes with Bentley. "I would have never cut you off, but don't tell Brant that. The man's more unhappy than you and Brock put together."

"Hate to break it to you, but he already knows that, too," Bentley admitted. The thought of Brant alone, without Bentley protecting him, sank like a rock in the pit of his stomach.

"None of that." Grandfather shrugged. "We've taken care of it."

"Brant isn't exactly—"

"We have our ways." Grandfather's eyes twinkled with amusement as he looked up at a still-silent Nadine. "Don't we, dear?"

"Oh yes." Humor danced in her eyes. "When Brock offered you and your brother as participants in the auction, I had to call in a lot of favors. Prudence has been worried about Margot for years. The only thing I could think of that made sense was a little visit from a long-lost best friend. And there's nothing better than getting a second chance at your one true love, is there?"

He nodded, emotion clogging in his throat again.

Grandfather chuckled and kissed Nadine's hand. "Well played, my dear, well played."

"I'll see you after I apologize for being a jackass."

"So, next year, then?" Grandfather joked.

Bentley rolled his eyes. "Hilarious."

"Treat her well." His grandfather stood, his lips trembling. "She deserves to be loved by someone like you."

"Thank you." Bentley's voice was hoarse as he walked around the large desk and pulled his grandfather into a tight embrace. "For threatening to kick my ass."

"It's what grandfathers do."

"Not sane ones."

"Touché."

"Go," Grandfather said gruffly. "We've got work to do."

Bentley laughed and then walked out of the office only to see Mrs. McCleery glaring daggers at him.

"I'm going to marry her," he announced.

She gasped. "Well, I suppose that would be fine as long as you start working on grandchildren immediately."

"Tough bargain."

"I'm sure you'll enjoy the process." She smiled, but it was a sad smile. "She's refusing to leave the house again."

"I'm headed there now." In the back of his mind, he realized he might still be feeling the effects of his whiskey fest, so even though it was going to kill him, he was going to have to hydrate and wait a few hours.

He only hoped he wouldn't be too late.

A sick feeling washed over him.

What if this time she didn't open the door?

CHAPTER THIRTY-NINE

A sick feeling settled in the bottom of Margot's stomach, and it had been there since she watched Bentley walk out the door.

The damn man had ruined her house. Even the door reminded her of him. It didn't help that the air lingered with his spicy scent or that every time she walked into the kitchen she thought of his stupid eggs and breathtaking smile.

It had taken him days to break down every barrier she'd put up for the past ten years. What a complete joke. She was back at square one.

Back to being alone.

Only this time she was painfully aware of her own loneliness and what it felt like to be a part of something bigger and better than herself—what it felt like when a man's kiss lingered just below her ear, or the taste of his tongue after he licked her skin.

With a gulp, she robotically went through her e-mails, answering as many as she could before going back to her manuscript.

There was nothing left but sadness.

And anger.

So much anger that he'd used her for his own personal gain. Then again, hadn't that been what she'd worried about all along?

A voice whispered that he wasn't like that—that he wouldn't hurt her—but the list proved otherwise.

The damn list.

The same list she had thrown into the fire and cast about a billion curses over while getting drunk on the same whiskey he'd favored his entire stay.

Yeah, she'd looked like a complete lunatic dancing in front of the fire while whiskey sloshed out of her glass and onto the floor.

The buzzing from her cell interrupted her dark thoughts. With a shaky hand she grabbed the phone and stared at the screen.

Her grandmother.

Of course.

Sighing, she swiped her thumb across the screen and held the phone to her ear. Avoiding her grandmother was impossible. It would be like ignoring a herd of elephants as they charged into her house.

Elephants.

Bentley.

Another sigh escaped between her lips, only it sounded like more of a hiss of pain. Felt like it, too, as her chest once again tightened.

"I know you're there, Margot."

"Are you there, God? It's me, Margot" was her only response, and even then she could only conjure up a little laugh.

"Why?"

Margot clenched her teeth and stared at the blinking cursor on her computer screen. "Why what?"

"Why did you mess up the best thing that's ever happened to you?" her grandmother asked.

"Hah, you mean the worst thing, right?" She could barely get the words past her lips without crying.

"You went outside."

Margot refused to acknowledge that truth. "We had lots and lots of sex, too, so there's that."

He grandmother refused to be scandalized. "So you could be pregnant with his child, and you still kicked him out?"

Leave it to her grandmother to fixate on that. "Not pregnant," she huffed out. "And *he* left *me*!"

You forced him.

He said he loved you.

The pain sliced through her fresh and new.

"A man like *that*"—it wasn't lost on Margot how her grandmother drew out the word *that*, as if to prove how amazing Bentley really was—"doesn't leave unless he feels like he's already lost."

An ache started building between her temples. Margot pressed a hand against her head and tried to count to three so she wouldn't snap or yell or say something she might regret.

"Look," she tried again. "Had he not had the 'seduce Margot' list, he would have probably hung out in his room getting drunk the entire time. But no, his crazy grandfather set him on a task, and guess what? He accomplished every single thing on that list."

"And you're upset?"

"He threw it in my face."

"Seems he must have had a reason to confess to you that he'd been working off a list."

Margot groaned. "I don't know! He was upset!"

"And what would make a man, one who wanted to save animals—"

Oh good, bring the animals in, lay it on thick! Whose side was she on?

"—that upset?"

Margot chewed her fingernail and stared out the open window. She hadn't had the heart to close it, not after he left. Maybe she was having a nervous breakdown, but the idea of being alone in her house suddenly made her feel trapped. Maybe it was because he'd given her a taste of life again, a taste of freedom.

The last thing she wanted to do was rehash the fight they'd had.

The things they'd said in front of the doctor and—

"Margot? I'm waiting."

"He was upset." Margot hated reliving that moment, the moment he walked out of her life, the moment he looked at her like she was a stranger, like a man defeated.

Defeated?

She frowned. "I think we were fighting about the doctor visit."

"A doctor?" Grandma shrieked. "Are you okay? Do you need to go to the hospital? What's wrong? Why didn't you tell me?" Margot pulled the phone away from her ear while her grandmother rattled off every disease known to mankind, including malaria—twice.

"Are you done?" She shook her head in annoyance.

"Are you sick?" Grandma fired back.

"No, no." The doctor had been so understanding, so kind, and she'd snapped at him, at Bentley. Cringing, she destroyed what was left of her thumbnail and answered. "Bentley wanted to get me a new prosthetic, one that fit better, so he paid for one of the best doctors in the country to make a house call." Well, when she put it that way, it made her sound like a complete bitch, so she was quick to add, "But he only did it because one of the items on the list was to give me something irreplaceable."

"A leg isn't irreplaceable," Grandma said softly.

"But—"

"No!" Grandma sounded disappointed. "I went to his grandfather, and I stood up for you. I'll always stand up for you, but Margot, do you think, perhaps, you were too harsh on him?"

"He broke my heart! And he left again! Just like I knew he would."

"And there it is." Grandma sighed. "It seems to me that you quit first, to protect yourself, and now both of you are nursing broken hearts. You need to learn how to trust again. How to love. Do you think your parents would want you to be unhappy? Untrusting?"

"I—" Emotion clogged her throat. "I'm happy."

"You're getting by," Grandma corrected. "Believe me, there's a huge difference between being happy and getting by." She cleared her throat. "In all the time you spent with him, did he ever seem the type to purposefully lead a woman on, gain her trust, make her fall for him, only to laugh in her face when things were said and done?"

Her pride begged her to say yes and hang up.

But that stupid, nagging thing called a conscience kept screaming in her head that even though he could be cruel and he had a list and he made her want to strangle him, his eyes said something else entirely, even while that wicked mouth of his was moving.

"It's too late," Margot finally said, slouching back into her seat and staring at the now-black computer screen.

"It's never too late," Grandma said.

"Grandma?" Margot blurted through thick blurry tears.

"Yes, dear?"

"Is he... I mean, how is he?"

"Maybe it's about time you asked him that. Good night."

The phone went dead as a hot tear slid down her cheek and dropped onto her bare legs.

The same legs she would have never been caught dead exposing to the world—that was, until Bentley Wellington bulldozed his way into her life.

And allowed her an out—when all she ever wanted was to be in.

CHAPTER FORTY

Bentley waited longer than he would have liked, mainly because Brock refused to leave his side until he deemed him sober enough to drive. So Brock sat at the table while Bentley chugged water and made a pot of coffee—the caffeine made him shaky, which just made Brock assume he was still drunk.

"Look." Bentley held up his hands. "I can touch my nose with both fingers and walk in a straight line. Don't make me say the ABCs backward."

Brock glanced up at the ceiling. "You could do that even if you were half dead and inside a barrel of whiskey. Honestly, sometimes you're even smarter when you're drunk; how the hell am I supposed to know if you can drive?"

"Straight lines." Bentley ignored him and started walking in a straight line then hopped on one foot. "Z, Y, X—"

"Fine." Brock sighed and tossed him the keys. "It's been at least four hours since your last drink."

Bentley caught the keys in midair and nodded. "It's not like I had a lot to begin with. You ruined my plans, remember?"

"You're welcome that I didn't let you get so drunk off your ass that you wouldn't have been able to see your girl until tomorrow."

"Did I say thank you?"

"You thought it," Brock said with slight irritation. "So why the hesitation?"

Honestly, Bentley had no idea. With keys in hand, and eyes on the door, he was ready to go. Ready to storm the castle—or really, in his case, break into the castle and force the woman to reason with him.

"None of that." Brock waved a hand in front of his face. "Just get the hell out already."

"What if she—?" Bentley clenched the keys harder. "What if she rejects me?"

"You sound like an idiot." Brock placed both of his hands on Bentley's shoulders and shoved him toward the door. "And nobody likes a weak man. Knock on the door." He shoved Bentley one last time. "And kiss her. Use the word *sorry* between kisses, and try not to make an ass out of yourself."

"Sorry between kisses?" Bentley repeated. "You make it sound like I'm kissing her better."

"Would you rather kiss her worse?"

"Huh?"

The door slammed in Bentley's face.

"You realize you're in my apartment, right?" he called through the door.

"Don't care!" Brock's muffled yell was followed by cursing before he opened the door a crack and shouted, "Go already!"

The door slammed again.

"Fine." Suddenly sweaty, Bentley smiled at the closed door and then turned and ran.

Images of Margot's face caused a slow burn to build in his chest—he had to see her. What the hell had he been thinking? Throwing the list in her face? Why? Because his pride was hurt? Because he was pissed?

No. Because he was scared.

He was a serious jackass.

He jerked open the door to his sports car and shoved the key in the ignition.

He needed to see her. Now.

And kiss her senseless.

Bentley was in a hurry.

So it only made sense that the universe would fuck with him.

Every light was red.

And when he was almost out of the city, a police officer pulled him over for having a taillight out.

A drive that should have taken forty minutes turned into nearly an hour by the time he neared her house at breakneck speed.

Angry rain pelted the hood of his car as he turned the corner. The roads were slick with oil, making them more treacherous than usual, so he slowed down to a speed that wouldn't get him killed and jammed his hand against the steering wheel when his car rolled to a stop behind a garbage truck that clearly had all the time in the world.

Thank God, it finally turned off onto another road. Bentley hit the accelerator and sped by.

Everything happened at once.

The car drifting into his lane.

The overcorrection.

The sound of metal crunching and twisting against guardrails.

And then the impact.

CHAPTER FORTY-ONE

Something was wrong.

Margot shivered and pulled the blanket tighter around her body. The house seemed to come alive at night, and it didn't help that for the first time in years she was aware of her own loneliness and how much she actually missed having another person with her in bed—in her house—in her life.

Just call him.

What would she say? Beg him to give her another chance?

She could go to him.

She had a car. She just never drove it.

But for him?

To go after him?

Maybe she could.

Damn it!

She would!

Her movements were jerky, shaky with nerves, as she threw on a sweatshirt and grabbed her Nike tennis shoes.

Just do it, they seemed to whisper.

She didn't have his address, but she knew her grandmother would be more than happy to give it to her—after all, this was her fault to begin with! Besides, if worst came to worst, she could always contact Brant, right?

Within minutes she was ready to go, but when she glanced one last time at herself in the mirror, she cringed.

Pale skin from being indoors.

And her sweatshirt was on backward.

She really should put on some makeup, too.

No! There was no time, but why did she suddenly feel the need for urgency? The hole in her stomach grew to epic proportions as she grabbed the keys to her Jeep Cherokee. Hopefully, the SUV would start. Then again, her grandmother had always told the groundskeeper to run the car throughout the year just in case Margot ever needed it.

Fear trickled down her spine as she slowly walked out the back door and into the garage.

Swallowing her nerves, she flicked on the lights. Her red Jeep looked recently washed. It was shiny and completely terrifying as it sat in the middle of the too-large garage and mocked her.

This is ridiculous. I'm being ridiculous.

But for some reason, she felt like she had to do it—had to take that initial step toward Bentley—even if he rejected her.

Honestly, what did she even have to lose other than her own loneliness?

"Keep me safe," she muttered aloud as she clicked open the door to the Jeep and slid onto the leather seat.

Margot gripped the steering wheel so tight her fingers turned a pinkish-white color. She released one hand and tapped the garage door opener, then very slowly slid the key in the ignition and turned it. The engine roared to life.

"You've got this, you've got this." Great. She was going to keep talking to herself, wasn't she?

With a sigh, she peeled out of the garage—accidently; it wasn't like she'd had a lot of practice driving in the last ten years. She tapped the brake and found out the hard way that it was more sensitive than she would have liked as the Jeep jerked to a stop, thrusting her against the steering wheel. She drew a shaky breath. Lesson learned.

Slowly, she inched the car down the driveway and then burst out laughing as memories of Bentley flooded into her consciousness.

His driving like a maniac.

His smile.

Everything about him.

"God, I'm such an idiot."

And now she was driving.

For the first time in ten years.

She was just about to pull out of the driveway when a large garbage truck sailed by.

After looking both ways, she took a right toward the city.

Just as a loud bark interrupted her concentration.

"Scar?" she cried out in surprise and, with a jerk, the steering wheel went right, then left.

And everything went black.

CHAPTER FORTY-TWO

Wake up, asshole." Brant's voice sounded like it was muffled behind something. A pounding ache pressed between Bentley's eyes like he'd stuck his head in a door and slammed it a few times just for shits and giggles. "Seriously, Margot's in worse shape than you. And you look like you've been run over by a truck."

"Too soon." Brock made a strangled sound.

Bentley squeezed his eyes tight and then opened them to see both Brant and Brock leaning over him with concerned looks on their faces.

"Told ya it would work." Brant grinned and held out his hand.

Brock slapped cash in it and grunted. "Or maybe it was just good timing?"

"The hell?" Bentley tried to push himself into a sitting position but his body was so weak it refused to respond. "What's going on?'"

"This?" Brant pointed between him and Brock. "Just a

simple wager between brothers." He flashed an easy smile. "I said you'd live."

Bentley's eyes narrowed, the motion increasing the throbbing ache in his head. "And what? Brock bet I'd die?"

Brock shrugged. Bentley let out a moan and tried to touch his head, but his hand was heavy with something. He looked down. White bandages covered his arm from his elbow to his fingers.

"Looks worse than it is," Brant pointed out. "How do you feel?"

"Like my brothers want me dead."

Brock winced. "Your car was sideswiped by a Jeep."

"Yeah. I know." Why wouldn't the pounding stop. "I was there."

The guys fell silent while Bentley flexed the fingers in his left hand—at least that wasn't bandaged up. And his legs seemed to still be attached, since he could move his toes.

"Hell, my head hurts," he grumbled.

"You hit it," Brant said helpfully.

Why were they there, again?

"Oh, good!" Jane, Brock's fiancée, opened the door to the room. "You're alive!"

"Hey, Jane." He waved with his bandaged arm. "Care to make me all better?"

"She would kill in a nurse outfit." Brant eyed her appreciatively.

"No." Brock shook his head slowly then studied Bentley. "Clearly you're feeling better."

"I got hit by a Jeep—" Bentley stopped talking and then looked around the room. *Margot*—hadn't someone said her name? "Is she here?"

Guilty looks appeared on everyone's faces while Bentley

searched for someone to offer up any piece of information that would help him.

"Seriously?" Anger surged through him. "I'm in the hospital and she still won't come? Is this payback? I didn't visit her. I didn't fight for her. Karma sucks."

Heart pounding, he stared at Brock with clenched teeth, ready to yell, ready to say things he'd regret later when he was more calm and rational, but when he opened his mouth Brant interrupted him.

"She was in the red Jeep."

"What?" He snapped his attention to Brant. "That's not funny."

"Am I laughing?" His twin's face darkened. "Apparently she had the dog with her and she swerved, though nobody's really sure if it was because of the dog or because of the rain. The dog's okay, but Margot—"

"—is fine," Brock answered for Brant. "She's in surgery."

"*Surgery?*" His gravelly voice sounded foreign to his own ears, like he'd been holding in the scream that kept threatening to come out every time he thought about Margot nearly dying—or being dead.

"She's out," Jane interjected. "The doctor just put her in Recovery. I came in to tell the guys—"

"I want to see her." He was already struggling to get up. "Now."

Brant let out an agitated sigh. "Bentley—"

"*Now!*" he roared.

"Okay." Brant pulled the blanket back and helped him to his feet. "But keep everything covered. The last thing we need is you flashing one of the nurses and getting arrested or something."

"It's not illegal if it's their job," Brock pointed out.

"Good to know." Brant grinned. "Storing that morsel of

information for later. Oh nurse, I have a pain, here let me just unzip my pants and—"

"You're going to burn in hell." Brock walked around the bed to Bentley's other side and held him up. "Remember, Margot doesn't know yet, so... let her down gently."

"Or..." Brant shrugged as they slowly moved out of the room. "You can take my advice and get angry at her. She's going to feel guilty enough, so if you attack her first and then forgive her, it might be easier for her to forgive herself."

Bentley stopped walking and looked at him. "Who *are* you?"

"What?" Brant shrugged. "She's a woman. That's what they do."

Brock grunted.

Leaving Bentley to wonder if his twin was actually right. Margot was going to blame herself—just like she did with her parents' death. And look how long it took her to get over that?

The thought haunted him the entire laborious journey to her room.

And when he opened the door and his brothers abandoned him—

He knew he had his answer.

CHAPTER FORTY-THREE

Margot stared at the white ceiling, the square panels that covered the room. The smell of bleach and medicine made her want to gag, but worst of all, her right arm was in a cast, and her leg hurt.

The one she was missing.

Because being back in the hospital reminded her body that yes, at one point she had a leg and it had been removed on this very floor.

The same floor they took her parents to when they'd died.

God, she hated hospitals.

"You're so lucky you're alive!" If she heard that one more time from another nurse or doctor, she was going to scream. Thankfully, the car had only rolled once before slamming into another car, which had just slowed down.

Had the car not slowed down...

And had she not overcorrected...

So many things could have happened.

She could be dead.

Scar could be dead.

Thankfully, the puppy had made it through without a scratch. How had she not seen him hop into the car after her? She'd held the door open only for a few seconds; he must have snuck in then.

Her head pounded with all the what-ifs.

Her grandmother had been called.

And was probably freaking out.

But worse of all—Bentley.

She was ashamed to call him. Fearful that he'd get mad at her for trying to drive when she wasn't confident behind the wheel. And fearful he'd reject her when he discovered that her only game plan was to get his address and stalk him until he accepted her apology.

Hot tears ran down her cheeks as the sound of people outside her room grew louder. She just wanted to be left alone. Was that so much to ask for?

"Knock, knock," came a familiar voice.

Margot jolted to a sitting position as a banged-up Bentley slowly hobbled in. His entire right arm was covered in bandages, he had two black eyes, and a cut across his right cheek.

"Oh God!" She covered her mouth. "What happened to you? Are you okay?" Tears spilled over her cheeks until she couldn't wipe away the moisture fast enough.

Bentley finally made it to her side and sat on the bed, then pulled her into his arms and kissed her. "I got in a fight with an angry husband, jumped out a three-story window and into a bear cage. You should see the bear, though. I fucked him up good."

"That's not funny." She sniffled against his chest. "What really happened?"

He pushed her away and smirked. "The true story, huh? No pretenses, no lists?"

"No lists," she repeated with a shaky voice. "Only truths."

"I met a girl." He shrugged. "A really pretty girl with a wicked mouth and beautiful legs." Oh great, now she was crying again. "And she terrified me."

"What?"

"She finally agreed to be my friend, then made me feel like she was using me for sex," he added with a wicked smirk. Leave it to Bentley Wellington to be completely gorgeous even with two black eyes, the bastard. "And I let her, because I liked her."

"That was stupid." She sniffled.

"So stupid," he agreed, leaning in and wiping the tears from her cheeks. "Because everyone knows that you can't sleep with your friends and keep it just about sex…" He sighed, touching his forehead to hers. "You end up falling…"

"Are you still falling?" she asked in a hopeful voice.

He ignored her and kept talking. "You fall and then you realize you're afraid of heights, so you look around for a parachute or a branch—hell, anything to hold on to—only to realize you've got nothing. And then a voice whispers that if only she'd catch you—everything would be okay. Except, what if she doesn't?"

Margot's breath hitched. "Then she doesn't deserve you."

Silence blanketed over them, as he took her chin between his fingers and brushed a soft, much-needed kiss across her lips.

"I was afraid. And fear makes you stupid. So I made her believe it was all about a list, when really it had always been just about her—about seeing her smile, and hearing her laugh. The list prompted it—and I wanted to finish it, until I realized that she'd always push me away, wouldn't she?" He pulled back from her as if mimicking what she actually did.

It was a painful reminder of how much she had hurt him. "So I let her."

"So stupid," she said between hiccups.

"She really is." He nodded seriously. "She's also a shit driver—nearly killed me."

Margot's stomach sank and she blinked in confusion. "No, no, what? *No*." She refused to believe it.

"I was in the other car," he whispered. "I was coming back for you, but nope, you couldn't just let the guy sweep in and storm the castle, you had to go and run him over." He glared. "With a fucking car."

She laughed.

She couldn't help it.

His expression.

The black eyes.

And then her laughter turned into sobs again as she leaned against his chest and said "sorry" over and over until her voice grew hoarse.

"Well, the good news is I'm not pressing charges, but I do have a list of demands."

She jerked back. "A list, huh?"

"Think of it more like...payback? You hit me with a car and nearly kill me when all I want to do is love you and—"

"You still love me?" she whispered as heat spread through her body. "Me? Are you sure?"

"All of you." His clear green eyes flashed while he placed a hand on her thigh.

"But"—panic flooded her system—"I almost killed you just like my—"

"Item number one says you can never say, 'I almost killed you just like my parents.'"

"But—"

"Item two says, 'Don't argue.'"

She glared. "Where is this list? I don't see anything."

"Up here." He tapped his head and then winced. "So basically, you have to just trust me. Think you can do that, Margot? Think you can trust the playboy with your heart?"

"Can you ever forgive me?" She hung her head.

"Can you ever forgive yourself?" He tilted her chin toward him. "Because that's the real question. You know I'd forgive you anything—unless you decided never to get naked again—I refuse to forgive that."

She burst out laughing. "You're impossible."

"Impossibly charming." He nodded. "Impossibly sexy." He stood and turned so she could see the part of his hospital gown that was open. "And impossibly naked, so..."

Margot covered her face with her hands. "Okay, that's enough of that."

Bentley gasped. "Item number three: Never turn down a naked Bentley. It's rude and completely wasteful."

"Yeah, we're going to have to put a number cap on this list."

"Shouldn't you just be happy I'm not suing you? Pressing charges? Taking you to court and demanding that you become my legal sex slave?"

"How hard did you hit your head?" she teased.

"Kiss me." He grinned. "We have to seal the contract."

Her lips met his tentatively at first. She was so worried she was going to hurt him, but the minute their skin made contact, it was impossible not to kiss him harder, to grab his biceps and tug him closer until their chests were pressed to one another.

Moaning, Bentley kissed her neck. "Need you."

"I need you, too."

"Now." He cupped her breast. "I need you right now."

"But we're in a hospital room."

"Exactly. We're trying to heal."

"Sexual healing? Really, Bentley?"

"I'm here all night." His deep laugh had butterflies erupting in her stomach as he trailed another lingering kiss down her jaw and then locked eyes with her. "It's just sex, right?"

"Too soon," she grumbled.

"Fine." His hand slipped lower. "That's a nice surprise, you're naked, too..."

"Bentley!" she hissed. "I have a broken arm, you're all bandaged up, and oh..." She bucked off the bed. "That's... Bentley Wellington!"

"Shout a bit louder, I want Brock to hear how good I am at this."

"Bentley!"

"That's the spirit!" He moved his hand in a perfect rhythm while he kissed her lips and made her forget all about the accident.

And all about the past.

CHAPTER FORTY-FOUR

Three weeks later

No." Margot shook her head and crossed her arms. "We can't."

"But think of the children."

"We don't have children!" He had to give her credit, she still hadn't cracked a smile, but her lips were twitching.

"But we could. In the future. I'm just saying, don't be selfish."

"So now I'm selfish because I don't want another dog to take care of?"

"He's sad. Besides, we only have three, and three isn't an even number," Bentley argued.

"We only have three," she repeated in a dry tone. "You rescued the other scrappy ones last week, bought a goldfish because"—she made air quotes—"it was on sale."

"It *was* on sale!"

"And then you adopted a cat because dogs and cats need to learn how to get along, right? Wasn't that your reasoning? And now, another dog." She pointed at the bulldog puppy in his arms. The thing was so fat and heavy that Bentley was pretty confident he would sleep most of the day away and passing gas would be his exercise.

Bentley set the dog down. Immediately, it went to Margot, looked up with its beady little eyes, and gave out a yawn.

Margot put her hands on her hips. "It's like you're Dr. Doolittle and you communicate with them. I swear they know my weakness." She leaned down and rubbed the dog's ears, only to have him turn onto his back and expose his spotted belly. "Ugh, he smells like a puppy, too. He's warm and—" She glared at Bentley. "I won't fall for it."

"Remember, item number three hundred and seventeen says you shouldn't say no to me when I'm trying to build my own zoo."

"You were drunk when you made that one up, and I thought you were kidding about the zoo thing?"

Bentley shrugged. "Just an idea." Actually, he was already working on plans to better the local zoo and had donated part of his trust fund money toward the endangered species project.

The zoo had immediately jumped on the opportunity to have a Wellington as a partner, and he soon found himself being offered a position on their board.

Which meant he actually looked forward to going to work.

It was a really strange feeling.

Growing up.

And since Margot loved her house—and found out she didn't like the loudness of the city—he offered to move.

Something she was probably regretting every time he brought home a new animal for them to adopt.

"Fine." She squeezed her eyes shut. "We can keep him."

"It's your turn." Bentley bit down on his lower lip and waited. "Which character do you want to use?"

Margot named the pets after the characters in her books, which meant they all sounded like Regency lords and ladies.

"How about Lord Langely?"

The dog barked.

"Lord Langely it is." Bentley pulled her into his arms and kissed her roughly across the mouth. "I love you."

"Because I'm keeping the dog?"

"No." He wrapped his arms around her waist and lifted her into the air. "Because you kept me."

"Same thing."

"Well, the list did say something irreplaceable—"

Margot gaped and then smiled so brightly his chest hurt. "You gave me you."

"I wish I could say I had it planned and that I'm really that romantic at heart."

"We'll say it was subconscious."

"I like that." He captured her mouth again and silently thanked his grandfather for being a meddling bastard—otherwise he would have never tamed the beast.

So yeah, apparently he was the beast after all—but hell, if it meant that the story would end this way?

He was all for it.

Beauty and the Bachelor.

Huh. He had to wonder what Grandfather had in store for Brant. Whatever it was—it wasn't going to be painless.

"Come on." He tugged Margot toward the master bedroom.

A bark interrupted his thoughts as Scar tried to follow after them.

"Not this time, buddy." Bentley covered Margot's mouth

with his and kicked the door shut, leaving the dog whining outside.

Margot pulled away from Bentley and grinned. "You know he's just going to keep whining until you let him in."

"Nobody gets to see you naked but me." Bentley pouted, but he was already working on pulling her T-shirt over her head and tossing it to the floor. "No bra, hmm?"

She grinned and lazily wrapped her arms around his neck. "It's just one more thing you have to take off. I figured it was easier this way."

"Mmm." He bent down and kissed the side of her neck, loving the way she tasted and how her body was already responding to his as he slid his hands down her sultry curves and cupped her heart-shaped ass.

Their lips fused as heat built between them like it always did whenever they touched—like an explosion of fireworks—like her hot-as-hell fire engine hair.

It was never like this with anyone but Margot, and now he knew why—because he loved her.

So much that sometimes it was hard to breathe when he thought about life before her and how painfully stupid he'd been.

The whining outside the door got louder.

Margot laughed against Bentley's mouth. "Told ya."

"Not now!" Bentley yelled, capturing her lips again while kicking his jeans to the floor and pushing her toward the wall. He pinned her arms above her head with one hand while wrapping the other behind her neck, and he brought her mouth harder against his.

Margot arched toward him with a whimper as she rubbed against him.

His hips jerked as he bit back a curse. "I love you."

Margot smiled against his mouth. "I love you, too."

"And not just because you're really good at sex," he teased.

"Good, because I've been worried about that." She reached for him and giggled.

"Damn," he panted. "Yeah, I can tell."

"Bentley?"

"Hmm?"

She arched a brow then shoved him backward toward the bed. He stumbled, his back coming into contact with the fluffy down comforter.

She followed after him and nestled herself across his lap and guided him inside her. Head tilted back, exposing the soft column of her pale neck, she looked like an Irish goddess, like a faerie.

He gripped her hips, controlling her movements so it wasn't over before things even really started.

Slow.

Heated.

Thrust after thrust.

With the sound of her pants.

And a dog whining outside his door.

It was just another one of his favorite moments, holding her in his arms, bringing her pleasure, but knowing that this connection they had—it was special and it was forever.

Margot gripped his hair and whispered his name like a prayer.

"You feel—" he quickened his movements "—so good."

Her body shuddered. "I think I'll have to write this."

He pumped into her harder, faster, unable to control himself or any of his thoughts. When he felt her walls tighten around him a second time, he let go as she fell apart in his arms screaming his name.

Panting against his chest, Margot pulled back and leveled him with a curious stare. "Just one more pet?"

"Even numbers, sweetheart." Bentley brushed a piece of hair away from her face and laughed. "Think of Scar."

"Oh, you mean the dog you left crying outside the door so you could have your way with me?"

"Well, it's weird when he watches."

She lifted a shoulder and nodded. "Most of the times he's sleeping on his bed in the corner."

"Whatever, I know the way his mind is. Dirty little bastard shouldn't get to see you naked."

"You're weird—you know that, right?"

"You love me." Bentley couldn't help himself, and he kissed her again. "So, another pet?"

She rolled her eyes. "You just had sex with me so we could get another pet. That's what this was, hmm?"

"No." He slapped her ass. "I had sex with you because I love you and because I could see your nipples through your T-shirt." He grinned shamelessly. "And you looked cold, so what type of gentleman would I be if I didn't do my best to warm you up? And everyone knows that skin-to-skin contact is the best way to do that, so basically, I just saved your life."

She burst out laughing. "I'm glad you're still a jackass."

"Tigers rarely change their spots."

"I think you mean stripes."

"So about that pet..." He started tickling her sides as he changed the subject.

"Fine!" She burst out laughing. "I give!"

He joined in her laughter, pulled her back against his body again, and threw a pillow at her face.

He could stay in bed with her all day.

And probably would if he didn't have a meeting with the zoo.

And his brother.

His smile fell.

Brant had been ignoring him.

And Bentley knew why.

Because Grandfather had saved the best and most painful for last.

God help them all.

Because Brant needed all the help he could get.

CHAPTER FORTY-FIVE

Nadine stared Brant down, her crystal-blue eyes like laser beams, making him shift in his chair before turning his attention to his grandfather. "You wanted to see me?"

"Your number's been called," Nadine answered for him. "And I won't be made a laughingstock, or a liar."

Brant rolled his eyes and let out a bitter laugh. "Which really is quite interesting, since you've been known to be both."

Her eyes narrowed.

Grandfather placed a hand on her arm.

"So what now?" Brant stood and placed his hands on the mahogany desk. He really didn't have anything to lose at this point. All he wanted was to be left the hell out of whatever matchmaking ideas they had.

He was happy.

He was fine.

Totally fine.

The pills in his pocket said otherwise.

The pounding in his head reminded him he had blacked out last night.

Fine.

Totally fine.

Neither of them said anything.

"You've acquired another ally in the McCleerys." Brant nodded to Nadine. "So that's more money for you, but my ex-wife isn't all that rich, not by your standards. She has nothing you need or want." He shrugged. "Ergo, you guys lose." He smirked at his grandfather. "You can't take away my trust fund, because there is no chance in hell I'm actually going through with the auction date. So if we're done here?" He didn't wait for them to say anything, just stomped out of the room and slammed the door behind him.

*   *   *

Nadine jolted at the sound. "He's an asshole." Her smile grew as she turned to Charles. "Reminds me of my grandsons—kind of makes me miss those little bastards."

Charles rubbed his temples. "I can't force him. He's right. He had a lawyer look at everything. As long as you're paid money and both parties agree not to go on the auction date, our hands are tied."

"Rubbish." Nadine winked and tossed a folder onto his table. "Because Titus Enterprises is fully prepared to sue the shit out of Wellington, Inc., if Brant Wellington doesn't go through with the auction date."

Charles grinned. "You're out for blood, aren't you?"

"No." She swallowed and sat on his desk near his hand. The warmth of his fingers sizzled the skin beneath her skintight white wrap dress. "I just happen to have a crush on a man who deserves some good after a hell of a lot of bad." She patted his shoulder. "Let me help you with Brant, and maybe then you can stop focusing so much on the mistakes of your past and focus on our future."

Charles tilted his gorgeous, well-groomed head. "'Our'?"

"Of course *our*!" She tilted his chin toward her. "I never make a deal without asking for something in return."

"And what do you want in return?"

"You, silly." She gently kissed his mouth. "And more great-grandchildren. Besides, Brant needs you...and his brothers need him. To be healthy. Strong. Virile..." Her voice lowered. "Sorry, I got carried away." She coughed. "He'll do what you say, because we aren't giving him a choice."

Charles was quiet and then nodded. "Do your worst."

"Oh, I plan to." Her lips curved into a greedy smile. "I plan to."

BRANT WELLINGTON TELLS
EVERYONE THAT HE'S SINGLE,
RICH, AND HAPPY. INSTEAD, HE'S
RUNNING FROM A PAST HE CAN'T
FORGET. BUT ALL IT TAKES IS ONE
UNFORGETTABLY HOT NIGHT WITH
HIS EX TO TURN BRANT'S PAST
INTO ONE COMPLICATED—AND
TEMPTING—PRESENT . . .

A PREVIEW OF *THE BACHELOR
CONTRACT* FOLLOWS.

PROLOGUE

Colorless shapes moved in rapid succession as the roar of the crowd grew louder by the minute. Nikki clutched the auction paddle with a sweaty hand while making sure to keep her wineglass secure in her left.

She wasn't sure what was louder.

The people.

Or her heart as it pounded against her chest.

At least she didn't have to *see* him.

Then again, she'd never had to see him to feel his magnetic presence. Brant Wellington was and always would be a larger-than-life figure to her, a person who didn't just live up to the hype—but out-hyped the hype.

He'd been her hero.

And then he'd fallen.

And stayed down.

That was the worst part.

When people fell, they got up—it was simple logic. You fall down, and you fight to stand again, you fight with everything you have to make sure you can find solid ground.

Not Brant Wellington.

He'd fallen down.

And he'd been on the ground ever since.

"The next item for auction!" the loud voice boomed. It was happening. It was actually happening.

Nadine Titus had given her strict instructions. And because she was out of her mind—she'd said yes.

"Brant Wellington!" the voice announced as a hush fell over the crowd.

And then the bidding began.

Heart in her throat, Nikki waited for paddles to lift—though she couldn't exactly see them, she supposed the announcer, Charles Wellington, would keep everyone up to date with how much was being bid.

A cough sounded to her right.

And then a second loud cough.

That was her cue.

Hand still shaking, she raised her paddle into the air and spoke in a reserved voice. "Twenty-five thousand dollars."

"Going once," the voice boomed. "Twice." Her pulse soared into dangerous territory while her mouth went completely dry. "Sold! To, sorry, what is your paddle number?"

"Zero-zero-five." She'd memorized it the minute Cole, her companion, had let her know the number.

She stood and forced a smile she didn't feel. A practiced smile. One that would convey her excitement at winning one of the most notorious bachelors in the country.

But she knew the truth behind that smile.

The hurt that still remained. The rejection that haunted her day and night, and still, she couldn't shake the feel of his hands on her body, or his hot kisses and how they always managed to make her melt into a helpless puddle at his feet.

Maybe it was better that she was legally blind.

Because when she stood, she didn't have to see the look on his face.

The look that would solidify how horrible an idea this had been.

Because she was pretty certain that look was almost identical to the one he'd worn the day he had walked out of her life.

And never come back.

CHAPTER ONE

Present Day

Get the hell out!" Brant roared as he threw a vase across the tiled floor. It landed with a crash as it exploded into hundreds of blue glass shards.

Bentley stared at the mess then stepped over the shattered pieces, and still, he made his way over to Brant. "A vase, man? Have you turned into a chick? Is this our first fight? You might as well have thrown a bra. Oh, also"—he walked around the couch while Brant retreated backward—"you missed."

"I'm drunk."

Bentley's clear blue eyes flashed. "You're always drunk."

Brant's ass collided with the wall. Trapped. He was completely trapped.

In his own apartment.

With the most annoying man on the planet.

Who just so happened to look exactly like Brant minus a few key muscles and a very unsavory personality flaw.

"Just go." Brant wiped his hands across his scruffy face. "I'm fine. I just need to sober up."

Bentley snorted. "And if I had a dollar for every time that phrase came out of your mouth."

Pain—raw, familiar, all-encompassing—wrapped itself around Brant's throat until he felt like he was going to choke. "Why are you here?"

Bentley slowly turned his head and looked around the apartment. Brant knew what his twin saw. Empty pizza boxes. Empty beer bottles littered across every flat surface. A few empty fifths of whiskey. Clothes strewn across the couch, and white powder on the coffee table.

"It's not mine," he said quickly. Guilt stabbed him in the chest at his brother's disappointed look. "I swear."

"Would it matter anyway?" Bentley asked in a quiet voice. He slowly walked over to the table and grabbed one of the small plastic packets, then disappeared down the hall.

A toilet flushed.

When he returned, a tense silence crackled through the air as Brant waited for the yelling, the accusations, more pain.

Because if there was anything he knew without a shadow of a doubt, there would always be more. A human's capacity for pain was limitless.

He would know.

Damn it, he wasn't drunk enough if he could still feel the pain, if he could conjure up images of her jet-black hair and red-lipped pout.

If the air still smelled like her skin, no matter how many times he told himself it was a trick of the imagination.

God, he hated her.

But not as much as he hated himself.

SIGN UP FOR RACHEL'S NEWSLETTER HERE:
RACHELVANDYKENAUTHOR.COM

AND FOLLOW HER ON SOCIAL MEDIA TO KEEP
UP-TO-THE-MINUTE ON HER NEXT RELEASE:

FACEBOOK.COM/RACHELVANDYKEN

TWITTER @RACHVD

ABOUT THE AUTHOR

Rachel Van Dyken is the *New York Times*, *Wall Street Journal*, and *USA Today* bestselling author of Regency and contemporary romances. When she's not writing, you can find her drinking coffee at Starbucks and plotting her next book while watching *The Bachelor*.

She keeps her home in Idaho with her husband, adorable son, and two snoring boxers! She loves to hear from readers!

Want to be kept up-to-date on new releases? Text MAFIA to 66866!

FALL IN LOVE WITH FOREVER ROMANCE

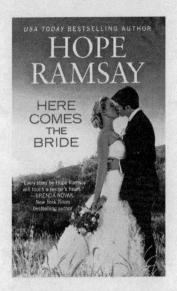

HERE COMES THE BRIDE
By Hope Ramsay

The newest novel in the Chapel of Love series from *USA To-day* bestselling author Hope Ramsay will appeal to readers who love Jill Shalvis, Robyn Carr, and Brenda Novak.

Laurie Wilson is devastated when she is left at the altar. How long will it take her to realize that Best Man Andrew Lydon is actually the better man for her?

FALL IN LOVE WITH FOREVER ROMANCE

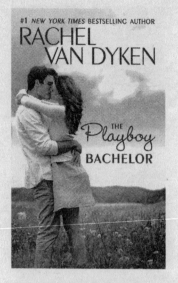

THE PLAYBOY BACHELOR
By Rachel Van Dyken

New from #1 *New York Times* bestselling author
Rachel Van Dyken!

Bentley Wellington's just been coerced by his grandfather to spend the next thirty days charming and romancing a reclusive red-haired beauty who hates him. The woman he abandoned when she needed him the most. Bentley knows just as much about romance as he knows about love—*nothing*—but the more time he spends with Margot, the more he realizes that "just friends" will never be enough. Now all he has to do is convince her to trust him with her heart...Fans of Jill Shalvis, Rachel Gibson, and Jennifer Probst will love this charmingly witty and heartfelt story.

WHEN THE SCOUNDREL SINS
By Anna Harrington

When Quinton Carlisle, eager for adventure, receives a mysterious letter from Scotland, he eagerly rides north—only to find the beautiful—and ruined—Annabelle Greene waiting for his marriage proposal. Fans of Elizabeth Hoyt, Grace Burrowes, and Madeline Hunter will love the next in the Capture the Carlisles series from Anna Harrington.

FALL IN LOVE WITH FOREVER ROMANCE

HARD JUSTICE
By April Hunt

Ex-SEAL commander Vince Franklin has been on some of the most dangerous missions in the world. But pretending to be the fiancé of fellow Alpha operative Charlotte Sparks on their latest assignment is his toughest challenge yet. When their fake romance generates some all-too-real heat, Vince learns that Charlie is more than just arm candy. She's the real deal—and she's ready for some serious action. Don't miss the next book in April Hunt's Alpha Security series, perfect for fans of Julie Ann Walker and Rebecca Zanetti!